EYRIE

GRYPHON INSURRECTION BOOK ONE

K. VALE NAGLE

STET PUBLISHING

This is a work of fiction. Names, characters, organizations, places, events, and incidents are either products of the author's imagination or used fictitiously.

No part of this book may be reproduced, or stored in a retrieval system, or transmitted in any form or by any means, electronic, mechanical, photocopying, recording, or otherwise, without express written permission of the author.

Cover art by Jeff Brown.

Interior artwork by Brenda Lyons.

Interior graphics by Crafty as a Coyote.

Author portrait by Murphy Winter

Published by STET Publishing, LLC, Denver

WWW.STETPUBLISHING.COM
WWW.KVALENAGLE.COM

Trade Paperback Edition
ISBN: 1-64392-000-6
ISBN-13: 978-1-64392-000-9

10 9 8 7 6 5 4 3

BELAMURIA
ALABASTER EYRIE
REEVESPORT
WHITEBEAK
CRESTFALL PALACE
DUCKBILL
ABYSSAL NAZE
ARGENT HEIGHTS
CRAC S
NIGHTSKY
NEW EYRIE
ALWREN
CI RA
JADEBEAK MOUNTAINS
EMERALD JUNGLE
FLOWER OUTPOST
SUNKEN EYRIE
STORMFALL
KING'S REACH
RAFTWORK
SUBMERGED FOREST

BLACKTALON
MOTHFEATHER
EYRIE
BLACKWING
EYRIE
PITOHUI
EYRIE
GLASSWORKS
GLACIER
PRIDE
POISONMAW
KLING
EA
CRACKLING
SEA EYRIE
REDWOOD VALLEY
EYRIE
OVER
NCH
KJARR
NESTS
TAIGA
WEALD
STRIX
PLATEAU
KJARR
S
LUMINAIRE

For Sare, who wanted more novels with gryphons and fewer novels with people.

HATZEL

GRYPHON

REEVE BREVIN
OPINICUS

1

ZEPH

Halfway up a tree that reached sixty feet in height, a gryphon clung beak-down and surveyed the forest floor. Several large, flightless ground parrots pecked at crushed berries. Violet stains covered their green plumage. The berries were casualties of a conflict much higher up. Two flying squirrels fighting on the sunny tree tops had dropped them, splashing the gryphon with juice when the fruit landed.

While the rush of sugar the berries offered had been tempting, that was short-term thinking. Instead, Zeph had groomed the juice from his feathered face, left the area, climbed one of the many massive redwoods, and glided back to a good vantage point—the one he now occupied. The local ground parrots had become wary of fresh scratches on trees that marked the climbing habits of gryphons. Not that ground parrots were particularly bright birds. The species, as a whole, survived mostly by virtue of laying many eggs, foraging effectively, and running away at the slightest provocation.

A plump parrot, a full four feet in height, shouldered its competition out of the way. There were a few squawks of indignation, then the birds all froze and looked around to see if anything had heard them. Zeph remained unmoving against the tree, his banded brown fur and feathers matching the slits of light against the bark. Backward-facing dewclaws on each paw held him in place and even allowed him to slowly climb higher, should the need arise.

Several more parrots peeked out from the overgrowth and jostled each other to peck the last of the berries. Just as the original plump one took a swipe at its rivals, Zeph pounced from the tree, crushing the bird on impact. The other parrots fled in all directions, *skraarking* with alarm, and Zeph set off after the next largest.

Thick ferns blanketed the dimly-lit forest floor, providing cover if his quarry slipped out of view. Heavy storms normally provided lightning to burn away the ground cover during the summer months, but this year there hadn't been any fires, and the vegetation was at its thickest in living memory. The parrot squeezed under a rotting log. Zeph leapt over it and spread his wings, gliding in pursuit. Thick vines and branches bred agile forest gryphons with hollow, muscle-covered bones to enable flight.

Bones that broke easily if they caught on something.

He did his best to drive the parrot towards the edge of the redwoods. Once it was in the grasslands between the weald and the eyrie, it would be an easy catch. Right as well-groomed feathers, the parrot burst out of the forest, and Zeph pounced. He held it down with his ever-useful dewclaw and snapped its neck with his beak.

The sun beating down on his wings was a pleasant change from the shade of the forest, so he spread out his plumage and looked towards the eyrie. The opinici had built a large city at the northern tip of the Redwood Valley, nestled against the mountains. The forest around the eyrie was well-maintained, and they'd cleared a large swath of trees between them and the weald to create grasslands for capybara herds and farms. Ground parrot was tastier and healthier than capybara, but parrot meat's unique flavor made it worth significantly more than just its nutritional value to opinicus merchants. The parrots around the eyrie had fled when the opinici cleared out the undergrowth, and the untamed gryphon lands were the only place to get them now. Zeph looked to see how the capybara herds were doing.

Instead of large rodents chewing and lazing about, the ground was soaked in wet blood. The fence at the edge of the grasslands had been destroyed, and a trail of dark red led into the weald.

He grabbed his kill in his beak and retreated to the safety of the trees.

Zeph returned to the smashed berries to find Hatzel standing over his first kill. A full five feet at the shoulders, she dwarfed him. Her feathers were a brown so dark they appeared black this far down the canopy. Only at higher tiers would the light reveal where her feathers stopped and her dark fur began. She was built for strength, bulky by gryphonic standards, and her beak had jagged edges on either side that resembled saber-like fangs.

"Zeph." She trilled a greeting to let him know she'd seen him.

He put the second parrot down. "Hatz-el."

Their names played together like the call of a songbird. She bowed a little in front of the plump parrot. He nodded to her and returned the second kill to his beak. They dragged the parrots through the brush, back to the nesting grounds. Years of helping each other transport food had taught them to talk with their mouths full. More specifically, it had taught them to understand each other's muffled sounds.

"The capybaras in the field nearest here are all dead," he said.

She tilted her head to the side and asked a muffled, "What?"

"It's just blood and broken fences," he continued. "Someone got in there and killed all of them."

Hatzel's brow furrowed. "Someone? Not something? You don't think it was monitors?"

Large monitor lizards were known to sometimes break fences while trying to dig under them. Though they tended to feed on carrion, they weren't above hunting. Early summer was a time of plenty, and monitors were more likely to take reckless chances when failure held little risk of starvation.

Zeph hopped over an abandoned parrot's nest. He nearly missed his landing with the additional weight in his beak. Only spreading his tailfeathers to rebalance kept him upright. "There was enough blood, I think someone got the entire herd. They were dragged into the forest."

Hatzel made a noncommittal sound, but her tail—tufted and unfeathered—whipped back and forth. Zeph knew her first instinct was to pick a fight, but the world had changed over the last five years. The grasslands development project had changed the dynamic between the weald and eyrie.

There were things you could fight, like a monitor, and things you couldn't fight, like an opinicus.

They continued their journey in silence.

2

OPINICUS

The undergrowth soon gave way to a rocky glen, the nesting grounds of Hatzel's pride. The leaves and branches of the redwood canopy above had been cleared to allow some light down to the forest floor, sunning rocks had been painstakingly transported from the mountains. On the tops of trees, branches woven together into the shape of gryphons were covered in feathers soaked in violet berries. Young gryphons, who could fly and climb as soon as their feathers came in, were taught to make their way above the tree line if lost and locate the blue feathers to find their way home.

The markers also served as a way of telling other gryphon prides that this hunting ground was claimed. From the heights, on a clear day, Zeph could see up to the taiga prides and down to the southern coast where the strange fisherfolk lived. Even if it was overcast, he could usually make out the dark red marker of their neighbors, Merin's pride, the only gryphons who could match Hatzel's strength.

Hatzel had chosen her nesting grounds for their proximity to the river and the abundance of rocky outcroppings.

While the pride and nesting grounds were hers, none of the eggs had been for years now. The grounds housed a half dozen gryphlets each year, with the pride's adult population numbering around thirty-five. While some pride leaders chose to lead and have young, she hadn't chosen to lay any eggs in Zeph's lifetime, and he wasn't much younger than she was. He assumed she'd given it up when she took control of the pride. With the canopy cleared and the under-growth beaten back, the nesting site was relatively safe. In the sky, gryphons had no natural predators. Only on the ground could monitors sneak into camp if the eggs or gryphlets were left unattended. The well-lit, rocky glen had been chosen to keep skulking lizards at bay.

Zeph got to work pulling the feathers from the parrots and enjoying the sun while Hatzel went inside one of the two caves to check on the gryphon guarding the gryphlets. When a shadow fell across his parrot, he looked up and saw an avian shape circling the camp. He let out a chirp of caution, and Hatzel came out to greet the newcomer.

The opinicus had colorful green and blue plumage with splashes of red, which faded into chestnut-colored fur painted with green spots to create continuity before the feathers began again at her tail. Her back legs were gryphonic, if thin, but her forelegs were taloned like a bird's. Their sharp tips had been sanded down to allow her to grip things with help from one backwards-facing talon. She was wearing a vest-like harness with several pockets.

"Is Hatzel here?" she asked. Her voice was pleasant, with a humming quality, but her words were terse.

Zeph's feathers perked up in annoyance.

"How may we help the eyrie?" Hatzel asked, rising to her full height. Opinici tended to stand taller than gryphons due to their long necks, but Hatzel towered over this one.

"I'm Kia." The opinicus's head was level with the fangs on Hatzel's saber-beak. "There was an incident at the grazing lands today, and I need to ask you a few questions."

Zeph followed Kia's eyes as she looked around the nesting grounds. There was no sign of the missing capybaras. There was also no sign of Hatzel's other hunters, most of whom were north dealing with an explosion in the snake population. If a gryphon were going to steal from the opinici, surely, they wouldn't bring their illicit goods back to the nesting grounds.

"I heard as much from Zeph. He was hunting nearby." Hatzel's voice was measured, but the tips of her claws stuck out from her paws. "The others are up by the Snowfeather River."

Kia made a move towards the caves, but Hatzel stood in her way, an impassable wall, so the opinicus turned her attention back to Zeph. "You saw who did it?"

"I only saw the broken fence and blood." His ears were back in agitation, a feat opinici couldn't replicate with their lack of external ears. "I was busy tracking ground parrots."

Kia's foretalons clenched reflexively. Opinici loved ground parrots but were terrible at catching them. "Did you see anyone else while hunting?"

Zeph continued his grooming. He hadn't seen anyone, but he'd heard several gryphons earlier in the day. At least, they'd sounded like gryphons. A gryphon's beak had more give to it than an opinicus's, being hard and sharp only along the edge. This gave them more flexibility when it came to language and made opinici sound like they were speaking with an accent, though opinici would say the same about gryphons. Still, after a few years of working with the fisherfolk, many sea-loving opinici were able to imitate a gryphon accent. The one or two gryphons who lived in the eyrie with the opinici were ostracized upon returning to the forest until they lost their *opi trill.*

"I didn't see anyone, no," he replied, "but I heard several others over the course of the morning."

"Did you recognize them?" the opinicus asked.

"No." He thought back. "None were close enough."

"Gryphon or opinicus?" she pressed.

He shook his head. "I couldn't hear a trill from where I was at."

She took out a small notepad and scribbled something down. Zeph's eyes were drawn to a magnifying glass sticking out of her harness pouch. In the eyrie, glass was rare. In the weald, it was unheard of. He wondered what she used it for. It was amazing the things opinici could do with their talons. Each of them was taught to read and write at a young age. Only about half of the weald gryphons could read. The farther one lived from the eyries, the less likely they were to learn. There were gryphons in the deep mountains who never learned to read.

When Zeph had realized that trading ground parrots for other goods was lucrative, he'd learned to read and write. He couldn't grip a pencil or a quill pen—an innovative sort of recycling he had to admire—but he could scratch into bark or dirt with a single claw extended.

Hatzel had gifted him a pouch with sand and a wooden box. It lacked the permanence of using ink on paper but allowed him to practice and check the figures when trading in the city. Most merchants were honest, but some would misrepresent the taxes to pad their coffers. Being able to show he knew how to calculate the price kept them honest. When times were lean, and lean times always returned, the ability to trade with the eyrie kept Hatzel's pride strong.

Their reputation for being literate and willing to trade

was probably why Kia had come here first and by herself. It would take an insane opinicus to visit Merin's pride alone and make accusations. For a pride directly across the grasslands from the Redwood Valley Eyrie, they acted more like kjarr gryphons, coveting the easy life of the eyrie. Zeph thought this was silly. If they loved the city life, why not go live there? A few gryphons had, but he knew it wasn't that simple. Life in the city wasn't easier for gryphons, only for opinici.

Kia broke him out of his thoughts. "I'd like for you to come with me to look around."

He looked helplessly to Hatzel, who shrugged.

"Why?" he asked.

"I need another pair of eyes." She pointed her claw at his flexible beak, specifically his nares. "And you smell better than I do."

Hatzel, out of Kia's view, snorted her disagreement with that sentiment but didn't protest the escort request. "You've hunted for the day. Go, show Kia the forest. We'll be fine here."

HATZEL AND ZEPH had dragged parrots through the forest faster than Kia was making her way through the brush. Part of her problem was that she was ill-suited to forest flight. She'd made the journey from the eyrie to the forest easily enough because the skies were clear. There was nothing to dodge or watch for along the way. Under the canopy, vegetation and wildlife filled every empty space. He'd already had to untangle her once. The second half of her problem was that she had to investigate everything. Her inquisitive nature was probably why she'd been assigned to look into the problem in the first place, but in the forest, suddenly, every-thing became interesting.

When she jostled a nest of flying squirrels, she stopped to take notes on how they glided, asking questions and making comments he'd never considered.

"None of the early surveys of the weald include squir-rels," she'd said. "I don't think they had them when we settled the valley."

When pulling vines off her startled a snake, which flung itself to a nearby tree, she began to ask questions about how many types of snakes could glide. When she had to take a break, she chose a low branch, and he advised her to move up higher to avoid monitors. Then she asked about the types and numbers of monitor lizards and how many attacks there had been over the last fifteen years. He'd always thought of himself as an inquisitive gryphon, but he found himself taxed by the time they reached his morning hunting spot.

"This is where the berries fell, so this is where I was waiting when I heard the sounds." To his relief, she didn't ask about the types of berries and where they grew and the different types of birds that ate the berries and the history of the ground parrot and why did ground parrots not fly but snakes and squirrels could glide.

Instead, she switched to a professional mode, grabbing a new notebook and putting the other one back into her vest. "You said it was a few of them. How do you know it wasn't just one gryphon talking to himself?"

"It sounded like at least three different voices," he replied. "One was rougher, one was higher pitched, and the other was lower. There could have been more, but I feel like there were three. And they might not have been gryphons."

He saw the conflict weigh on her face: the need to be an

impartial recorder of facts coming up against the casual racism of *but it's the weald, who else would it be?*

"So, the other hunters, at least three—" she began.

"I was hunting," Zeph interrupted, "but they might not have been hunters. They were talking loud enough that I could hear them this far away. Obviously, they weren't worried about scaring the game."

She scribbled it down. "So, three unknowns talked loudly east of here in the mid-morning. They were probably not hunters and may or may not have been gryphons."

His ears were forward to show he agreed, but when she didn't pick up on them, he nodded.

She chewed on her quill pen. "But why would opinici be in the forest?"

"Why would gryphons talk so loudly in hunting grounds?" he countered.

"Have you ever seen an opinicus in the forest?" she pressed. "Do they ever come out here?"

"I'm with an opinicus in the forest right now," he countered.

She sighed. "Other than me."

He thought back. It was uncommon to see opinici in the forest, but this year had been uncommon. Usually, they would fly overhead and arrive at a pride's camp before descending. Opinici *inside* the weald were more unusual. There was forest land around the eyrie before the grasslands began, but it was well-cultivated and sparse, making it easy for opinici to fly through it. It had started out just as untamed as the weald, but the reeve had created rangers to manage it. Now it was considered the Reeve's Hunting Grounds, by appointment only. But he was sure he'd heard opinici in the weald several times this year. He hadn't thought anything of it. His predatory instincts often warred with his desire to stay out of trouble. What had they been doing here? Gryphons kept away from the contested areas between prides, which was where he'd heard the opinici.

"There have been several groups of opinici in the forest since spring, but I don't know why," he answered at last. "I've heard others say the same."

Kia looked incredulous but made a note. "So, you attacked your ground parrot here, then followed it to the grasslands?"

"I killed one here, then followed another." It was important to him that she represent his hunting skills accurately in her journal.

She made him reenact the whole thing, taking out her other notebook to draw how he looked upside-down, stalking his prey from the tree, before following the parrot path to the weald's border.

3

FISHERFOLK

Zeph and Kia came out from the forest and into the late afternoon light. Having kept her wings tight against her body after the incident with the vines, he allowed her a moment now to stretch and give her feathers a cursory check.

"You're sure this is the exact spot?" she asked.

He'd stopped being offended by her questions when she asked him about the history of monitor attacks and he realized he'd started forgetting how many there'd been. Instead, he just pointed at one of the massive redwood trees. Twenty feet up the trunk was a scratched circle with wings and the number eleven.

"What's that?" she asked.

"In the fog, fledglings can't always see their way back," he explained. "The markers help them figure out where they're at. The numbers start closest to Crater Lake and count up from there."

"What happened there?" She pointed her beak towards another tree further down. The winged circle with a thirteen next to it had been scratched out. An angry beak and ear tufts with the number one had been drawn above it.

Zeph twitched his feathery tail. "Merin disagrees with where our hunting grounds end and his begin."

"I didn't realize anyone in the Merin pride could read or write," she said with a sniff. "Next thing you'll tell me is that they've developed manners and scholars."

"I wouldn't go that far, but no pride shares all the same plumage," he explained. "Askel and Triddle helped us out a few years ago when there was the terrible flooding. They're smart when it comes to rivers and diverting water. Especially Triddle. Askel is more of a forest fire kind of gryphon."

Kia's feathers ruffled. "They're the ones who flooded the grasslands that summer! They caused a lot of irreparable damage. They're criminals."

"Criminals?" His ears went back. "They saved our nesting grounds from being flooded. Eggs are irreparable. Grass is not. No one *lives* in the grasslands."

That wasn't necessarily true. The growth of the livestock trade had drawn a few permanent residents and one makeshift group nest along the plains. To Kia's credit, she didn't speak what was probably on her tongue. Opinici were often of the opinion that gryphons bred too much. In fact, he would guess that there were fewer gryphons than opinici. No weald pride had a hundred gryphons in it. They maintained genetic diversity by interbreeding with other prides. Only half of the gryphlets grew to adulthood. Forest life was full of danger. That's why culling the snake population now was so important, before they grew large enough to feed on hatchlings.

The year Hatzel was born, a slow-gestating disease from monitor meat killed every hatchling save three. What was dangerous in adults had been fatal to the youngest. It was one of the few times the deep mountain gryphons, with their spotted white coats, had come down and sought help. Hatzel still sent gifts to them in the fall out of a bond that had formed between her and one of their gryphlets that had also survived that year. Even today, a gryphon would have to be starving to eat a monitor, though there were no cases of the strange disease after that year.

But the opinici couldn't see the gryphon population. They were mysterious forest creatures living in the untamed wilds. Who knew how many there were? Since destroying some of the shared forest to create the grasslands, the opinici had whispered of a possible gryphon retaliation. Their justification had been that no one owns the forest. After that, gryphons started putting up wooden banners and marking trees.

Kia picked up a fallen black notebook next to the marker on the tree. Several golden feathers stuck out from the blood caked on its cover. Some of the pages had been pulled out. She shivered.

"Can Merin read?" she asked.

"Yes," Zeph replied.

She looked into the thick underbrush of the woods, then up to the tops of the trees two hundred feet in the air. "I need to get back to the eyrie. This is important. Will you come with me?"

He cocked his head to the side but assented.

"We need to hurry," was all the explanation she gave.

As OUT OF place as Kia had been under the tree line, Zeph felt even more exposed in the sky. She flew effortlessly, aided by her slight build and long hours of past flights. He was muscular and used to running, climbing, and gliding. Gryphons were designed to wait and pounce, not to fly long distances. He found himself annoyed at being asked to tag along on this errand because it made him feel unfit.

She seemed unaware of his discomfort and kept looking below or behind them. What she was looking for he did not know, but she wasn't looking at him. When they stopped to drink on the other side of the grasslands, she shied away from a group of fisherfolk.

He found this incredibly rude and was careful to chirp a happy greeting at them. For all their strange, sandy homes, they were social while on vacation, their term for coming to the Redwood Valley Eyrie to trade. This group was particularly brave, having several children who lacked ear tufts or non-avian forepaws.

Opinici and gryphons were not as distinct as politics may lead one to believe. When they interbred, the offspring were defined by which characteristics they had. Ear tufts and non-avian forepaws meant the child was clearly a gryphon. If it only had ear holes and taloned foreclaws, it was clearly an opinicus chick.

The confusion came from individuals who had one and not the other. In most eyries, one needed to have talons that could grip a pencil and write in order to be an opinicus. Among gryphons, a lack of ears made it hard to tell emotion. Many bonds were formed over annoyed flicks of ears. Where tone and stance didn't change, being able to see someone's ears full back served as a warning. Gryphons weren't used to opinicus mannerisms and their strange lack of ears.

For the gryphon-opinicus offspring that had forepaws and no ears, the fishing villages were the only places they'd be accepted without challenge. To a fisherfolk, everyone was a gryphon and everyone was an opinicus. It made them exceptionally cheerful and happy to talk to anyone when they traveled. While it seemed like a recipe for disaster, the one thing that triumphed over the bigotry of gryphons and opinici was both sides' deep love of fish.

"Hello!" chirped a tall fisher from across the fountain. She had the look of a heron about her with a black beak, light blue face, and grey feathers that blended with her fur. She left her compatriots and flew over to them.

"Hello, yourself!" replied Zeph.

Kia added something noncommittal but polite. Her attention was taken up by the strange mix of gryphons and opinici relaxing together. While some had come from prides or eyries and now wore fishing harnesses, there were species only ever found along the coast, too—petrels, terns, and cranes.

"I'm Gressle, but call me Gress. Would you be heading into the city to trade, by chance?"

"I'm Zeph, and this is Kia. We're actually on official business, just heading back to report in. Did you happen to see anything suspicious in the grasslands this morning?"

The fisherfolk's eyes widened in surprise. Kia's did similar in annoyance. Not many people outside of his pride were aware of his propensity to take a small amount of adjacent authority and apply it to himself.

"No, no we didn't," Gress replied. "We've been in the city all day. We're just getting ready to head back. Is it safe?"

Zeph gave his best grin, careful to keep his ears happy. Gress may lack ears, but she'd certainly been around enough gryphons to recognize what friendliness looked like. "I'm sure it's perfectly safe. Right, Kia?"

The eyrie opinicus was caught off guard. "Yes, yes, I'm sure it is."

"But to be extra safe," he continued, "they should probably cut southwest instead of straight south on their way home, shouldn't they?"

Kia rolled her eyes but played along. "Yes, when you hit the end of the grasslands, look for a mark on the tree line with a circle and wings. You'll want to follow that to the violet clearing."

"I hear they have ground parrots to trade," he added.

Gress perked up. "Thank you for the information!"

She started to turn away, but then fished two salted tuna bars from her vest and gave them to him. He had to sit back to hold them in his forepaws.

"For you and your pretty mate," Gressle said and flew back to her people.

"Wait, what did she say?" Kia asked, but Zeph was already scarfing down his fish.

"So salty," he said with watering eyes, "but so good."

Kia's tears also flowed, and she nodded. "We need to get back. It'll be dark any time now."

4

REDWOOD VALLEY EYRIE

Opinici had once lived in small nests called eyries built on the tops of trees. At least, that's what Zeph had been taught as a gryphlet. As their population grew, the border between one family's eyrie and another's disappeared. Then, as their ability to use tools improved, they expanded above the tops of trees and built higher, sometimes securing dead trees to live ones to serve as supports. Their cities now reached into the skies.

While there were several of these mega-eyries in the world, Zeph had come to think of the Redwood Valley Eyrie in the forest as *the* eyrie. He'd never had reason to travel across the mountains to see the others. He understood that the eyries had trade amongst themselves, but he'd never personally met an opinicus from another eyrie, though it was said the fisherfolk were made up of gryphons and opinici from across the world.

Even having seen the Redwood Valley Eyrie before, he was still overcome with a feeling of danger and awe when he looked up at its spires. They were three, four, maybe five times as tall as the tallest trees. Wind chimes hung from family domiciles and created a constant music that interfered with his instincts. It was all noise, pretty noise.

The ground beneath his feet wasn't dirt or rock but just another platform. He'd learned to guess the strength of branches, but he had no idea how the platforms were built or how safe they were. His muscles maintained a level of tension that would enable him to leap into the air and glide to safety if it all fell apart. Someday, he was certain, it would all fall apart.

From the skies, the platforms resembled a colossal mushroom patch. Homes existed on the underside of platforms and along the edges of the city while shops, schools, and other things he had not identified were on top. Some system that Askel and Triddle might understand, but Zeph did not, pulled water up from Crater Lake and created bathing pools on top of one mushroom cap.

Though the city center stood proud and clean, things became dirtier the further one traveled from the center. Lizards of the non-gliding variety and pigeons infested the city. There were no snakes to keep them at bay—opinici hated snakes. He shuddered to think what the ground level looked like. He'd never seen it, never asked what was down there. A twenty-foot-high fence kept it from view as he flew closer. Maybe that's where the few gryphons lived.

Kia brought him to a building near the market. It was meant to resemble a redwood, but no trees grew this high. The craftsmanship was impressive. He looked at his paws. No matter how much practice he put in, he'd never be able to create something like that.

She chirped a greeting and short message to an opinicus whose only job seemed to be to relay messages to opinici who were more important, leaving Kia and Zeph waiting outside.

Zeph's ears twitched. "What're they waiting for? Did we interrupt dinner?"

"I'm sure they're wondering why I brought you along and trying to figure out what to do about it," she said.

He wasn't sure if she was joking or not. "Why did you bring me?"

"It seemed important this not be about opinici and gryphons."

He weighed her words. "What is this about?"

"I don't know." She kept worrying at a golden quill pen. "Something bigger or smaller than that."

He ruffled. "It's always about gryphons and opinici. There's no getting around that. You think gryphons killed and ate your herd. I could hear it in your questions. Gryphons know that strange groups of opinici are coming into the forest. If you want gryphons and opinici living in peace and laying gryphon-opi eggs together, you'll have to catch up with Gress's band of fisherfolk and fly all the way to the ocean to make that happen."

She bristled at his choice of the word *opi*, but he felt confident she'd heard and said far worse at his expense inside the city.

"There are gryphons here," she retorted. "And I'm sure they're quite happy to stay in the city."

"You'll have to show me these gryphons," he said. "I've been here many times and never seen an eyrie gryphon."

"I will tomorrow." She stretched her neck up and cocked her head to the side like she was listening for something, but without ears it was difficult for him to be sure. The eyrie was full of so many sounds, he couldn't tell what she was listening for.

After a moment, she continued. "Look, if we get separated and you get sent home, you should probably know this. Normally, I work for the university. We've been working on keeping different types of livestock. That's why I got sent out. They thought it might be an animal attack."

He nodded his head, unsure why he was being entrusted with this information.

"The notebook I found is Cherine's." Her talons tightened on the golden feather. "He was working out there, taking notes, doing research. The eyrie can't sustain much more population growth if we don't find better ways of raising food."

Zeph remembered the blood on the journal. "I'm sorry. Was he a friend?"

"No. Yes," she corrected. "It's complicated. I like him. He chose to be kind when it was not easy. But this is important: from what I read on our flight back, he was trying to follow the opinici sneaking into the woods to see what they were doing. There's a note in here about pressure from someone to increase the size of the grasslands."

"That would require cutting down—" he started to say before she silenced him with a hiss. Whatever she had been listening for earlier, she must have heard it because a moment later several opinici descended to their level. A tall one with a circlet and more jewelry than he'd ever seen— metallic jewelry, not beaded—spoke first. She had a long, thin neck and green feathers. She was flanked by a military-looking opinicus in a faded army harness and a spoonbill-shaped opinicus with a pink harness. To Zeph's surprise, she recognized him.

"Zeph Parrotbane," the opinicus in charge stated. He prayed no one ever called him that again and was thankful Kia was too awed by the peafowl-opinicus to laugh. "You've provided the meals for my table many times in the past.

We'll make sure you're settled in for the night and comfortably fed before you leave in the morning."

"Thank you," he replied.

"Apprentice Kia," the peafowl continued, "you'll be coming with us."

"Yes, Reeve Brevin," Kia said.

Zeph stiffened. While the reeves ostensibly served at the behest of some leader far away, in reality, they were the monarchs of their eyrie city-states. He didn't know the proper way to address a reeve, but his response had not been it.

Kia flew off with the reeve and her assistants, leaving Zeph alone with the opinicus who resembled a spoonbill.

Zeph relaxed once the reeve was out of sight. "So, what's for dinner?"

For all the talk of fish and parrots, dinner turned out to be less exciting fare. Zeph's guide, Jonas, took him to the far end of the market where several braziers were lit. While Jonas's plumage reminded Zeph of the blue herons that migrated through the weald in winter, his beak was closer to an elongated duck's bill. It was a common face for opinici, but less so for gryphons—fisherfolk offspring being an exception. His back half was grey, almost blue. His harness had a pink fish on it and seemed to be made of a nicer material than what most merchants wore. The symbol meant nothing to Zeph, but it made him wonder where Jonas fit into the pecking order of the eyrie.

The wind changed, and the smoke stung Zeph's eyes. It struck him as foolish, or perhaps arrogant, to leave braziers around on a city built on the tops of trees. When they landed, he pushed his claws into the flooring. They stuck to the special coating before retracting.

"What do you do if someone knocks over a brazier?" Zeph asked.

Jonas pointed to bags the same color as the ground coating placed conspicuously close to each brazier. "They're filled with a powder that chokes the flames out."

Zeph looked up and followed the lines of the aqueduct overhead. The waterworks pulled water in and up from a large lake created by the dam at the Snowfeather River that Triddle was always going on about. While the dam itself had statues of a peacock and a cobra, Triddle was more impressed by the waterworks. Zeph could only imagine the trouble Triddle could get into here.

"Why not just put a spigot on that?" Zeph asked.

Jonas made a *tsk* sound with his beak. "Because the braziers have mostly oil in them. The water is as likely to spread the fire as put it out. It's leftovers from the butcher's shop."

Zeph could smell their destination from here. The butchery was a large building with braziers made for cooking instead of illumination. Processing meat had started as a way of transporting goods across the goliath bird pass to other eyries, but when word of the monitor disease killing hatchlings had reached the Redwood Valley opinici, the popularity of cooked meat grew exponentially. Butchers cooked, salted, and stored the meat here for later. It was large enough to be a factory instead of a store, but it kept a shop front.

A generation of opinici grew up with a taste for cooked meat and a love of salt, hence the healthy trade with the fisherfolk, who set up a saltworks to capitalize on the trend. While the flickering lights interfered with his normally excellent night vision, he thought he saw several other columns of smoke across the market he hadn't noticed in past visits.

Other butcheries processing and storing capybara meat? he wondered.

Jonas took a line of tiny, metal beads and paid the butcher. He returned with two salty, warm plates of meat for himself and Zeph. Zeph did his best to smile. Smiles were equally important among friends and adversaries, and there was no way to know which Jonas was.

Zeph winced a little at the salinity of the first bite. Between the salted tuna bars and the butcher shop's meat-of-the-day, he'd be crying out this salt all day tomorrow.

"So, lived here long?" he asked.

Jonas was startled by the question, piquing Zeph's curiosity. "Yes, for maybe two years now. You're from the Hatzel...eyrie?"

Zeph's interest grew. "Yep. My mother was from the taiga prides, but I never had the fur for the heavy winters up there, so I joined my father's. What brought you here?"

Jonas sawed through a piece of gristle. He enjoyed himself so thoroughly that Zeph suspected the funds for dinner had come from the reeve and not Jonas himself.

Or perhaps food is scarce where he comes from?

"I grew to hate the water," Jonas said at last. "The Crackling Sea is beautiful. At least, in the summer it is. When the thunderstorms cross the water, the crackling jellies that give the sea its name light up in response to the lightning. There's nothing like it in the world. But the Crackling Sea Eyrie is a quarter of the size of this one, the inland sea is frozen all winter, and I hate fish. Eating fish, catching fish, smelling fish, fish oil: all of it. I guess, like you, I wasn't cut out for the environment I was born into. I used to lead the goliath birds along the trail to trade with the Redwood Valley Eyrie. When my mate and children died, this was the first place I thought to come."

"I'm sorry for your loss. It's nice to see the world, though," Zeph agreed. He was trying to enjoy his meat now that he knew it wasn't meant as a slight. "I still go to the mountains sometimes when it starts to warm up. Though I'm still discovering a lot of interesting things in the weald I'd never have guessed at."

Jonas and Zeph traded travel stories into the night. Jonas spoke of the domesticated goliath birds, flightless like ground parrots, but much larger, who pulled supplies through mountain passes to reach new eyries. Zeph talked about the mountain goliaths that stood three gryphons tall and were all white and fuzzy. He talked about how the alpine pride dug up large frogs from the permafrost during exceptionally warm summers. The frogs normally tasted like, well, frogs. But when they froze solid, they turned sugary sweet. The taiga pride dug them up before they defrosted and ate them. He talked about how a hatchmate, Mignet, had once waited so long to eat hers that it defrosted and hopped away and into the forest. Jonas seemed particularly interested in that story. Everything was going well until the last question.

"You seem different from the other gryphons I've met," Jonas confided.

"What're the gryphon prides like by your eyrie?" Zeph asked.

Jonas's answer sent a shiver up Zeph's spine. "There are no gryphons by my home eyrie anymore."

5

EGRESS

The next morning, Zeph wiped the crusted salt from around his eyes. Jonas had excused himself, citing the late hour, when chimes played from the center of the city. Louder chimes played during the day at set intervals, but the opi trick to keeping time eluded Zeph.

When he could help it, he'd often come into the eyrie in the morning and leave in the afternoon. The few times bad weather had caught him off guard, he'd stayed in a hotel off the market. He was always given the same room—was in that exact room even now—which made him suspect that it was reserved for the few gryphon guests who showed up.

Despite his deep-seated suspicion towards opinicus currency, he always made sure some of his payment for the parrots he traded came in the form of a string of beads. Hatzel disapproved, but Zeph worried a time would come when they'd need supplies or medicine and not have ground parrots to trade for them. It also helped on the occasions when he was stuck in the city. If he'd brought a bracelet of beads with him now, he'd be searching out the least salty breakfast in town. Since he hadn't expected his journey with Kia to last this long, he hadn't brought beads with him.

He stretched, confirmed with the hotel owner that his stay had been paid for, and wandered out into the city to explore.

Lacking direction and trade incentives, he decided to get a feel for the layout of the eyrie. He saw opinici flying up to a structure above him and assumed it must be open to the public. The top of this platform was less like a mushroom and more like a sinkhole. From the center of an amphitheater, a red-plumed opinicus with black markings around his eyes was shouting. Zeph stayed behind the crowd and hung upside-down from the shadows of a higher platform to watch the proceedings.

"While we're starving, they grow rotund on the weald's bounty. While we struggle to find food, they let it rot in their larders, forgotten."

Zeph wondered at all the salted meat being processed at the butcheries. Was that not going to feed the eyrie? He had to hunt for his game. These people picked off pieces of jewelry and traded them. How did they earn their beads?

"The fault doesn't lie in the forest. It lies with us. We let them come here and trade their fish and parrots. They bring disease and spread it to the populace. They unleash their bloodlust on the eyrie. Do we really believe the missing guards and rangers were killed by opinici? They steal our loved ones and take them to the ocean to live like heathens. They don't mate for life. They don't mate for love. They put the eggs into a communal pile because they can't figure out who the parents are. Is that any way to live?"

Zeph began to realize that coming here might have been a mistake. Surely these opinici had been warned about gryphons skulking under every branch, ready to eat chicks and steal spouses. The more he stayed out of sight and eavesdropped, the more he fed into that myth.

"While we live in the slums of the underbough, the beautiful lands have been taken. Gryphons rut in the great forests, denuding them of their game through irresponsible population growth. The corpses of parrots and monitors litter the forest floor, picked clean by starving gryphlets forgotten by their parents, if they even know who their parents are. Meanwhile, responsible opinici worry about the future for their chicks. Will there be enough food in five years' time? Ten? If we don't do something now, will it be too late?"

Zeph hissed a little against his better sense. While some of the crowd seemed disinterested, fully half of them were leaning forward, engaged. They were worried about their children and had probably never chirped a single word to a gryphon. He knew relationships had long been strained, but he didn't know things were like this.

"It's not a question of *if*. It's a question of *when*. Do we wait until our children are starving and dead? Do we wait until the gryphons decide they've ruined the weald and need our lands, too? If we double the size of the grasslands, we double the future for our offspring. The reeves don't want you to hear me saying this. They want peace. They've already grown fat like gryphons, preying upon their own. They're okay watching the rest of us starve, knowing they'll be fine, their offspring will be fine. But I don't say this to spite them. Not at all. They'll get their comeuppance when the gryphons run out of food and come after ours. No amount of beaded wealth will save them then. No, I say this for all of you: the reeves cannot save you. The future is bleak. Only by acting now can you save your children. We must act while there is still time to act."

Zeph decided it was time to leave. He needed to get back and let Hatzel know how bad things were here. He was no longer willing to believe that the opinici coming into the forest were simply tourists hoping to take in a bit of nature. Hatzel's pride included a pond, the river, excellent ground parrot hunting grounds, and it formed the northwestern border of the grasslands. If the eyrie was looking to expand, Hatzel's pride were a prime target.

He wondered if Kia knew about this but couldn't believe she'd be ignorant of it. And he'd told her about the markings along the trees. Only now did he realize his mistake. Gryphons would need a language of their own and not just a simulacrum of what the opinici used. He'd leave a note for Jonas and fly back to the pride.

"Look at the Crackling Sea opinici," the orator's words commanded. "They've already purged the gryphons from their lands and live a life well beyond our meager existence. You want proof? They are the proof! They had the strength to do what was necessary for their future."

Zeph crawled along the platform and away from the crowd before leaping and gliding away.

KIA, Jonas, and Reeve Brevin had all flown to a higher elevation when they'd left Zeph. He decided to descend into the depths of the eyrie and find a route out from there. What he'd come to think of as the middle of the city had open spaces around a market, university, public area, and other places of interest. Above were several nicer nests. He wasn't sure what was lower, but he'd always felt more comfortable below the canopy line.

As he left his perch, he caught sight of Jonas entering the

inn. Zeph ducked behind some boxes marked with circles. Jonas left a few minutes later, feathers puffed up in annoyance. He whistled, and two opinici wearing official-looking gold and blue vests flew down. Together, they went off in the direction of the amphitheater. Zeph waited until they had passed his hiding place, then ducked under the market.

His eyes adjusted to the dimmer light. Below the market was another market without the glitz and bright colors of above. A disheveled opinicus purchased squirrel meat. Two chicks followed behind him, chirping with hunger. There was a butchery smoking meat down here, too, but this time several large opinici stood guard to dissuade theft.

Zeph did his best to stay out of sight. The pattern-recognition center of his brain noted that even in the sublevels, all opinici wore harnesses. He pulled some of the vines—no one seemed to care enough to clear them out—and did his best to wrap two around himself. At a distance, at a glance, maybe no one would notice his ears or forepaws.

The opinici kept to themselves. Few were in the company of others, and so far, no one gave him a glance. He descended further. He hoped deeper meant safer, but this underbough raised many questions. These opinici were emaciated. They were eating squirrels. Did the smoked meat just feed the heights? They were starving down here.

Light played on a glittering harness and Zeph ducked behind an abandoned nest stuck to the side of a tree and peered out. The sparkle came from a polished pink medallion with a fish on it, similar to the one Jonas had worn. Its owner was a gryphon, not an opinicus.

Her feathers were varying shades of brown and grey with a golden crest atop her head, framed by two black, tufted ears. His first thought was that her tail was short, but he amended his assessment. Her tail was a little short, but her back legs were also exceptionally long.

The strange gryphon, along with two opinicus guards, made her way to the ground. With no other gryphons around, she stood out. She was making no effort to hide her forepaws, despite the stares of opinici as she passed. The gold spot on her head made her easy to follow. She didn't seem to be escorted by the guards but also didn't seem to be free to divest herself of their company. Zeph's hunting instincts kicked in, and he followed the trio down.

For the last twenty feet before arriving at the ground, the underbrush was even more congested than the weald. Dried vines draped over rotting vegetation and the beams connecting each redwood to the others in its support network. He'd seen this before.

If a long period of time passed without a forest fire, the next time it happened would be significantly worse. This year, it seemed like every time lightning struck, the flames would give up within an hour, leaving behind strange white ash. If the summer passed without a fire, there was already talk of setting controlled burns. The only concern was that it might be too late. Hatzel's pride had a winter nesting site along the western edge of the valley where the weald met the taiga, but most prides lived in the redwood forest during the winter and had no place to evacuate to if a wildfire got out of control.

The eyrie was a city that had forgotten it used to be a forest. What would happen if someone knocked a brazier off a platform and it reached these depths? The whole place would go up.

It took too long for Zeph to prowl through the dried tangle; he lost the gryphon and her escort. He glided to where he'd last seen them and looked around. Vines, angry pigeons, a tree infested with ants.

Ah, a break in the undergrowth. He slid into the path like he was tracking a ground parrot. The smell of opinicus was cleaner here and included the spice of gryphon. No, *gryphons.* He followed it until he heard noises. He recognized an opi trill, but there were also familiar sounds. He flattened himself against the ground and crawled around the corner.

Several opinicus sentries talked amongst themselves. He could see the back of the gryphon's head as she entered the compound. Thick, wooden walls blocked Zeph's view. Painted against a section of tree in red juice was graffiti of a gryphon, wings not yet filled in. He shivered and backed around the corner. His hackles prickled. Whatever was going on here, it was past time for him to leave.

6

ORLEA

When Zeph reached the wall that circled the eyrie, he worried he would have to ascend to a higher level to escape. He'd never had a good look at the barrier when flying to the market but had assumed it existed to discourage ground-bound predators from getting inside. Every decade or so, a large number of lace monitors, having grown to an enormous size somewhere to the north, would migrate across the Redwood Valley and pose a danger to anyone caught on the ground. With the wall looming before him, he understood that whatever its previous purpose, it now existed only to hide the lower levels from view.

It'd probably been solid when it was built. It was made from thick, treated planks that were covered in hanging moss, vines, and dirt. The wood was too old to have come from the trees cleared to make the grasslands. Rickety gates appeared at set intervals. Perhaps, in better times, there had been a path for goliath birds to carry goods into the city from the shore. There was an overgrown trail and bridge that wound through the weald to the southern shore that made little sense for airborne inhabitants.

Most of the gates were now in a state of disrepair. The one in front of him showed signs of scorch marks, and the door itself was in shambles. Anything metal had been pried off and stolen by some enterprising thief. He pushed aside the vines, disturbed a nest of leaf-nosed snakes that rattled their tails angrily in the dry leaves, and crawled out of the city.

He was still full from the meal the night before, though tear stains cascaded from his salt glands. He decided to stay under the tree line until the grasslands no longer afforded him their protection.

He'd heard the eyrie's forested area called the Reeve's Hunting Grounds, and it was preternaturally quiet. Forests of all types offered several levels of silence, based upon what predators made themselves known. A mature monitor would quash the *skraarking* of ground parrots until it passed. The glided flight of a snake leaping from one tree to another might quiet the squirrels. When Hatzel struck, it silenced all prey larger than a squirrel, but the buzzing of insects would continue.

Zeph wondered if this forest had predators he was unaware of, or if starving poachers had killed everything large enough to be eaten. It was impossible to guard an entire weald, as the recent opinicus infiltrators attested to. Maybe the university scholars had frightened off the game with their food experiments. Maybe it was something else. All he knew was that this section of the forest should be full of turkeys but was empty.

A scream cut through the silence, followed by cruel laughter. Zeph stopped at a tree. He needed to get word back to Hatzel, but he'd never heard an opinicus scream for help before. What if it was Kia? He climbed higher and glided from tree to tree until he reached the sound.

A cardinal opinicus, grey except for her red beak, crest, and sections of her wings and tail feathers, hung by a wing in a large net spread out between the trees. Four others looked on from the ground. One, crane-like and still laughing, was wearing the same gold and blue harness as the guards from the market. The other three had pins of a matching color. These must be the rangers: hunters and trappers under a reeve's employ. They resembled falcons.

"Such a pretty voice!" the guard crooned. "We were hoping to catch a fat bird for dinner. You're large enough, but you look like you haven't eaten for a week. Come onto the reeve's land to steal away a few turkeys for yourself? These are the eyrie's turkeys. When you steal one of them, you steal from all of us."

Two of the guards threw lassos in an attempt to catch her forelegs before she freed herself from the net. Her talons had been sanded down and were struggling to saw through the rope.

"If these are the eyrie's turkeys," she snapped, "why have I never had them? Do you think any of us have ever eaten turkey?"

The guard laughed again. "Such a beak! How could I eat such a loquacious songbird such as yourself? You must go and explain yourself to Reeve Brevin. I'm sure she'd love to hear your plans for food distribution. It would be a shame for you to take those with you to the grave."

The two trappers were good at what they did, and the lassos soon caught her foretalons and hind legs. The rangers started to untie the net.

For Zeph, the calculation was simple. The rangers were not necessarily military but were more likely to be skilled fighters than the guard was. It would be dangerous and require a lot of effort to incapacitate all four opinici. They'd likely remember who he was when they awoke. The question, in his mind, was this: was he willing to kill four opinici to save one? It felt overly altruistic, but this *songbird* may be able to provide answers about the eyrie if he helped her. She might have context he lacked to understand what he'd seen in the underbough. The world did not seem like it would be a worse place if it lacked these four. He'd seen lizards with better personalities.

The netted opinicus made the decision for him. One of the lassos came loose, and she lashed out, catching a trapper across the neck and face. Only the dull nature of her claws kept his head in one piece.

Zeph dropped like a boulder on a distracted ranger. The opinicus's spine punctuated the forest's silence with an audible *crack* as it snapped. Zeph sprang from that corpse to the next closest opinicus whose lasso had held. That one tried to move out of the way, but he had wrapped the rope around his talons to make sure it held. His ribcage broke as he crashed against the tree and Zeph severed his neck.

Zeph slashed the ropes holding up the net and chased after the guard who had taken flight. Zeph ran along the ground, pushing up when he was below the opinicus. He caught a back paw and then folded his wings. His weight caused them both to drop to the ground.

The guard tried his best to hold them both aloft, but a loud pop in one wing showed that he didn't have the muscle. Zeph let go when the opinicus's wing gave and spread his wings, gliding to the floor. The guard hit with a *thud*.

"The reeves will tear off your wings for this. They'll

break every bone in your body just to watch them reset in strange new shapes. The horrors that await you—"

Zeph tore out his throat and went to check on the other opinici.

The last trapper, it seemed, had become entangled in the net with the grey opinicus when Zeph cut the line. The songbird had gotten behind her captor and was pecking at him mindlessly when Zeph arrived and put the trapper out of his misery.

"He's dead. You can stop," Zeph said.

She looked up. Her heart was pounding, and she was close to hyperventilating. Zeph chewed through the ropes and detached the dead trapper. Then he began to work on untangling her, careful to stay away from her claws. He'd seen trauma do strange things.

"I'm Zeph. Who are you?" he asked. "How bad is your wing?"

For a full minute, she said nothing. Then, quietly: "Orlea. I can't fly, but I still have feeling."

"Well, Orlea, you have two choices." He licked his paw and used it to wipe away some of the blood staining her beak. "If you want to walk back to the eyrie, I won't stop you. I don't know what life is like for you back there. Or, if you want, we're at the border of the grasslands. If we can get into the weald, I can have someone look at that wing. There's an old medicine gryphon who specializes in wings on the edge of our hunting grounds. Which would you prefer?"

She looked up at him, finally seeing his ears and paws. "You're a gryphon?" She began to laugh, high-pitched but not shrill.

"Hey, hey, you're okay. I'm not going to hurt you. You're okay now." He made a calming, purring noise. One ear was facing her, the other scanned the forest for rangers.

"Okay?" She balked. "I'm starving. I can't afford to have this wing fixed. They killed my mate over a year ago. Most of the rangers were reassigned across the mountains, and I thought maybe, just maybe, they wouldn't be watching the forest for poachers anymore. I was so hungry."

He moved next to her and groomed her feathers until she stopped shivering. "You'll be okay. I'll make sure you're fed and fixed up, but we can't stay here. Someone might be looking for me. We need to get across the grasslands to safety. Can you walk?"

She got up, took a few steps, then nodded.

"You start heading towards the plains," he said. "I need to clean this up so the next opinici to arrive don't know a gryphon killed these rangers. Maybe they'll think it was poachers."

He grabbed a frond and walked backwards, covering his non-avian tracks. When she just stared at him, he added, "I'll cover yours when I finish here so they don't see where you went. Don't worry. You'll be safe."

She gestured at a rocky outcropping in the distance. "There's a monitor den over there. If you leave a trail, they'll handle the bodies."

He nodded, and she began her walk to the grasslands.

HAVING CLEANED UP HIS TRACKS, Zeph bit off the guard's foot and used it to create a trail to the monitor den. In his ideal scenario, the monitors would come out and drag the opinici back to their dwelling. At minimum, he hoped they should chew on the corpses enough to make it unclear what had happened.

The taste of opinicus in his mouth made him uncomfortable. He'd never killed a sapient creature before. He expected to feel something deep, for there to be some strong physical reaction. Instead, his stomach growled. It'd become accustomed to hunting and then eating.

He stole the harnesses off two of the trappers and the guard, then loosened the fourth to make it look like the monitor lizards had taken them to chew on. He searched around until he found their camp. There were makeshift nests for four opinici, suggesting they'd planned on being out here for a few days. He left it intact, except for some stolen jerky to calm his stomach, but noticed several crates marked with circles.

He sniffed at one. It smelled desiccated, like salt and bat guano. He poked and prodded the crate but couldn't see a way to get it open that could be blamed on lizards or squirrels. Finally, he grabbed a branch and backed down the path Orlea had taken, obscuring their prints as he went.

"COMING UP BEHIND YOU," Zeph called to Orlea. She'd made better time than he expected, and the ground was more vegetation than dirt now.

She turned to look at him. He was still walking backwards and using a branch to obscure the tracks.

"Why not just let your tail hang down and do the work for you?" she asked.

"I'm banking on opi nostrils not picking up any scents from our path," he replied, "but if we leave little fluffs of down along the path, they might catch on."

"Gryphons and opinici don't smell that different, if they smell different at all," she said.

"Oh? Did I just save a fisherfolk?" He took a moment to

reevaluate her. Red beak. Brown and red plumage. No hint of ears. Well-defined, taloned forelegs.

She chirruped her displeasure at his gaze. "I didn't lop off my ears, if that's what you're looking for."

"Ah, sorry." He blushed.

They walked in silence until the tree forest gave way and revealed the grasslands that lay between them and the thick, untamed weald to the south. Zeph climbed a redwood and scanned the skies behind them. He didn't see anyone from the eyrie headed in their direction. A few opinici flitted about, but none with gold and blue harnesses. The wind picked up.

He looked at the path ahead but didn't see the long blades of grass bending around any large shapes. A clever hunter would be hiding next to a rock or tree, but there wasn't time for him to scout it all. "It looks clear, but we should be quick."

"Why don't we wait until dark?" she asked.

"Because the sooner we fix your wing, the better the chance it'll heal quickly and without complication," he said. But privately, he added, *Because a wounded animal limping through the forest floor at night will attract more monitors than during the day. Because helping a limping opinicus through the forest floor would look like conspiracy to some prides. Because one opinicus has already gone missing in this area.*

She hesitated.

"If they're looking for us—" he began.

"Yes, I know," she snapped. "Better to be in that forest than this forest. I'm just tired. Let's go."

He placed himself under her injured wing to support it. She spread her other wing. At a glance, they might just look like one gryphon. One gryphon with a wing that was shorter on one side than the other going for an evening stroll. It wasn't the worst plan.

He pushed her to pick up the pace, and she whimpered in pain. He thought he heard a flutter coming from the canopy but didn't see anything when he looked around. They made it across the grasslands, past the marker, and into the forest.

7

HATZEL

Hatzel reached up high with her forepaws and scratched down the trunk of a tree to leave behind her scent. Several of the gryphons who'd gone snake hunting, led by Xavi, had returned. Zeph would be relieved to find his magpie-colored friend back when he returned from the eyrie. Zeph's non-hunting responsibilities in the pride consisted of taking over as Hatzel's second-in-command when Xavi was busy elsewhere.

From the perky ears and swishy tails, the campaign to cull the snake population at the northern border was a success. Xavi was busy helping store some of the snake meat for later, but the mission was more a matter of pride safety than food gathering. On their way back, they'd run into Triddle from Merin's pride, and he'd tagged along.

"I'm supposed to be following the Snowfeather River, but it went underground forever ago, and I never found it again," Triddle confessed. "I've been flying in circles all day."

Since arriving at her nesting grounds, he'd been resistant to returning home. He snacked on a ground parrot and looked around with an interest that surprised her. He'd been here before, and the layout was simple—a redwood clearing, two caves going into the rocky outcropping, and nests above.

While Triddle hadn't done anything to help with the snakes, Zeph had always insisted that both Triddle and his inseparable other half, Askel, be afforded every courtesy. Being able to solve problems with water was too valuable a skill set to lose access to from impoliteness. Hatzel was just discovering that without Askel to rein him in, Triddle was one of the more talkative gryphons in the weald.

"Did Zeph catch this one? I bet it was Zeph," Triddle said between bites. "Or maybe it was you, Hatz? Did you catch this one? I bet you both caught it together."

She took a deep breath and remembered that practicing patience was a method of improving hunting skills that could be done at the nest. She chewed on some dried mint to calm her nerves. "I caught one. Zeph caught the other two."

"Oh! He's fast. That's why I like him." Triddle paused to think. "But if there were like a super-giant parrot, then he'd have to run away. That's why I like you."

If Zeph were faced with a giant parrot, she was pretty sure he'd think of something. The largest parrots were already pretty big compared to him. He'd probably drop a branch on its head. He was cunning when he was hungry.

"Is Merin expecting you back?" she prompted.

Triddle missed her implication. "Oh, maybe. I don't know. I wasn't paying attention. Where is Zeph?"

"He left yesterday." Hatzel resolved herself to having Triddle here for at least a little longer. "There was something wrong with the herd squirrel things on the grasslands and an opinicus asked for his help."

"He's not back yet?" Triddle sounded genuinely worried. His crest and blue hackle feathers were up. While he had the hooked beak of most of Merin's pride, he didn't have the size of Merin's immediate offspring.

"They were probably just held up," Hatzel assured him. "Or he stayed overnight at the outpost there. I don't think she ate him or anything."

Triddle looked alarmed.

"A joke. I joke." She'd never seen Triddle so on edge. His tail swept back and forth and his crest wouldn't stay down. She turned all her attention to him. "Are you okay, Triddle? Did something happen to Askel?"

"No, nothing like that. I just... I have something to show you, but I need you not to tell Merin I showed you." Triddle looked up, gauging the late afternoon light.

She tilted her head to the side.

"Here, come with me," he said and bounded south into the forest.

HATZEL ALLOWED Triddle to lead her through the dusky forest, far from where the others had picked him up, to where her territory met Merin's. They were within walking distance of the taiga. It was here that the Snowfeather River disappeared underground.

A length of rope and a harness lay abandoned along the shoreline. By their age and quality, Triddle had probably scavenged them from the eyrie trash pile.

"I hope you're not going to ask me to put that on," she said.

"Oh, no," he replied. "That one's not for you."

"I hope you're not going to ask me to put that on you," she rephrased.

"No, it's for—." He stopped. His back leg twitched.

She let the silence do the work for her.

Triddle filled the quiet with more words. "Okay, they have a prisoner. We have a prisoner. I don't know."

"Askel...?" she asked.

"No, not Askel," Triddle hastened to say. "But I'm worried something bad will happen to him if I act. I need your help because I'm not strong enough, and you're strong and not scared by Merin."

She nodded but wasn't sure what to say.

"I'm too hollow-boned and stringy for this," he continued. "I've traced the river's route. I think this is the same one that flows into the cave below, and then goes deeper into the earth before arriving at Glacier Run's rapids. I've run some tests with floats and string. They're holding him down there. I don't think he has long to live if we don't do something. I think Merin is going to do something to the prisoner tonight or tomorrow at the latest. Even if Merin doesn't do something, he's not in good shape."

Hatzel's eyes widened. She'd never heard of a gryphon holding prisoners before. "What do you need me to do?"

Triddle finished preparing the harness. "I'm going to lower this one into the water. The float should bring it up when it gets into the cave. He's supposed to tug five times when it's securely fastened. When that happens, I need you to pull as hard as you can until we get him out. I think he can hold his breath long enough, but maybe not. He's been in there for two days now."

It turned out when Triddle said the harness wasn't meant for her, he'd meant that the harness *with the float on it* hadn't been for her. There was a second harness designed for her musculature. She slipped into it and prayed she didn't get pulled into the water. He let the float go, and they watched it disappear underground. A minute passed. Two, three, four minutes. Then the tugging came: exactly five tugs.

"Pull!" He was behind her, pushing.

She yanked as hard as she could. It took almost a full minute, but finally the float and harness popped out of the river. She dug her claws into the bank while he ran over to help the prisoner onto the shore. Once the two of them were out of the water, she squeezed out of the harness and joined them.

The prisoner was in bad shape. Broken, golden feathers matted over deep cuts and bruising. The very tip of his beak had been broken off. He held one of his talons at an unnatural angle.

"He's an opinicus?" Not just an opinicus, *the* missing opinicus, she'd wager.

"I'm Cherine," he gasped. "Thank you."

They unhooked his harness just as a cry of alarm came from the direction of the cave mouth.

"Don't worry, they'll be heading to Glacier Run," Triddle said. "They won't think to look upstream. Well, not at first. You'll have plenty of time to get him to the medicine gryphon. Oh! They'll expect me to help with the search." And with that, Triddle flew off, leaving her alone with the opinicus.

"What's...what's your name?" Cherine managed.

She gave serious consideration to responding with Zeph. "Hatzel. Now keep quiet and hang on."

She got under him and lifted his wet, damaged form onto her back. Then she made her way through the forest, out of Merin's hunting grounds, and towards the mountains.

8

CHERINE

The chittering of squirrels went silent as Hatzel stalked through the forest. A monitor or two peeked out from behind the trees but decided not to risk messing with her. Even grounded, she still had a saber-toothed beak and sharp claws.

Cherine would need food soon, but she hadn't found a safe place to leave him while she hunted. Her stomach grumbled a reminder of all the parrots she'd plucked but not eaten back at her nesting grounds.

The monitors may be keeping their distance for now, but if she left him on his own, they'd come looking for dinner. So, when she turned a corner and found a dead parrot with recent chew marks, probably from scavengers scared away by Cherine's mumbling, she had an idea.

"Don't eat the parrot," she warned him.

He looked around, unsure of where he was. They were in a glen, on top of a small boulder.

"It could have been monitors that chewed on it," she explained. "The mountain monitors, lace monitors we call them, are venomous and may have left their poison on it. So don't eat it, just sit tight and whimper."

He looked confused but obliged.

She ran off like she was chasing something, then doubled back quietly from a greater height. As she suspected, in her absence, several of the monitors that had been tailing them came out from hiding and converged on Cherine.

The largest was six feet from snout to tail—much bigger than she'd planned on. It was accompanied by two smaller lizards, probably its offspring, around three feet long each. They had blue stripes running down their heads and onto their backs that would fade as they matured.

Hatzel pushed off from the tree, then dropped straight down at the parent. The monitor was quicker than it looked and leapt out of the way. Hatzel hit the ground hard, sending a shock through her limbs that should have been absorbed by squishy lizard flesh.

The monitor hissed loudly. Hatzel hissed back. The juveniles seemed unsure if they should help or flee. One backed away, the other moved closer.

Hatzel had always considered herself a surprise-attack hunter. With her opening gambit a failure, she looked up at where the medicine gryphon lived, farther up the mountain. If she were bitten, would she make it that far carrying Cherine before the venom overtook her? She couldn't leave him here. Her little experiment had proven he was monitor bait.

She drew herself up tall and spread her wings to their full width. The juvenile that was backing up turned and sprinted away in full retreat. The other two were unfazed.

Keeping her wings out, she moved so that she was closer

to the juvenile. She flicked her tail, its tuft attracting the attention of the little one.

When the lizard pounced, she impaled it on her beak, not waiting to see if it was dead before she tossed it aside and flung herself into the air to prevent the adult monitor from taking its revenge.

The adult hissed in rage. Hatzel flapped her wings and landed a short distance away. The plan for dealing with a large monitor was to sneak up on it when it was asleep and kill it in one blow. Actually facing off against one was ill-advised. Being stronger was not always better when an opponent was venomous.

She slashed out with her claws to get its attention and feinted towards its throat.

The monitor swung its tail faster than she could register and hit her square in the chest. She tensed and fell back a few feet. The front half had teeth, the back half was a whip. Perfect. This was why she never let the monitors in her hunting grounds get this large. She'd have to have a word with Merin if she could ever explain why she'd been in his territory without his knowledge.

The monitor gave chase, and Hatzel flew up to a low branch of a tree. It slammed the tree with its tail in annoyance. It could climb up after her, but she'd just fly to a new perch. It hissed and spat, but only enough to keep the saliva flowing. It wouldn't do to bite with dry mouth and not get venom all over its target.

Hatzel weighed her options. She might be able to get the branch to fall on its head. It seemed pretty limber for a lizard, however. Maybe she could tire it out. Or convince it to go elsewhere. The body of its dead offspring sat unmoving across the glen.

No, probably not.

She heard a *crack* and worried it might be her branch. Then she looked down and saw the monitor turning to look behind itself. Off in the distance, on his boulder, was Cherine, throwing rocks. The first one had skipped off the rocky ground near it. The second hit its flank. It hissed and turned around, crawling towards him.

Hatzel jumped off the branch, and this time, the *crack* was the sound of the branch giving way and crashing to the ground. Caught between a rock to the face and the sound of a branch crashing to the earth, the monitor was a moment too slow to move out of the way.

She landed on its back and bit down on its neck as hard as she could. It thrashed around, managing to catch her once or twice with its tail, but the jagged nature of her beak helped her hold on.

It stopped moving.

"So...is that dinner?" Cherine rasped.

AT SOME POINT during the scuffle, the monitor with the tendency to flee had circled around and absconded with the body of its sibling. That left Hatzel and Cherine to split the large one. She felt as hungry as he looked, but when she opened her mouth, her beak refused to close on the meat.

Some diseases, once survived, gave the survivor a defense against them in the future. Others worked like wasp stings, deadlier with each recurrence. Even having pulled Cherine from the river and killed two monitors, she couldn't make herself eat the lizard.

"Did you know that monitors aren't actually venomous, they just have really bad germs in their mouths?" he said between mouthfuls. He had mistaken the reason for her hesitation.

She motioned towards the mother's severed head with her beak. "You can clearly see the venom sacs."

"What? Oh, yeah, I guess." He seemed disappointed to have been proven wrong so quickly. The fact that he was well enough to show disappointment was heartening.

"Wait, so is this poisonous?" he asked. He didn't stop eating but looked alarmed.

"No, it's just...the prides were hit hard by the monitor plague," she explained. "Among all the local prides, I was one of three gryphlets who survived that hatch year."

He nodded. "That's when the university began its own research. I lost a brother. While the Reeve's Hunting Grounds claim they're for turkeys, the few remaining birds attract monitors that're killed and processed for food. I actually got my start working at the butchery. Headmaster Neider, then just a scholar, came and taught us to cook and salt meat to keep it safe to eat. The next year, on a scholarship he arranged, I joined the university. That's how I got assigned to the grasslands."

"You're a food scholar, then?" she asked.

Cherine perked up. "Yes, that's right."

"So, you were looking for new foods in the weald when you were caught and held prisoner? What did you do, steal some eggfruit from Merin's hunting grounds?" Just mentioning eggfruit made her stomach growl. Eggfruit trees grew wherever light slipped past the redwood canopy. Its name came from its size and shape, which resembled that of goliath bird eggs.

"Oh, didn't Triddle tell you?" he asked.

Hatzel rolled her eyes. Triddle had not been forthcoming on details. "He just said he needed help."

"I'm surprised you were willing to risk betraying Merin," Cherine commented.

Her hackles rose. "I am not one of his pride."

He looked closely at her for the first time, noting how the shape of her beak formed two saber-like fangs. "You're muscular in the same way. Actually, I think you're bigger than he is. I just assumed you were related. Who did you say you were again?"

"Hatzel."

He took a moment and seemed to be reading through a mental guide of the weald. "Oh! I'm so sorry. You own the tiny strip of forest south of the Snowfeather Mountains, between the taiga and the grasslands."

She used the same tone she normally saved for scolding gryphlets. "No one *owns* the weald. But yes, the section with the best ground parrots and access to clean water."

He held up his open talons in the way opinici did to show they were unarmed, not realizing it meant the opposite to sharp-clawed gryphons. "I didn't mean to offend."

"You are terrible at being rescued," she grumbled. "Of course, *I* end up with the rude opi. I bet Zeph is having more fun with Kia."

"Kia!" Cherine said. "Is she okay? Did she come looking for me?"

Hatzel filled him in on what she knew, the little she'd already told Triddle and Xavi. "So that brings us back around: why were you prisoner?"

Cherine preened at his muddy feathers, realizing for the first time that the tip of his beak was broken. "I've been out here helping raise capybaras." Her eyes showed no recognition to the word capybara, so he continued. "The rodents about twice the size of a gryphon that graze on the grasslands."

"Oh, the herds." She thought of how she'd describe them to another gryphon. "The large, chunky squirrels."

"Yeah, that's about right," he admitted. "We've been importing them to feed the eyrie. It's growing too fast. There's only so much meat you can raise when a city is growing up instead of out. We tried keeping goliath birds like the other eyrie, but that didn't work out."

Hatzel recalled the stampede of goliath birds that crashed through the weald years ago. "So Merin's pride stole the herd squirrels and kidnapped you at the same time? They're behind the massacre at the grasslands?"

"Yes. No. Sort of. So, they did kidnap me and—" he paused. "Wait, what massacre at the grasslands? Are my capybaras okay?"

She chewed on some mint growing from a crack in the boulder to assuage her hunger, careful to avoid the red fern next to it. She needed a clear head. Her grandfather had complained about the squirrels first appearing when he was a fledgling. The prides wouldn't be happy to find out the furry animals wandering the grasslands were just incredibly large squirrels. Gryphons and opinici both liked being the only fuzzy thing for miles. It's why they didn't get along with each other.

"Zeph said he found a lot of blood and no herd," she said at last.

"Did he find my journal? Merin didn't have it. I thought I left it in the grass by the herd." He sighed when she shook her head. "I put it down because I've been watching opinici in ranger harnesses wander into the forest all season long. Most of them are Crackling Sea opinici who showed up to serve Reeve Brevin last year. They've been carrying crates, not easy to do over long distances, and hiding them in the forest along the borders between prides, in the grey areas gryphons avoid. I thought maybe it was related to agriculture, but when I asked the university if they'd share their data with me, the headmaster's assistant said he didn't know what I was talking about. So I went out to find the crates on my own."

Hatzel bristled a bit at the thought of things being hidden in the weald. None of the hunters had mentioned it, but Merin's volatility over borders meant both of their prides gave each other a wide berth, creating a no-gryphon-zone around each hunting ground. The large monitor had likely been nesting in the same safe area the rangers were using.

"What did you find?" she asked.

"I opened one up," he replied, "and I think it's saltpeter."

She shrugged at him. First capybara, then saltpeter. Like all opinici, he was full of words she'd never heard.

"One of the scholars, Felicio, found it while searching for new caves," Cherine explained. "If you add a small amount of heat to it, it explodes."

"I don't get it," she said.

He shrugged helplessly. "I don't, exactly, either. But I think you could use it to start and spread several fires at once in the forest. I had a flint and tinder I use sometimes while watching the herds. I wanted to be sure, so I took some of the powder and, well, it's saltpeter all right."

He held up a talon that was scorched black.

"We need to get you to a medicine gryphon." She just remembered why they'd come out this way instead of going back to the nesting grounds, other than the fact that she didn't want Merin to find his prisoner there. She hoped Xavi had taken charge in her absence. He was smart enough to deflect questions if someone came looking for her.

"No. I mean yes," he corrected, "but I need you to know

that I didn't know what was going on. I still don't know for sure. But Merin's gryphons were watching me. When they saw what happened, they took me prisoner. They didn't know that I was just then finding the crates. They thought I was with the rangers."

9

OLD MEDICINE GRYPHON

The redwood trees finally gave way to the rocky path leading up to a set of caverns that had once housed the gryphlets dying of monitor plague. Hatzel had made friends with one of the two other survivors, a taiga gryphlet who'd lived atop the mountains that separated the eyrie and weald from the bog.

Seeing them grow to be so close, their prides had hoped that they'd pass along the gene that gave them resistance against disease. With his beautiful white plumage and black spots, she'd been more than happy to try, but it looked like the disease had left them both sterile.

The thought of bringing Cherine to a place that meant only sickness and death to her was upsetting, but she knew the entire cavern had been scoured with fire, and it'd been, well, nearly her lifetime since the last outbreak.

She paused her climb and listened. The opinicus was still breathing, but no longer awake.

She pressed on. Her unfed body threatened to give out with Cherine slumped atop her, but they made it to the caves where the medicine gryphons lived. As she dropped him at the cave mouth, a familiar voice greeted her from above.

"You two make a cute couple," Zeph teased.

"Skulking about?" Hatzel asked her pridemate. "Did you track the missing capybaras here? Or did you get that poor, helpless opi girl hurt?"

He bristled. "I don't know about any capybaras, but I got tired of eyrie hospitality. Especially the food. So much salt."

She preened some of the salt off his face. Blood speckled his fur.

"Are you injured?" she asked.

"No, I'm fine. Tired." He noticed her shaking. "What about you?"

"I just need something to eat and a chance to rest," she replied. "There was only monitor meat, so I let him have it. He's in worse shape than either of us."

Zeph lowered himself in front of her, and she slid Cherine onto his back. Cherine was larger than some of the songbird opinici, but compared to even a small gryphon like Zeph, he lacked the weight of muscle. Cherine's golden wings wilted down Zeph's sides, hiding the gryphon from her view.

"You go rest," Zeph suggested. "I'll bring you something tasty after he's settled. Oof, did you have to feed him? What did he eat, the entire monitor?"

Hatzel flicked a pebble at Zeph to stop his complaining.

As they passed the arches and entered the cavern, the sounds of an opinicus crying out came from farther down the cave.

"Kia?" Cherine awoke and tried to stand up.

"Oh, parrot scat," Zeph said. "He weighs more when he's awake. Who *is* he?"

"He's our missing opinicus." Hatzel shook her head

when Zeph started to open his beak. "I'll explain later. Let's get him inside before we attract the wrong sorts of attention."

ZEPH RAN AFTER CHERINE, who slipped off the gryphon's back practically fell into the room.

"Kia, are you—Oh. Who are you?" Cherine asked.

Orlea looked up, but she seemed more concerned with the gryphons working on her wings than with the strange new opinicus. If he'd been wearing a harness instead of mud, Zeph might have been concerned he was from the Reeve's Guard or rangers.

"Or...lea," she managed between gasps.

One elderly gryphon, her eyes unfocused, monitored three younger apprentices who worked on Orlea's wings. Like most medicine gryphons, she'd come from the Feather-mane Pride. Her eponymous mane of feathers dragged along the ground when she walked.

"Please wait over there." Her voice was honey on bark. "Hatzel, Zeph, if you would get her clean?"

"I'm a him," Cherine protested.

"It's tough to tell with opinici," the medicine gryphon said.

"It's really not," he began, but Zeph and Hatzel moved him to a raised stone across the room. The cave was lit by a fire tended by an apprentice. The small gryphon, still a fledgling, was covered in a greasy mixture to keep from catching fire himself.

"Why does a healer live so far from the nests?" Cherine asked Zeph.

"She doesn't like gryphons stopping in with their

hunting wounds," Zeph speculated before going off to the larder in the corner to find food. There were some parrots in the corner wrapped in leaves, preserved by their own fat and marked with feathers to identify the meat.

Cherine looked confused.

"Ever since her eyes started to go, she prefers to train rather than treat," Hatzel added.

Zeph returned with a parrot. Hatzel managed a few bites before joining Zeph in his attempts to clean the mud from Cherine's feathers. Cherine looked embarrassed to be preened by two gryphons. He was ticklish and kept fidgeting, forcing Hatzel to use one of her giant paws to hold him down while Zeph did the hard work.

"Who is Orlea?" Hatzel took another bite of the preserved parrot, but made a face that suggested all she tasted was the mud she'd preened from Cherine.

"And what happened to Kia?" Cherine added.

"When we arrived at the eyrie, Kia went off with Reeve Brevin. I was given lodging, but there was some kind of anti-gryphon mob outside, so I ducked out early and came back. I found Orlea in a ranger's trap. Her wing was broken, so I brought her here. I don't know what happened to Kia after we parted."

Cherine tried to click his beak, realizing again that the tip had been broken.

Hatzel gave Zeph a look, but Zeph shook his head. Not in front of the opinicus.

"You're looking pretty clean," Zeph said. "Let's go find some drinking water and food for you."

"Oh, we had monitor," Cherine mumbled. His energy seemed to be linked to his chances of seeing Kia. "It was good, if unseasoned. Did you know that mountain monitors have venom sacs? Water would be nice."

Zeph motioned for Hatzel to follow him. As they left, he could hear Cherine saying "Do you know you're covered in grease?" to the fire keeper.

"I can see why Triddle and him got along so well," Hatzel muttered.

OUTSIDE THE CAVE, Hatzel spoke first before Zeph could open his beak. "I think they're going to blow up the weald."

Zeph blinked. "What?"

Hatzel's ears went back. "Cherine was tracking several opinici. He said he saw dozens of teams take crates into the forest. They have this saltpeter stuff in them that explodes."

"Salt...peter?" Zeph asked. "The crates I found smelled salty and like bat guano. They were bringing more crates through the eyrie. Oh! The eyrie. Look, things are not good there. They're producing tons of food, but it isn't getting to the poorer opinici."

Hatzel tilted her head to the side.

"I saw starving chicks fighting over squirrel meat," he continued. "Orlea hadn't eaten in days, and the rangers were going to kill her for poaching. Kia tried to warn me about something, but I don't know what. Then I found tons of opinici who think that we're stealing their food. There's talk of expanding the grasslands. I thought that they might try to push into the weald a bit more, but what if they plan on burning down the forest?"

Zeph socialized with other prides and the eyrie more often than any other gryphon Hatzel knew, but he'd always taken a paws-off approach to the squabbles about hunting grounds. She suspected it was because he hadn't been born in the weald. Until his mother's passing, he'd gone to visit her every summer in the taiga. Afterwards, he'd redoubled his hunting efforts but still hadn't concerned himself with who was in charge or where their decisions were taking him. That was why Xavi served as Hatzel's second-in-command and not Zeph. Zeph was capable but feared interfering with the lives of others.

"They could wait until we left for the winter. We'd come home to nothing," she said. The harsh winters had forced them to use caves along the weald's edge or risk freezing. Some prides had cave systems in the forest. She wasn't sure how they'd fare if the entire forest burned. She found herself thinking of all the underbrush that should have burned away before now. The redwood forest thrived on small fires, but with a wildfire large enough, she wasn't sure anything living in the forest would survive except for the trees.

Zeph shook his head. "I don't think they plan to wait that long. I think they want to burn the forests down with all of us in them. When I talked with an opi from the Crackling Sea Eyrie—long story, it's across the taiga somewhere—he let slip there are no gryphons where he's from anymore. What if they killed them? When was the last time we talked with the prides outside the weald?"

It took her a few moments to remember. "We talked with your kin," he bristled but hopefully knew she'd meant ex-kin, "not long ago. Last year, I think. Maybe two years. Xavi spotted one of their scouts patrolling the skies along the taiga's edge, but whoever it was didn't come near enough to say hello. Otherwise, I haven't seen anyone from the kjarr pride since I was a fledgling. Even then, it was several bog refugees who decided they'd rather be fisherfolk. I can't even tell you what prides exist past the bog. We have a lot of room to spread out here in the weald. We've never needed to travel. Really, if it weren't for the sickness, I don't think we'd even know there were non-weald gryphon prides out there."

"Maybe there aren't anymore." He moved his head back and forth, his ears plastered straight back. "We need to tell the other prides. There's still time to find the saltpeter and move it before it's too late."

She frowned. "It might be tough to convince them without proof. We can't use Cherine, Merin was holding him prisoner and thinks he was the opinicus planting the crates. One of Merin's pride saw Cherine lighting some of the saltpeter to see what it was."

ORLEA FIDGETED. The strange gryphon-doctor and most of her entourage had moved on to help the new opinicus patient, leaving Orlea with a single sleeping gryphon watching over her. The gryphon, poor dear, had a blue face with black bars and then yellow haunches with black spots. With coloring like that, it was no wonder she'd turned to healing instead of hunting. She was fit only for hunting a blueberry bush at sunset. She looked like one of the sillier songbird-opinici had mated with one of the gryphons that came with the Crackling Sea Eyrie delegation. Her face had a constant surprised look that slumber did not erase.

Even now, Orlea found herself wondering what the mismatched apprentice was dreaming of. Perhaps the sun setting over a field of blueberries.

Orlea knew her grumpiness wasn't because of her wing sprain. Once treated, she'd been told it would heal quickly and without permanent damage. No, it was because she'd never been around so many gryphons before. In her wealthier days, before the forests of the eyrie stopped being public hunting lands and became the reeve's lands, she'd seen one or two fisherfolk gryphons come to market to sell salt or fish.

With her current state of affairs, she'd gotten to know some of the refugees at the bottom level. She'd even made some beads helping watch their fledglings when they reached the age where they started to try to fly. Everyone in the lower levels was hungry, but the fledglings' insatiable curiosity was endearing. It was better than dealing with opinicus chicks, who took their cues from their elders and treated her like part of the lower class.

She stretched her good wing and flapped it slowly.

"Careful there," came the voice of Hatzel from behind her.

Orlea tensed in surprise, then in pain.

"Sorry, I didn't mean to startle you." Hatzel frowned.

Orlea rubbed her wing joint. "I'm not used to being around so many of you."

"Oh, there's only one of me," Hatzel said. "You can't throw a rock without hitting ten Zephs, however."

Zeph looked up from where he'd been napping along the edge of the room. "I don't think you could hit one Zeph with a rock."

"Just let me find a rock." Hatzel flicked a tiny pebble, perhaps an acorn, at him. He gasped and pretended as though he were dodging a boulder, flattening himself against the ground.

"You must be glad to have him back," Orlea said. The medicine the apprentice had given her was finally starting to take hold. "Did he escape from the army? You're lucky he made it out before they cut off his wings."

Hatzel and Zeph looked at each other in alarm.

"Before they did what now?" he asked.

10

KIA

After being separated from Zeph, Kia was questioned for an hour by Brevin. The reeve was polite, making a show of her relief that Kia had made it home safe. Brevin's long neck meant that her beak was always hovering above the apprentice's eye line.

Kia found herself staring at seven delicate chain necklaces of varying sizes that cascaded down the reeve's neck to her chest. They caught the fire like starlight on a field of green feathers. Each necklace clasped in the front with two serpents intertwining. She'd never seen such delicate metal work before. She wondered if anyone at the eyrie had the skill to make something so small, so detailed.

"Kia?" Brevin prompted.

Kia looked up. She'd been lost in the swaying of Brevin's neck. "Yes, sorry. It's been a long day. I seem to have dozed off for a moment. Please forgive me. You were asking about the gryphon?"

At Brevin's nod, Kia explained that Zeph had been assigned to her by the pride and turned over her field note-book. The reeve seemed unsurprised by the gryphon territorial glyphs but commended Kia on her attention to detail.

Behind the reeve stood the commander of the eyrie forces. With just the two of them, he looked like her bodyguard. Kia tried but couldn't remember his name. He looked like he wanted to ask her some questions, but the reeve put a jewelry-adorned talon on his shoulder and then told Kia to go home and get some rest.

Kia was grateful for the dismissal. When she exited into the brisk, moon-bathed night, she perked up. A cool breeze pulled smoke past her nares. The brazier light danced against the spires, illuminating some while others fell into the night. The flighty shadows of moths chased each other along the walls.

A gryphon with black ears and a circle of yellow feathers on her head passed Kia, heading inside. The stranger bowed slightly as she passed. She wore a harness with a pink fish on it.

For a moment, despite the wrong plumage and build, Kia thought the female gryphon might have been Zeph. She'd meant to find him, but the hour was late, and she didn't know where they'd have sent him. To live with a refugee family? To stay in the diplomat's quarters? She finally gave up and headed back to the university.

The guards stationed at the border of the Reeve's Nest building and the university grounds were stopping and questioning anyone out this late. Ahead of Kia was a cockatiel opinicus hopping from side to side. He was black, maybe midnight blue, with a little red stripe under his bloodshot eyes.

A red-leafed fern, once limited to a fairly secluded valley along the mountain pass to the Crackling Sea, had become popular for opinici to grow in the shaded sections of the eyrie once its mind-soothing qualities became known. In small doses, it calmed the nerves and served as a contraceptive. In larger doses, hallucinations and paranoia were common. It was too valuable to forbid outright, but it was still a good idea not to get caught in possession of it while out and about.

The cockatiel's beak was starting to chatter. He slipped his harness off and shoved it behind a decorative plant. When the guards were busy questioning another opinicus, he tried to slip out of the line and back the way he'd come. His back feet stepped on Kia's feathered tail, and she squawked.

Several guards turned and chased after him. She watched him dive straight down into the deeps of the eyrie at break-neck speed and prayed he wasn't too wobbly to dodge the branches and herb-drying lines on the way down.

By the time Kia arrived at the front of the line, they saw her university-issued, many-pocketed harness and sent her on her way.

KIA WAS FLYING up to her small nest when she passed by an open door. Under other circumstances, she'd have ignored it. Some opinici preferred a cold nest even this high, and others were up late studying and wanted to let in the moonlight.

Braziers were available in the common areas on campus for late-night studying, but candles in the housing nests were prohibited. Fire provided a great boon for working late, but until the spires were rebuilt with nonflammable materials, a project whose funding had dried up, candles were out of the question.

Two things caused her curiosity and concern to overcome her fear. The door seemed to be hanging at an unusual angle, and it was Cherine's home. There was enough light from the moon to let her see inside, so she pushed her way in to look around.

Cherine had always been a bit of a magpie, figuratively speaking. She'd seen his parents' place once, and it was the cleanest nest she'd ever set foot in. Whatever quality caused them to clean every day had not been passed down to their youngest son.

Youngest living son, she corrected herself. On one bookshelf were several feathers that had once belonged to his little brother nestled between a goliath bird egg re-creation and several pouches of grass seed.

The only way to know for certain that something had been taken in Cherine's nest would be if the place had been emptied out. IIe took his work home with him and treated his hobbies like they were a second job. One rounded wall was filled with books, a quality he had inherited from his mother instead of her cleanliness, as her own spotless nest housed a fancy bookcase with thick volumes that weighed more than an opinicus chick.

The scribes often worked at a major library, and for a fee, they would make a copy of a book. The fee was large, but the university offered researchers a stipend for any books related to their work. With this many books, Kia thought he was probably keeping at least one scribe flush with beads.

She looked for any familiar titles, *A Treatise on Feather Dynamics* or perhaps the ever popular *What Does Your Plumage Say About Your Personality*, but didn't see either. Taking a book to the door and holding it under the moonlight revealed that these were all ones he'd written himself based on the observations in his field notebooks.

They seemed fairly tame—this one was on the ratio of grass consumption to manure production in capybaras—though the gaps in the shelves suggested that many of them were missing. Maybe the library had them and was making copies of the more interesting tomes for use by other researchers, or perhaps he'd taken them with him to the grasslands for reference.

They were so heavy, he'd have had to bring one or two with him at a time. These all used the older vellum and weighed a good bit. As she'd once heard Cherine's mother say, it was the kind of book you could have killed a lace monitor with if you had to.

A dozen vials of ink looked undisturbed on a short, makeshift desk. Several feathers, converted to quill pens, were resting upright in a cup. Only two looked like they'd been his, the other four didn't match his golden eagle hues. One green and blue feather looked suspiciously like it'd come from her own plumage. She blushed and left the house, doing her best to wrestle the door closed.

Kia's own domicile was two stories higher. Having a high-altitude home meant that there was no one above her. She opened the roof and let the moonlight settle in before unhooking her harness and letting it fall to the floor. She started to head to her sleeping nest but remembered she had a few questions she didn't want to forget for tomorrow. She reached into her harness for her field notebook and, just as she remembered she'd given it to Reeve Brevin, she pulled out Cherine's bloodstained book from the grasslands.

Sleep was going to have to wait.

11

HEADMASTER NEIDER

Daylight came early with the open roof. Kia left at once for the university. The headmaster—an opinicus who embodied his title so well that his hatching name, Neider, was nearly lost to history itself—had sent Cherine to the grasslands to do research and had sent Kia after him. She wanted to know how much he knew about what Cherine was up to. Neider had university staff more skilled than her, more trusted, but she'd been sent instead. She'd assumed it was because no one was more invested in Cherine's well-being than she was, but was that why?

The sun warmed her wings even as the early morning winds chilled her face. She shared the skies with two young opinici—siblings, judging by their matching upturned scythe-beaks and similar build. Housing formed a rim around the classroom buildings, which were several stories shorter than the surrounding area, giving her a nesting feeling when she traveled this route.

The university grounds did, in fact, resemble the ground. The tops of buildings were covered with a small layer of soil and seeded with variants of the same grass they used to feed the herds on the grasslands. What started from the necessity of science had become an aesthetic choice. The scythe-beak siblings joined several apprentices who were already fully awake and going through different sections of the grass, picking weeds and recording their type and frequency in their notebooks.

The imported capybaras found several native berries and flowers poisonous, so efforts were underway to determine which types of grass encouraged which types of weeds to help keep their herd rodents safe. As far as Kia knew, there was no discernible difference in weed frequency, and this was all a plot hatched at the highest levels to get the apprentices to keep the grounds looking nice.

They were used to seeing her come and drop by with breakfast, so they perked up when someone noticed her bright colors. She was embarrassed that she'd forgotten and promised to bring something by for them tomorrow. They accepted her apology graciously, and she continued on her way to see the headmaster.

She ran a talon along the chimes outside his office. The heavy, water-proof curtains—imported from the Crackling Sea—parted, and a brown owl's face stared out at her. She'd heard he was in his office before daybreak, but from the blinking of his eyes, she suspected he was either still awake or newly awake.

"I'm quite busy this morning." he hooted. "Could you come back later... What was your name again, apprentice?"

His forgetful owl act was just that: an act. She was certain he could name every opinicus in the university from memory. After spending weeks on assignment at the Crackling Sea Eyrie to trade saltpeter for seeds and capybaras, he hadn't missed a beat when he returned. His mind was as sharp as a ranger's trap.

His assignment had been necessary because the initial attempts to domesticate the goliath birds for use on the grasslands had only created a feral goliath herd that rejoined their fuzzy kin in the mountains. Capybaras were supposedly easier to care for.

In lieu of words, she unlatched a pocket on her harness and pulled out Cherine's bloodstained journal. Headmaster Neider squinted but seemed to recognize the handwriting.

"Ah," he said. "Come in."

The headmaster's room was as ceremonial and decorative as it was functional. It contained paintings and plumage of past headmasters and notable graduates. While an apprentice's good standing outside the university was linked to the master whose tutelage they had endured—and often depended upon their master's reputation remaining intact —the university's multiple-teacher system had allowed its graduates to remain inoculated from the transgressions of any one master.

It even seemed to thrive upon a certain level of scandal, as the paintings attested to. Felicio, nicknamed *The Phoenix,* had pioneered techniques that were used today for heating and luminescence. His nickname was appropriate for a life full of near-hits and at least one accidental self-immolation. His death, most likely but not definitively accidental, had come heralding experimentation in saltpeter. His son, Bario, had taken over the work and still had a scorched section of wall with the blast shadow of his father hanging in the flameworks outside of town.

Other paintings included Impir the Mad, the blue peafowl opinicus whose research continued from jail. Mally the Nighthaunt, who had fled the city with a dozen eggs but left behind excellent research in the form of the *Nachlass Mal* still used today, and even a single gryphon who had helped set up the university. The gryphon painting's picture frame was unusually high at the bottom, covering his paws to protect the delicate sensibilities of modern opinicus scholars.

She looked from the gryphon painting to the headmaster's owl foretalons, which had been left shaggy. Most owl-taloned opinici trimmed back their fur-like feathers to keep them from being mistaken for forepaws. The headmaster was lazy, obstinate, or perhaps just recognizable enough on his own that he felt no need for such shearing.

The books along the walls were beautiful and practical, just not for reference. *Opinici Lacuna: Lexical Gaps in Native Eyrie Populations Volume IV* was a dense book that no one ever referred back to. What the eyrie really needed was a term for research so esoteric that even the university shied away from it. The books, heavy curtains, and thick walls provided a barrier against the incredible auditory senses some opinici possessed.

"I had a letter from the reeve this morning. It didn't mention Cherine's notebook." The headmaster's words floated on the air like bees. Whether he was discussing the most horrific plague or a beautiful flower, his words remained weightless.

Kia considered asking him about the gryphon she'd seen outside the reeve's building but decided not to muddy the water on tangents. "I didn't know I had it until I got home. Look, here. He was doing math on the herds and how many opinici he could feed with them. He determined that we're already producing far more food than we need to consume here in the eyrie. Is this right?"

The headmaster recoiled a little from the blood on the

journal but pulled it over to him and glanced over the figures. "His math is correct. He just fails to see the scope that the future holds."

Neider walked to the wall and pulled back one tapestry to reveal a map of the valley and surrounding areas.

"Are we expecting a rise in chicks?" she asked. Their eyrie was small on the map. The area between the coast and the mountains, the weald and the fishing villages, was small enough that she could cover them all with both forelegs. The tapestry must have been at least a decade old because the grasslands were still forest, and the weald ran unchecked from ocean to eyrie.

"Most of our food is sent to the Crackling Sea Eyrie. Jonas is here to serve as trade ambassador. In return, they keep watch on the mountain pass." Neider traced a talon from the forest eyrie through the mountain pass to the Crackling Sea in the northwest.

"Did something happen to their fish?" she asked. "Why does the pass need watching?"

"Another eyrie attacked." He touched a claw on several other eyries marked in the north and west. She couldn't name half of them, didn't know if they'd interacted with any of them in her lifetime. The mountains allowed for isolation. The single goliath bird pass permitted the Crackling Sea Eyrie, which traded with the other eyries, to then transport any notable goods on to the Redwood Valley Eyrie with significant mark up. One eyrie far north had a recent circle scratched around it. It drew her eyes.

"No, we're not sure which one. The markings on their harnesses aren't ones we've seen before. The Crackling Sea opinici managed to fight them back." His claws lingered on the blue water, the inland sea that gave the eyrie its name. "Feeding on the bodies of so many opinici turned the wildlife of the Crackling Sea into something different. Something violent."

Strange as it was, the logistics of running an eyrie fascinated Kia. "It's not all fish, surely. There are a lot of fruits grown up in the cold climate, aren't there?"

"The eyrie was only the first attack," Neider continued. "While the opinici fought in the skies, the local gryphons slipped in low. At first, they contented themselves with stealing fruit and crops. After some were caught and strung up, the next time the opinici were busy with the invaders, the gryphons came in and salted the farm lands. Most of their fields will no longer grow crops."

Kia's beak was open and dry. She'd never heard of such a thing.

"We sent what help we could, but we had to keep our own eyrie safe." He paced while he talked. "We raised a new army of sorts, sent food, and helped some refugees set up a small fishing village on the far side of the sea. We even quelled most of the gryphon uprising. A few attempted to escape and reunite deep in the peat bog. I don't know if they made it or if the rangers caught up with them. There are still small attacks, but that could be the taiga pride. They enjoy the benefit of being able to disappear back into the mountains."

"Did Cherine know about this? Is this why he was taken?" Kia asked.

"Oh, no, dear. I would never have let something happen to him. I'm not sure what's going on there. But I do worry that his curiosity led him to some unfortunate places." The headmaster placed his talons on the map and sighed. "There's more, but I don't have the heart to tell you myself. It's probably safer now if you know, but first we need to turn Cherine's journal over to the Reeve's Guard. I'll make sure it doesn't contain anything that will hurt Cherine when we find him."

"Won't they notice if pages are missing?" she asked.

Neider walked to a window and opened the thick curtains, filling the room with sunlight. He plucked at a loud chime. The sound was like the resonate buzzing of a monstrous insect. "No, I suspect not. I have someone who specializes in this sort of thing. In your own field notebook, what did you say about Cherine's?"

"Nothing. Just that I found it. Oh, and it had blood on it," she said.

The headmaster nodded and selected a book from his desk with the same color binding as Cherine's journal. "Come back and meet me here tonight. I'll have a book for you to turn in to the Reeve's Guard. Then I think it's important you see something." The lightness of his words belied the weight she felt at hearing them.

As she left, she saw the same black cockatiel opinicus making his way to the headmaster's office. A rainbow of ink stains decorated his harness. He looked different wearing it, no longer naked like a wild gryphon, and the fact that he was here now suggested that the guards never caught up with him last night, and he'd been able to retrieve it from its hiding place.

Kia had no shame about going without her harness, but she would never be able to function without the associated pockets.

12

REEVE'S NEST

Reeve's Nest served as the capitol building for the Redwood Valley Eyrie. Despite the name, it was closer to a throne room and meeting hall. Kia didn't know if it contained a place for Reeve Brevin to sleep but suspected the reeve kept off-site housing in the reaches of the northern quarter with the other wealthy opinici.

Long strips of metal framed the building, showing off the opulence of the eyrie from the outside and catching the light. It was easy to spot during the day: it was the only building she couldn't look directly at. Now, at night, it was softer on the eyes. The headmaster nodded to the guards but stopped just inside the entryway once they were alone to have a word with her.

"It's safer if they think you already know everything you're about to hear." His owl-like face and droopy feathers hid his emotions well. He was less groomed than she remembered. She wondered if this was a symptom of his time at the Crackling Sea Eyrie or a recent development related to Cherine's disappearance.

"About the book or the Crackling Sea Eyrie coming

under attack?" She held a new journal with the same shape, nearly identical handwriting, and comparable blood stain to the original. The cockatiel, as relayed by the headmaster, said the blood was unlikely to have come from Cherine. Matching the hue of opinicus blood was easy, he claimed, so it probably came from one of the herd.

The forger was good at his job. The ink seemed to grow fresher, more vibrant as she paged through from old entries to new ones. Her closeness to Cherine caused a nagging sensation that the words weren't his, but she couldn't point to any example of what was incorrect. Also missing were his figures and calculations about how much food they were producing versus how much the Redwood Valley Eyrie actually needed.

Neider waited for a Reeve's Guard to pass them by. "About everything. Brevin believes it's better with the growing unrest if we wait to release information about the Crackling Sea Eyrie attack and our aid until the food crisis dies down and we have some idea of who attacked them. I'll imply that you were one of the scholars who helped with the initial herd analysis, though not one of the ones who underestimated how hard it would be to keep goliath birds. Those poor fools are manning a way station on the goliath bird pass for the foreseeable future.

"Where was I? Yes, right, if we leave the reeve's perceptions of you to chance, she may assume you're working with that gryphon you brought back. Better to let this fall on Jonas. They need him and will grant him some leeway. Whatever you hear at the meeting, say nothing. Stay by my side and don't draw attention to yourself. What you're about to hear will be uncomfortable."

More uncomfortable than what you've already told me? Kia wondered, but she nodded and followed him through the foyer and into the massive, tall-ceilinged meeting room. Tapestries of past reeves lined the walls. Most prominent was a weaving of Brevin's grandfather, an emerald-plumed peacock of an opinicus standing over the corpse of a large serpent. The snake was symbolic, of course, but Kia wondered if Zeph would even bother to mention having had to kill a snake.

Neider motioned to her, and they settled into the meeting room. She sat well behind the headmaster and kept her beak shut. The meeting was already in session.

"Why chance burning down the entire vale?" a burly opinicus asked. He'd been by the reeve when Kia had been questioned. His harness had faded to a light blue and was decorated only with his military rank. The longest talon on his right foreleg had a metal covering which he tapped on the floor to reinforce his words. She'd seen this before on veterans and hunters who lost the end of a digit. Few refused the prosthetic, only those who wanted to make a point about the weight of their sacrifice to the eyrie. "Why not use the wingtorn to hunt them down? We run the risk of the fire spreading out of control."

"What risk?" Jonas asked, his words as slippery and charged as the jellies of the Crackling Sea. "We have more than enough of the fire suppressant powder stored in the grasslands to keep the flames from reaching the eyrie."

"And we don't know how many gryphons there are," Reeve Brevin countered. "As long as the untamed weald extends to the coast, it will harbor them. We're going to have to clear most of it anyway. This is just... expediency."

"We can't risk leaving the Crackling Sea Eyrie undefended even for a moment, and I don't think we can trust the wingtorn with this. I'm not sure they've been properly incentivized to clear out entire families." Jonas kept his head lowered as he spoke. His spoonbill nearly touched the cushions he set on, possibly a sign of contrition after Zeph's escape.

The guards in the hallway were still gossiping about it. He didn't look like he'd been disciplined—he wasn't part of this eyrie, after all—but he must be worried that word would travel back to the Crackling Sea about his misfortune. Kia wondered what rank he held at the Crackling Sea Eyrie. Most interesting was the medallion on his harness: the same fish from the reeve's mystery gryphon visitor the night before.

What's the connection? Kia wondered.

"They've certainly given up a lot not to feel incentivized. Surely the squeamish ones didn't make it this far." The burly one tapped his metal talon on the ground.

Kia leaned forward to try to get a better look at him in case it jogged her memory, but the headmaster pushed her back with a back paw. She was to be seen but not to draw attention to herself. He wrote the name *Commander Wolden* on a piece of paper and pointed to it. She nodded.

"They sacrificed so their children could have a better life." Brevin glanced at a green peafowl listening from the doorway, possibly one of her own offspring. "They may feel differently when they see that we're not offering their weald kin the same...kindness."

Jonas shrugged. "I won't claim some aren't having second thoughts. Losing your wings is a traumatic experience. Most are adjusting well to it. Having Jun in charge makes things easier. The gryphons here are used to obeying him. The others we left back home."

"Surely there's nothing we can do about that now," said Wolden.

"No," Jonas said, "but anger makes everyone do strange

things. It's better if you use their anger against opinici instead of other gryphons. At least until the new batch has settled in. Once their children can fly and integrate into eyrie culture, they'll be easier to control."

He seemed to have more experience with the wingtorn than any of this eyrie's opinici. Kia wondered how often he'd done this. She'd heard rumors that in past disputes some gryphons had agreed to join the eyrie at the cost of their wings. In return, they and their children became full citizens. The children's wings weren't clipped. She'd never seen the wingtorn herself, probably because the university was so high. She wouldn't want to risk the upper tiers of the eyrie without flight, either.

"Then we dispatch the wingtorn to the fishing villages." Brevin's voice was tinged with an agitation. "Once the coast is secure, we light the fires. They can clean up any gryphons who don't burn."

"Some of them will escape into the mountains instead of heading to the coast," the headmaster said. "The taiga has always been a safe haven for dissidents."

Hearing her mentor talk of genocide the way he spoke of plants or logistics made Kia uncomfortable.

"Go back to academia if you want a perfect plan," Wolden scolded. "This is our best, most effective option for securing the valley. We cannot afford to be fighting a civil war if another eyrie makes a move. The weald has remained wild for too many years. I can deal with a small insurgency in the mountains." He eschewed his metal tapping to stand this time. "I cannot defend the eyrie if an unknown army of ribald masses waits to rise up the moment we're under siege. That is the situation we're dealing with, imminent invasion. If you want to keep your own wings attached to your body, I suggest you live in reality."

"There have never been any reports of wingtorn opinici," the headmaster looked for assurances.

Jonas spoke softly. "It does happen sometimes."

A shiver rose in Kia. She remained quiet for the rest of the meeting, mostly talk of supplies going out to the Crackling Sea Eyrie and the troops housed there. Then she slipped out with the headmaster and headed back to her nest. This was time she should have spent looking for Cherine.

13

UNDERBOUGH

When the sun rose the next day, Kia stayed in bed. She'd been through a lot, and the adrenaline that had fueled the previous day had burned out, leaving her empty. The headmaster had flown her home but refused to talk about the meeting without his sound-proof precautions. She couldn't argue with that. Most of the night, she'd been forced to eavesdrop on a nesting dispute two floors down.

The triller of the two was upset with her mate, who had let their chick play too close to the edge. The chick had fallen but was mostly okay—a broken foreleg, a sprain on the other foreleg, but its wings were fine. Instinct had kicked in, and it had flattened itself properly, minimizing the damage from landing. Most adult opinici forgot how to fall from great heights, forgot that chicks are more resilient than their parents give them credit for.

Still, it'd proven impossible to make a case for conspiracy while eavesdropping. Kia had a lot of questions for the headmaster but suspected she wouldn't get more answers than she already had. She had even more questions for the reeve but was already flying too close to the sun there.

She went to the pantry, pushed aside the curtain used to deter flies, and pulled down some of the hanging meat for breakfast. Her father would have been horrified to know she'd slept in this late. She wanted to go search for Cherine, but being seen going to the weald, let alone talking to Zeph, would lead to her getting locked up. The meeting last night had painted him as a spy.

Yet the gryphons seemed unaware that they needed spies. There was a war looming, and they had no idea what was coming for them. Failing to warn the gryphons might be as good as killing them herself, but what did she owe them? She had so many questions, but no one would talk to her. The reeve, the headmaster, the cockatiel, Jonas, surely none of them would help her with Cherine. But there was someone she hadn't talked to, the strange gryphon with the Crackling Sea harness.

Kia finished her meal, switched into her non-university harness, repainted the green markings on her back half so her fur matched her feathers, and headed to the market to find out where the gryphons in the eyrie lived.

THERE WAS some sort of convention at the amphitheater, and the markets were nearly empty. Turquoise chimes and non-currency beads hung from every awning, singing in the breeze. The butchery remained packed as opinici went back and forth from the convention with salted meats. This was not their usual, upper-class clientele, and so the merchants found they had more time to chat with customers than was customary. Kia hoped she'd find information on an upscale gryphon in the upper markets but had prepared herself mentally to go down below if it became necessary.

Her first questions about a gryphon at the market yielded the information she'd wanted two days ago, where Zeph had been. The upscale market sellers all recognized "Zeph Parrotbane" because of his past transactions. When someone, even a gryphon, brings parrots at a reasonable barter, they remember what he looks like.

One of the opinici, a splotchy blue thing with a wistful expression, actually sighed when she spoke his name and kept talking about how the parrot meat was wrapped in leaves, and then feathers were used at the top to show what meat it was. "It adds that rustic touch the plumed elite just love!"

He may not currently be popular with the elite who ate his parrots, but he wasn't lacking in friends among the merchants whose harnesses he lined with beads. It became easier to ask about non-Zeph gryphons. Most of the fisherfolk used the lower markets, but even the more adventurous ones were there strictly to trade. Only their leader, a monster of a crane opinicus with a booming voice named Rorin, used the upper markets. He handled the luxury goods, dealing in ambergris, exotic shells, fine salt, and high-quality items that took merchants a while to offload on the wealthy.

Once the fisherfolk and Zeph were out of the running, there was only one gryphon important enough to get her food from the upper market, meet with reeves, and have a Crackling Sea medallion on her harness.

"Oh, you mean Satra," the splotchy blue opinicus chirped. "She's a bit stuck up when it comes to food. Those Crackling Sea types are uppity—but not important enough for parrot. Still, someone is keeping her happy. She eats better than I do."

Kia made a note of that. "What's she like?"

"Oh, who can tell with gryphons?" The merchant kept her sighs and blushing reserved only for copper hawk weald inhabitants bearing feathered gifts, it seemed. "She holds her beak high. Polite like she's one of us but keeps herself aloof. Comes with an escort most of the time. Usually takes her food with her."

Kia continued asking around and making small purchases. Most of the braziers were extinguished during the day, but a few still smoldered. Cherine's doorway was missing its chimes, so she purchased a set with turquoise interwoven into the design for him.

Asking around, always paired with purchases, led to another merchant admitting he had once delivered meals to Satra down in the depths. Kia paid him and attached packets of green and blue dye to her harness. There were few goods that weren't designed or packaged to be attached to a harness. She wrote down his vague directions, flew as best she could with her new goods to drop them off at her place, then mentally prepared herself to descend into the lower quarters.

KIA GLIDED below the market level, leaving the light behind. The mushroom-like platforms above blocked the sun, creating an artificial dusk as she descended. The vines this far down were brown and sickly instead of vibrant and green.

There was a feral look in the eyes of the people down here. She was grateful that she hadn't worn her university harness. It wasn't the poverty itself that flustered her but by the scope of it. The run-down nests and starving chicks ran more than twenty stories from the lower merchants to the bottom level. She'd never entered the city from below. It hadn't occurred to her that there was so much down here, so many opinici, all hungry.

Had Cherine known? He'd worked at a butchery salting food after the death of his little brother, back before he applied to the university. Is this why he'd kept the journal? She'd seen his estimated eyrie population. It seemed high then but accurate now. They could feed all these opinici if his math was correct but instead chose to send food to the Crackling Sea.

Gravity pulled Kia down, her vibrant form circling a beam of light determined to thrust itself as far as it could before being snuffed out by the shade of civilization. Many of the nests she'd presumed were empty had signs of movement within them. Flies and moths crossed the beam of light uncontested. There were no pigeons below the light to fend them off.

Did they need the light? she wondered. More squirrels than she'd ever seen in one place glided away at her descent. Was it only days since she'd been so excited to see the gliding squirrels in the weald? How could the university exist above while this existed below?

She settled on a branch that seemed public enough to keep her out of trouble and checked her directions. The districts had names and numbers. The level with the shops was marked zero, with higher elevations going up from there. The numbers on the trees here were negative, leaving her with the uneasy feeling that she could descend infinitely to a place without light, a place with only hunger.

Kia shook her head. No, she must be close now. She

closed her journal, put it into a pocket, and then felt the first bite. It was like she'd stepped on a thorn that slipped around the pads of her back paws.

Then it throbbed. When she looked down, she saw a whole line of large, red ants making their way out of the branch and onto her hindquarters. She tried to scrape them off with her talons, then leapt into the air.

The ants just clung on tighter with their venomous little mouths.

She landed at a clearing, finally at ground level, and shook them off as best she could, rubbing her hindquarters against a post. It was only when she was sure the biting had finished that she looked up and saw a startled gryphon in a pink harness trying not to laugh.

"Satra?" Kia managed, still a bit out of breath after the ants.

The gryphon nodded, her golden crest and black-backed ears wobbling a little with the motion. "Would you like to come in?"

THE ENCLOSURE WAS a round dome with an open, woven top and wooden walls that pushed back against the clutter and vegetation on the ground. Kia entered the building and was greeted with a tidal wave of fluff and feathers.

Her eyes took a moment to adjust. The light was dim down here despite the cage-like roof. There were thirty gryphons of varying degrees of youth climbing around the nursery. Most of them had black ears like Satra, suggesting they came from the same pride. Others resembled mocking-birds or shrikes in their plumage. Kia looked to an unlit brazier inlaid into a collection of stones.

"It's not safe to have the fire going with so much feathered down. They're still clumsy at this age." Satra turned to two newly-fledged gryphons. "Would you fetch the ointment?"

The two fledglings returned with a paste. Kia turned her head inquisitively at them.

"I've been here in the underbough long enough to recognize your little dance," Satra said. "Ants, right? Believe me, this will help. The gryphlets get into the ants often enough that I keep a supply within paw's reach."

Kia fought to stay still while a stranger applied ointment to her hindquarters and twenty gryphlets watched on. Her embarrassment was at its zenith, though some relief came from the fact that almost all the gryphlets were looking on with commiseration. It probably made them feel better to see that adults ran afoul of ants, too.

"I like your green fur paint," Satra said. "My sister used to use blue."

Kia was too shy to say more than a polite thank you.

Satra finished up and sent the kids to play at the far end of the enclosure. "I can't imagine you found this place by accident. Did the headmaster send you or was it the reeve? If it's the reeve, tell her I stand by my demands. The gryphlets need better food to develop properly. If it was the headmaster, tell him I don't care about his research. They may be hostages, but I will not let them be lab pigeons. They'll be full members of the Crackling Sea Eyrie soon enough."

Kia tried to sit down but immediately regretted it. Instead, she found a comfortable standing position. Whatever she had thought Satra was, babysitter to the kidnapped was not it.

"It's just me," Kia said. "No one sent me. You had food delivered here once, so I tracked it down."

Satra tilted her head a little, inviting Kia to go on.

"I know a little about what's going on here, about what went on at the Crackling Sea Eyrie. I just don't understand it," Kia confessed.

Satra laughed. It was a scratchy, worn sound. "It's simple enough. This is no bog wisp. They strung up a starving gryphon for taking some berries. We made sure they'd know what starving felt like. They brought in the Redwood Valley opinici to help them attack the kjarr while we were gone. They took the gryphlets and unhatched eggs. Some continued to fight, they died, and their children were killed. The rest agreed to have their wings cut and to fight for the eyries in exchange for their gryphlets remaining unclipped and granted full eyrie membership."

Kia couldn't help but notice Satra's mature plumage. Satra was an adult by any measure and had been for several years at least.

She seemed aware of what came next and spread her wings wide. "Yes, I am no longer a child. My father was good at killing and eating but not so good at having gryphlets. I am his youngest, despite my maturity. My mom and siblings chose to die fighting. The opinici had to make sure my dad would stay in line, so I got to keep my wings."

"Who's your father?" Kia asked.

"My father is Jun the Kjarr," Satra explained, "leader of the kjarr and bog prides, ravager of the Crackling Sea, blight upon the eyrie. He now leads the wingtorn."

"Tell me about the wingtorn." Kia knew she wouldn't like the answers that came next.

By the time she slipped away and back into the light of the sun many hours later, she was sure of several things. The eyrie's depths housed a large, hostile army that would soon march on the fisherfolk. If the kjarr gryphlets, most of whom couldn't fly, could be moved to a secure location, the eyrie would lose control of the wingtorn.

Someone needed to warn the weald prides before they faced a similar fate. To do that would require finding out where all the explosives had been planted. Cherine's field notebook had included a map with circled boxes, the alchemical notation for saltpeter, on it throughout the forest. If she was going to seek out Zeph Parrotbane, she'd need to get the original journal back.

14

THE FORGER

Kia knew of only one opinicus who regularly entered and left the headmaster's study: the black cockatiel with the ink-stained harness. In her own notes, she called him "The Scribe" or "The Forger." Breaking into the headmaster's study could lead to too much trouble, but the cockatiel's quarters should be much more accessible. She leaned upon several of the apprentices, promising them her notes and study assistance if they could track down the location of the black cockatiel.

Thankfully, like most functioning addicts, he would likely chalk up any paranoid feelings to his red fern consumption. She had apprentices following him for days. Despite his bloodshot eyes and disheveled plumage, he still maintained a clean and orderly hovel at the edge of university housing.

Kia would be the first to admit she'd led a sheltered life. She didn't know much about red fern abuse, but she'd heard that addicts could possess super-opinicus strength and speed when confronted. She wished she had Cherine here to ask. He'd at least have an opinion on the matter, even if it turned out to be wrong.

Her best bet, she decided, was to attempt to bribe the cockatiel first. The key to keeping an addict-scribe in your employ, she speculated, was to be the sole supplier of his fern. Since such appetites often grew, she hoped he'd be amiable to a bribe.

She went back to Cherine's home, taking a moment to hang the chimes she'd purchased for him. From their past relations, she knew he had a small supply of the fern in the back of his larder. It only took a small regular dose to keep male opinici infertile. She found the jar with the powdered herb. Its level was the same as last year when they'd broken up, far too little to bribe anyone with.

Standing in his larder while he may be dead, going through his contraceptives, she was overwhelmed by the invasion of privacy. She stumbled outside and flew away in embarrassment.

KIA FLEW AROUND the university district to help clear her head while she came up with a new plan. She had some beads saved up. She could try to find a fern dealer in the underbough who would sell to her. Underbough fern might be less potent than what the forger was used to. Would low quality fern be enough to buy his silence?

Probably not, she conceded.

Below her, the scythe-beak twins were weeding and talking about their lessons. The grass outside the botanical gardens was always under attack from *invasive flora*—the headmaster's term. Wire mesh let water and air through while stopping some of the birds and squirrels of the eyrie but often carried seeds out onto the lawn. Once they sprouted, they were returned to the gardens if they looked valuable or moved to compost if they were just weeds. The occasional red fern would sprout up on the lawn in the shady sections next to the botanical gardens but were returned while they were still small. At least, most of them were. She suspected some of the students sold them or tried to grow them in the forests around the eyrie.

Kia landed next to the twins.

"Hello, Kia!" the male scythe-beak chirped.

"We're just about done here, then we need to get to class. It's just slow going," his sister added.

"It's okay, I'm not here to scold you," Kia reassured them. "I thought I heard the chimes and wanted to make sure you weren't too caught up in your own discussion."

"The chimes!" The sister was surrounded by two piles. One was weeds that needed to be taken to compost and the other, smaller pile, was of precious plants to be brought to the botanical gardens.

"We're going to be late!" The brother looked at all the dirt on his feathers.

Kia pretended to think something over, going so far as to put a talon against her beak. "Well, you two have been so helpful, I suppose I could take care of things here. Just be sure not to track mud into the classroom!"

They both chirped a thank you and flew towards the main building, kicking dirt off their paws as they went and showering several junior apprentices.

Kia looked down at two piles of plants in front of her. She pulled the most gnarled, sun-dried plant she could find from the soon-to-be-compost pile and slipped it into the large pouch on her harness. Then she dug through the pile of valuable plants and pulled out three nascent ferns. The rest of the plants she combined with the compost pile and dropped it off on her way to the front entrance of the botanical gardens.

KIA LANDED alongside the botanical gardens and peeked around the corner. Two Reeve's Guards, an owl and a falcon, stood vigil. There were always opinici trying to sneak in to steal the fern, so it had an around-the-chimes watch.

"You haven't seen some of the weald monitors that sneak in after the turkeys," the owl was saying. "They're as big as Commander Wolden."

The falcon scoffed. "Even Commander Wolden would agree that nothing beats a lace monitor. Remember when that pack of them came through the underbough and we had to chase them all down? They're nasty little venomous beasties."

"Wait, cave monitors or lace monitors?" the owl asked.

The falcon bit off some salted meat and chewed. "Aren't those the same thing?"

Kia got a brisk pace going and came around the corner with her best scholarly look. "Good morning, guards. Just dropping off the latest batch of ferns from the apprentice weeders."

The guards spared a glance for the ferns she was bringing in and motioned her through. No one tried to smuggle ferns *into* the botanical gardens, so she hoped no one would stop her.

"Wait!" the owl Reeve's Guard called out.

Kia froze.

"Is a cave monitor and a lace monitor the same thing?" he asked.

She turned around and put on her best Cherine impression. "Yes! They also go by the name mountain monitor. Did you know that they may not be venomous at all? There's a theory in academic circles that the germs in their mouth from eating carrion cause them to spread disease to what they bite. I'm in the middle of writing a new tome on the subject and I'd be delighted to bring it by later if you're interested?"

The look on their faces suggested that they were not, in fact, interested.

"That's more than okay," the owl replied. "We wouldn't want to take up anymore of your time than is necessary. Sorry to have bothered you."

As she slipped away, she heard the falcon whisper, "Don't you know better than to ask a question of the university folk? They'll talk your ear off about nothing."

She smiled. Cherine might not think she listened to him, but she did. She had a weakness for the esoteric, even on subjects outside her expertise, such as monitor mouth hygiene.

The inside of the botanical garden was both wide and tall. The high ceilings allowed opinici to hang vines from them, and the extra width meant there was enough room to lift off and land without crashing into anything important. The only area with a shorter, opaque roof was where the ferns were kept. She walked past a scholar hard at work on something vine-related and slipped into the shaded section.

The new crop was doing well, considering the past failures. The fern didn't like to grow this high, preferring the depths of the weald to the heights of civilization. Even the forested area around the eyrie that housed the turkey population resisted fern growing efforts. Whether that was because the undergrowth had been cleared out or because opinici snuck past the rangers to steal it, she didn't know.

She looked around and found a fern that looked on its last legs. There was a hole in the roof and direct sunlight was killing it. She replaced it with the dead weed from the yard and slipped the sickly fern into her harness. She consoled herself with the knowledge that it would have died on its own. She was giving it a purpose.

The scholar didn't look up from his vines as Kia made her escape. The Reeve's Guards grunted thanks and went back to arguing, this time about sailfin monitors. Specifically, whether or not it was possible to hold the mouth of one shut with just their talons, an endeavor that would surely end in disaster. She was out of the botanical gardens and at her nest with no one the wiser.

KIA AWOKE the next morning before first chimes. She was certain that any moment someone would discover her deception at the botanical gardens and drag her off to jail. When she opened the door to her nest, she found a clay pot of ointment left at her doorstep. Inside of it was a note that was just legible with all the marks of a gryphon scratching into vellum.

They left last night on the old goliath bird trail south of the eyrie. -Satra

Kia frowned. She'd expected to have at least another day to sort this out. Still, the apprentices she'd talked to had said the cockatiel spent all night working. If she approached his hovel now, at the break of dawn, he might be at his most receptive after a night of forging.

She slipped on her harness, fern still inside, and flew to

the edge of the university district. Instead of ringing the chime, she pushed aside his door and walked right in.

The cockatiel looked up from his work. His feathers were stained with ink. His eyes had trouble focusing on her after staring at the written words for so many hours. She waited for him to speak.

"You...you're..." he stopped. "Who are you?"

"I'm Kia, university scholar."

He nodded. "Are you here to pick up the books for the headmaster?"

She looked at the pile of books next to him. They included copies of most of the forbidden teachings with new bindings. Was the headmaster setting up a new library somewhere outside of the university? Or were these gifts, perhaps for a colleague at the Crackling Sea Eyrie?

"Not the copies, but he needed a few of the originals to double check something," she lied.

"Sure, take what you need." He turned back to his current project.

Kia hesitated, then took out the stolen red fern. "Go easy on this, okay?"

Focus and recognition returned to his eyes. He seemed to understand that Neider hadn't sent her. She could see the war inside of the forger. Fortunately for her, addiction won. He took the fern and went into a back room to prepare it.

She opened the original version of Cherine's field notebook and carefully cut away the page that included his maps. Since the page contained a different map on each side, she hoped no one would notice it was missing. The reeve and headmaster likely had their own maps and didn't need Cherine's incomplete list. Then she closed the book and slipped away before the forger returned.

KIA PACKED LIGHTLY. She hid the map in the binding of a journal that was otherwise empty. Her other goods were all practical: food, but not too much of it; a container of ink; and a few quill pens. The quill pens were the only place she allowed sentimentality to slip in. If Cherine were alive, he could make her more. Just in case he wasn't, she took one of the pens he'd given her and slipped it into her harness.

She thought about going into his house and looking for something he might miss. Hadn't his mother gotten him a special harness? Maybe a book? But her earlier violation of his privacy had been too much for her. What if she found some keepsake she'd given him or a letter?

It was nearly midday. The skies would be most crowded now, so it was time for her to leave while she wouldn't stand out. She closed the skylight, secured the door to her nest against squirrels, and then flew off southwest towards Hatzel's section of the weald.

15

———

MERIN

When Merin was young, just after he'd taken on his adult feathers but before he'd grown to the near-Hatzel size he was now, he would watch his father to learn how to become a pride leader. While the young Merin felt impatience at everything, his father seemed impervious to the daily annoyances. As members of the pride explained their issues—more trifles than troubles —his father would listen, unmoving. His patience had seemed supernatural to fledgling Merin, something his father had just been born with. Even his father's tail remained frozen, a feat few gryphons could replicate.

Merin had once watched a forest spinner crawl across his father's tail. His father hadn't as much as blinked.

It seemed ominous, now, thinking back to the calm his father had shown right before his death. He'd stood his ground against a stampede of goliath birds, escapees from an earlier grasslands experiment, to protect a nest of unhatched eggs in the birds' path. Like with the spider on his tail, he hadn't flinched when the stampede trampled him.

Not that his death had been in vain. The lead bird had been spooked by its collision with the gryphon and turned just enough to keep from trampling the nest.

The eggs had been saved. The goliath birds were hunted down and eaten—mostly by his pride, though some were tithed to the medicine gryphons. It was much later when Merin found out that his father had been born as precocious as any gryphlet but had trained himself to be preternaturally calm after taking over as pride leader. Upon hearing this, Merin had spent years practicing a stoic look that replaced his underlying feelings of impatience.

Which brought him to the present.

Askel and Triddle were explaining rivers to him. Specifically, dropping things into rivers. They brought Merin—and his pride—a certain prestige because they fixed problems that gryphons would not consider fixable. He appreciated that, but he also thought they were lying to him.

Everything they'd dropped into the river in the cave had come out in the rapids that divided the weald into north and south. Whatever the underground river was, it must feed into the much larger glacial runoff, Glacial Run. If the opinicus's corpse was stuck, any of the dozen things they'd thrown in should have knocked it loose. The opinicus had probably escaped. They'd find him frozen halfway up the taiga, or his bones would be discovered regurgitated by a monitor during the spring hunt. Or, if he hadn't escaped the water, he'd been washed out to sea near the twin fisherfolk cities of Swan's Rest and Crane's Nest.

"I think if we maybe wrap it in a seed casing it might explode when we put it in the water and dislodge his corpse," Askel was saying. His reddish brown tail fanned like he was in flight as he jumped up to mime the explosion. With Triddle's plan being to throw things into the water, it didn't surprise Merin that Askel was trying to find a way to make that explode.

Hidden behind him and out of Askel's view, Merin's tail twitched. Merin stood much taller than the rest of his pride. Both his father and mother had been muscular gryphons, but not like him. He was more than the sum of his parents. Yes, his harpy eagle beak matched the rest of his pride. Its top curved down wickedly like an icicle at the tip. His colors, browns and golds, those had come from his parents, too.

But his size had come from somewhere else. It was like the forest itself decided there needed to be larger gryphons. Had there been a hook-beaked monster of a gryphon anywhere in the weald, the mystery would have been solved. Instead, his mother said that the weald itself had seeped into his egg.

While he felt he had no ancestors, he'd wasted no time in creating the next generation. Several of the gryphons wandering the nesting area were nearly his size at half his age and shared his hook-beak. He yawned, a long, drawn out affair, and Triddle took the hint and pulled Askel away. It was no use scolding them. Better to let them think he was bored of their excuses. Their minds would latch onto a new project soon enough.

What he really needed them to work on was a way of extending the pride's lands. He'd pushed the southern boundary as far as he could without risking the ire of the Feathermane and Fantail Prides. The runoff from the taiga and plateau that formed Glacial Run were too obvious a border. It was too bad Triddle couldn't shift the rivers south.

Merin had tried to push further into Hatzel's lands, but the border they shared was good parrot hunting grounds, and she wouldn't back down. For a pride of only thirty, she held onto her lands like a lace monitor protecting its young.

Moving east was its own hassle, as those prides were restructuring themselves. It was hard to know whom he could risk offending. And by the time he'd thought to expand north towards the eyrie, the opinici had taken advantage of the fire to create the grasslands.

What he needed more than anything was what he couldn't have: land. There was no point in growing his pride just to exhaust their hunting grounds. He'd even take a slice of the taiga if it weren't so frigid. He'd sent his eldest son along with four of his best flyers to explore the lands beyond the taiga.

They had yet to return, but he didn't expect them back for several seasons.

Once, the prides had talked more. There was some taiga stock, some kjarr stock in his pride. He remembered being a fledgling and traveling with his father once and looking up at gryphons who sparkled green like a pond on a sunny day. Now, he couldn't remember what they called their pride or where they'd come from. They'd looked at his size and recognized it, possibly from one of their own. He'd asked his son to find those gryphons before coming home.

He looked over at Askel and Triddle. They were nervously watching the crate taken from the prisoner. He shared their anxiety. They'd cleared a meeting area away from the nesting grounds, but having seen what the boxes could do firsthand, he wasn't convinced they'd cleared far enough.

The fire and ice couple had already forgotten Merin and were wrapped up in further discussions about the substance in the box. Triddle wanted to submerge it in water—the underground river, in fact. Triddle thought the water might make it safer; Askel thought the water might make it explode. Either way, they both wanted to try it and find out.

Merin had vetoed that idea but allowed them to experiment with the smallest of doses of black powder and the opinicus's flint and tinder. Askel had already found a replenishment for the tinder by drying what he now called tinder fungus. Or, more likely, he already had a stockpile of dried, flammable items that the flint had made exciting again.

A rustle overhead announced the arrival of several gryphons from the eastern prides gliding down to the meeting area. He recognized most of them, though he didn't see any from the Fantail Pride who lived in the southeastern corner of the weald. Hatzel's pride, mostly copper hawks and magpies, were also absent.

Strix flew down and settled next to Merin. Strix was a uniformly dark gryphon with only a hint of red on the underside of his wings. His owl face lacked the ear tufts of most gryphons, giving him the appearance of youth despite his long years, but he'd earned a reputation as an adept night hunter. When hunter training was in session, he'd make the new adults learn to hunt in the dark. If they fell asleep, he'd sneak in and kill something in their camp without them waking. He was twisted like that.

Merin bowed a little to him in thanks, understanding that Strix's vanity needed to be indulged for a meeting so far across the weald before nightfall.

All the prides expected to arrive were now here except Hatzel, who had asked for the meeting in the first place.

16

XAVI

Hatzel's pride lazed about in the afternoon, trading stories and gossip. Instead of circling down from atop the forest, Zeph glided in, tucked his wings, and crashed like a boulder into Xavi, sending them tumbling into a pile of fir branches. A leaf-nosed snake that was trying to sneak to the wood pile to check for bugs flipped onto its back and played dead as the gryphons crashed into its destination.

"Welcome back!" Zeph said.

"Oomph," Xavi replied. The fir branches cracked, leaking sap onto Xavi, who was on the bottom. Zeph hopped off, and Xavi attempted to stand, a small tree's worth of branches adorning his fur and feathers. Moving only spread the stickiness, so he stood still, looking like a scruffed gryphlet.

Zeph just grinned and began to groom the sticks and resin off Xavi. He was always happy when Xavi returned and he no longer had to bear his friend's responsibilities as Hatzel's second.

"How was your trip?" Zeph asked. "Did they teach you how to hunt? You're growing up so fast."

"I'm older than you," Xavi protested. "And I know how to hunt. This wasn't for beginners. I killed a snake!"

Zeph stepped back and put on his surprised face for Xavi to see. The leaf-nosed snake took advantage of the distraction to right itself and slip back into the forest. "A real snake, not just a vine? Well, I guess you have your adult feathers now. What did you fall in? You're sticky."

"It was a big snake. Like, bigger than three gryphons." Xavi looked around for a gryphon to illustrate the point.

Hatzel had glided down and was giving them both a strange look. A tiny gryphlet bounded up to chirp at Hatzel and see if she wanted to play. While Xavi was trying to point at Hatzel, Zeph sat back on his haunches and measured out the size of the gryphlet from shoulder to shoulder, then expanded that by three.

Xavi sighed. "No, like, three Hatzels."

"Now you're just telling tales," Zeph protested. "Nothing is as big as three Hatzels."

"This is why I throw rocks at you," Hatzel said as she took the gryphlet back to the nests.

"Where've you two been?" Xavi asked.

"I went to the eyrie," Zeph said through a mouthful of feathers and twigs. "It was big, like two and a half Hatzels big."

He was glad to see the nesting grounds in one piece. He'd bypassed them while walking Orlea to get help in case more opinici had been sent to look for either of them.

They'd left Orlea and Cherine with the medicine gryphons for the time being. Zeph liked his pride, but he didn't want to put them in the position of harboring fugitives. The medicine gryphons, on the other paw, were known for helping anyone in need. No one would hold it against them.

As relieved as Zeph was to be back, Xavi seemed even more relieved to let Hatzel take charge. She'd dispatched the fastest gryphons to call together the prides, asking Merin to host the meeting to keep the eastern flights from having to fly into the northwest corner of the weald. Once Xavi was deforested, she and Zeph were working out how to get Cherine and Orlea's information to the prides without revealing that they were hiding two opinici. The answer came via a greeting from above.

Blue, green, and red, Kia descended upon their nesting grounds for the second time. Zeph rushed up to her when she landed but seemed unsure of how to greet her— certainly not with a pounce into the fir resin. The sort of opinicus who painted intricate designs into her fur would not appreciate being covered in anything sticky. Not the way Xavi did. One exciting trip into the city didn't make for life-long friends, but she'd been in Zeph's thoughts. He'd worried that his extrication from the eyrie had caused her strife. She seemed to radiate color next to his brown bands.

She was out of breath, but once her beak opened, every-thing came out at once: the kjarr and bog prides were now the wingtorn, Satra and the kjarr gryphlets were hostages, and the wingtorn had left to march on the fisherfolk. Oh, and there were opinicus rangers planting boxes of saltpeter across the weald because everything was going to explode. Kia tossed Cherine's map down in front of them.

Why does the name Satra feel familiar? Zeph wondered.

Hatzel looked to him. Both looked down at the map. Cherine had told them he'd found several camps full of crates, but he hadn't known what they were for. His best guess was a new mining operation.

"We can't bring Kia with us," Zeph said before Hatzel could suggest it. "We've seen how Merin's pride treats opinici."

"They're going to ask us how we got this information and why they should trust it. Kia speaks to both of those things. With her, we have a reliable source without having to talk about our," Hatzel realized that most of the pride was staring at them and Kia, "well, our other source."

"Did you find Cherine?" Kia asked.

Zeph took her and led her away from the pride. "Why don't we get you some food and water, and I can explain along the way?"

As they walked away, Zeph heard Hatzel ordering Xavi to fly as fast as he could to the fisherfolk and warn them. As the quickest gryphons had already been dispatched to tell the other prides of the meeting, Xavi was their next best hope for getting word down there. Instead of waiting for supplies, he leapt into the air, his blue markings expanding as his black and white wings stretched.

17

MEETING OF THE PRIDES

Hatzel arrived at the meeting of prides to find the other leaders waiting on her. Not ideal, but she'd needed the time to bring Kia into the fold before coming here.

Both Kia and Cherine presented problems. Orlea could probably return to the eyrie without anyone the wiser, though she'd been on the brink of starvation there, but Hatzel worried that Cherine and Kia had burned too many bridges the moment Kia left with the map. Hatzel would offer them a place in her pride if no one else objected, but she couldn't imagine two minds as inquisitive as theirs being happy out in the weald, far from the university. Orlea might be an easier sell since she was a hunter by trade, but scholars were a different bird altogether.

Also, there's the small matter of them not being gryphons.

Hatzel landed and saw Triddle restraining Askel from waving and reconsidered her initial assessment. Cherine and Kia might find at least two kindred spirits out here, but that raised another question. What would happen if she took Merin's prisoner into her pride?

She nodded a greeting to Merin and Strix. Everyone was assembled in a circle. The canopy was sparser here, hinting at the past nesting site abandoned after the stampede. The sunlight's penetration over years had grown soft grass for them to lie on while they talked. In the center, someone had cleared the foliage away to form a stone-ringed dirt crater. Before Hatzel could begin, Merin took over.

"We have a problem." He stood when he spoke, giving the illusion that he was taller than her. "An opinicus problem. When they cleared the burned weald to make the grasslands, we didn't speak up. Now, their rangers hunt in the weald, stealing our game. We caught one of them, but he opted to drown himself instead of speak."

An elder from the Parrotface Pride, with a face and plumage that resembled a tired ground parrot, spoke up. "What of it? We capture them and send them packing. It's a game, nothing more. We used to sneak through the eyrie lands and catch turkeys when I was young. Is this what I was brought here for?"

The parrotface gryphons were known for being mild. This one must be cranky, Hatzel decided. They controlled most of the northern weald. Only the feathermanes, south of the river, had more territory.

"There's more to it than that. Askel, Triddle?" Merin prompted.

At Merin's command, the couple brought the smallest bit of saltpeter to the center of the circle of pride leaders and placed it on a rock in the crater.

"This is what they've been bringing into our forest." Merin held flint in his paw and struck it against the saltpeter, causing a burst of flame and noise. All the gryphons jumped to their feet.

"Irresponsible!"

"What is that?"

"Skraark!"

"Was that really necessary?"

Merin smirked and looked pleased that he hadn't burnt off his paw. Askel and Triddle must have spent all morning figuring out the right amount of saltpeter for his theatrics.

"I don't know why the opinici brought it here," Merin said when everyone had calmed down, "but I know we can't let this stand."

Strix, the only pride leader who hadn't settled down onto his stomach as was customary for meetings, was looking up into the canopy far behind Hatzel. His concave face allowed him to capture sound in a way that the others couldn't. "Why do we not ask them? I can hear that opi trill from here."

There was murmuring among the pride leaders.

"Calm your feathers," Hatzel scolded. "I've been doing my own investigation after the herds turned up dead."

She saw no sign from Merin but thought Strix was looking at her more intently now. It was tough to read his earless visage. Word of the slaughter must have traveled quickly to have reached even his far plateau.

"The eyrie is worse than we thought. Please show respect to my guest, as she has much to say about what's soon to come." Hatzel whistled.

Zeph and Kia descended. Hatzel had advised Kia to start strong, weather the storm of questions, and then leave with Zeph when the discussion turned away from her. It was too risky to take her to Cherine just yet. She'd have to stay with Hatzel's pride for the time being. Perhaps the fisherfolk would be a good haven for Kia and Cherine if Xavi's mission succeeded.

The opinicus scholar sat on her haunches instead of on

all fours, putting her well above the gryphons she spoke to. "The eyrie captured the kjarr pride, enslaved them, tore off their wings, and are going to blow up the weald."

Despite Strix's critique, Kia's words barely trilled. Like the explosion of the saltpeter, there was a long moment where all the air from the glen was gone. Even Merin seemed surprised at the revelation.

And then the arguing and questions began.

"Why the kjarr pride?" This came from the parrotface elder. She had several grown offspring with fathers from the kjarr pride.

"There was a dispute and the kjarr salted the fields, starving the Crackling Sea Eyrie," Kia explained.

"Jun never did have any sense of cause and effect," Strix mused. The owls had been the last pride to adopt the common language, and his accent made it hard to tell when he was being facetious.

"Why burn down the weald?" asked another pride leader whose feathers formed a mane. Even his calm voice felt like the precursor to a roar.

"They need to recreate the grasslands experiment on a grander scale to feed themselves and the Crackling Sea opinici," Kia explained. Hatzel had advised Kia to use *they* instead of *we* when speaking of the eyrie opinici in front of the gryphon pride leaders.

The feathermane leader considered this. "How much of this explosive have they brought to the forest? When will they set it off?"

"Soon," Kia replied. "The wingtorn were dispatched yesterday to raze the fisherfolk villages and set up a trap to catch any gryphons leaving the weald."

Hatzel pushed the map to Merin with her paw, who looked it over and gave it to Triddle. He and Askel cleared the rocks away and began to recreate the map in the dirt while Hatzel talked.

"We don't know for sure. Our contact—" with this, she nodded to Kia, who allowed Zeph to pull her away from the meeting and back to the nesting grounds, "was able to find a document with some of the locations."

The map came to life before them. Askel and Triddle were unusually adept at this kind of work. They often drew out what they expected to happen when they diverted a river—returning later to update their map with what had actually happened. Now, they converted the dirt crater into Cherine's map of the weald.

"The circles are the crates of explosives? They're mostly along the grasslands edge, then." Strix's pride was best situated if this were the case.

"These are the ones we know about," Hatzel explained. "We could be greatly underestimating how deep into the weald the rangers went. Think of the border areas between the prides and how deep they go."

No one wanted to think about opinici sneaking past gryphons in the deep forest, but the crate in Merin's hunting grounds had been there long enough to collect moss. Several other prides admitted to turning back opinici that were deep into their lands. Even the Fantail Pride's leader admitted to opinicus tourists being turned away.

"We also don't know if the wingtorn are carrying more explosives with them," Hatzel added.

"What time did they leave? Did your opinicus see them?" Merin asked. "The kjarr was a massive pride. Jun's father conquered and assimilated the bog pride, combining the nesting grounds, which now strech from the kjarr to the peat bogs to the edge of the goliath bird plains. Depending on how many kjarr gryphons were enslaved, these wingtorn could outnumber all of the weald."

"We don't know what time they left, just that it was at least a day ago. The information came directly from Jun's youngest, Satra." When the parrotface elder made an inquisitive skraark, Hatzel added, "She's being held with the other gryphlets. Her wings were left unclipped to keep Jun in line."

"They're insane to leave her alive," the parrotface gryphon said. What Satra had done was left unsaid, but the elder's love of the kjarr did not seem to extend to Jun's youngest daughter.

"Jun is her shackles. Satra always had a soft spot for her father. They'd better hope nothing happens to him. She would not stay her claws for a hundred gryphlets." Unlike the parrot-faced elder, Strix spoke with a hint of envy.

"If we can rescue the gryphlets and get word to Jun, could we bring them to our side?" Merin asked.

Our side? It was not lost on Hatzel that Merin had referred to the prides as one entity. In all her years as a leader, she'd never seen the weald prides as anything except independent groups who loosely agreed on hunting grounds. Nothing had brought them together, not even the monitor plague, goliath bird stampede, giant snakes, or lace monitor migrations.

When none of the other leaders spoke up, she weighed in. "I don't know if they would flee with their children or seek to join us. But it should at least remove the pressure from the fisherfolk if we can free Satra and her charges fast enough. Where we would house twenty gryphlets, I don't know. The whole forest could go up at any moment. We should be moving our own offspring."

"I will take them," Strix said. "You and Merin may be

better off heading up into the taiga, but for the eastern prides, your kin are welcome in my lands. The fire may climb the plateau, but it's still the safest place until we see how this plays out. If push comes to claw, we can watch the conflagration from some of the small islands off the coast."

18

RANGERS

Zeph and Kia's flight back to the nesting grounds was held in the upper canopy for safety and reminded him of their first trip through the redwood forest. This time, they didn't talk about the squirrels, parrots, or gliding snakes. Zeph wanted to talk about Kia. Kia wanted to talk about Cherine. They ended up talking about Reeve Brevin.

"After her ancestor killed the massive cobra," Kia slipped into her teaching voice, "he was made reeve of an eyrie. He was the final opinicus to be made reeve, and this was the last eyrie. I think they planned for another one where the fisherfolk live now and built a goliath bird trail to the shore, but it never came to pass."

Zeph thought this over. "So, does she still report in to the...king? Empress? Reeve lord?"

"Oh, no," Kia laughed. "It's been generations since anyone's been around to give orders. The reeves all seemed to become content with their autonomy. No one orders them around anymore, not since before the Connixation."

"None of the reeves went to find out what happened to their leader?" he asked.

"I'm not sure," she admitted. "It was a long time ago. What I think happened is—"

Zeph made a hushing sound and stopped. "Something's wrong."

He sniffed the air with his flexible beak. His ears were at full alert. It was quiet, but there was a pungent smell that didn't come from the plants in this corner of the weald. He motioned for Kia to stay back and hide in the canopy while he scouted ahead. He glided from tree to tree, landing against the soft moss in case anyone was listening for him.

The nesting grounds were silent. The gryphlets should have been taken to the safety of the winter caves, but there were no adult gryphon sounds ahead, either. There were a lot of food and supplies to be transported, and the two nesting caves here had to be secured so they didn't return to find snakes or monitors in residence.

He peeked around a tree trunk and saw a single gryphlet sitting next to the fir pile, looking quiet but nervous. It was the same one who'd greeted Hatzel, the one who was always wandering off. She seemed to have been tied to something hidden under the branches. The two nesting caves had debris covering their entrances.

He retreated and made a wider circle around the nesting grounds, approaching them downwind, from the north, this time. There was that smell again, not opinicus but a pungent weed that masked other scents. It was similar enough to soured eggfruit that an opinicus or even a distracted gryphon wouldn't notice the difference.

When he traced it, he saw the muddy-colored plumage of a camouflaged opinicus ranger holding a net. The scent was strong enough that he suspected there were two or three more rangers hiding nearby. They'd probably caught the last of the gryphons and gryphlets who were cleaning up. Since they'd left at least the one gryphlet alive, hopefully the other prisoners were wrapped up in the nest. He wished he had a better idea of how many there were and decided there was only one way to find out.

He silently backtracked a ways and then got a flying start, built up as much speed as he could get, and pulled his wings in, crossing the center of the clearing at top speed.

The gryphlet squealed with excitement. Two traps triggered but weren't fast enough to catch him. Two opinici threw nets. Two more gave chase.

Zeph spread his wings before he hit the ground, landing in a sprint, then leapt up again, gaining altitude and breaking through the canopy, into the sky, where he let out an alarm.

All four opinici were in pursuit. They were more agile flyers than he was and seemed confident in their ability to bring down a single gryphon. While they were better at flying than he was, they underestimated his impressive falling capabilities.

He looped back and let gravity bring him to his pursuers, and in the case of one, through him. The sickening sound of a wing breaking, nearly detaching, sent the first opinicus falling to the ground. The ranger's net and an alarming number of his feathers floated down after him. The other three scattered, then dove after Zeph, but lost him below the canopy line. They landed and looked around.

A cricket chirped once before being silenced by a forest spinner.

In the distance, the wounded opinicus, having survived the fall by some miracle, was calling for help. They turned in the direction of their fallen comrade and seemed to consider going to his aid.

Zeph, upside down on a canopy branch and covered by the leaves, released his dewclaw and pounced on the opinicus in the middle. One bite was all it took. He was now sandwiched between an opinicus with sickles for claws on his left and another with a net on his right. The one on the right threw the net, and Zeph flattened himself against the ground in the time it took to blink, becoming one with his shadow. The net caught Sharpclaws in the face. While he struggled to untangle himself, Zeph dispatched the thrower.

A scream came from far away. As forest-savvy as these opinici were, it seemed no one had told this one that making the sounds of a wounded animal in the weald was a good way to attract monitors.

With the penultimate opinicus facing his own demise, Sharpclaws made a dash back towards the nesting grounds. Worried he intended to use the gryphlet as a hostage, Zeph pursued.

Sharpclaws flitted between the branches with a practiced wing that would have made even the nearest gryphon proud—if that gryphon were not also chasing after him and trying to murder him.

Sharpclaws went over a tangle; Zeph slipped under it.

Sharpclaws pulled up his legs to avoid catching a stump; Zeph pushed off of it.

Sharpclaws came through the forest and into the nesting grounds likely expecting to find a helpless gryphlet; Kia stabbed him in the chest with her beak. He fell back into the pile of fir branches.

Zeph backpedaled his wings and landed. He looked down at Sharpclaws. The wound was too deep to try to save him, even if they wanted answers. The ranger coughed something that sounded like "Kia" but became a gurgle.

Kia had untied the few remaining pride gryphons. It seemed the only gryphlet to stay behind was this one, who had been hiding when the others left.

"Get to safety," he told Kia and his pridemates. "I need to check on Hatzel and the pride leaders."

The aggressive hiss of a monitor defending its meal could just be heard from a distance away.

HATZEL HAD FILLED the pride leaders in on all the information Orlea, Cherine, and Kia had given them without mentioning the former two opinici. There was some talk of reaching out diplomatically to the reeve, but only perfunctory conversation was paid to the idea. No one expected anything to come of it.

Reeve Brevin, unlike her father, had not taken the time to meet with the prides. Most of the weald gryphons had only seen her when the smoldering forest was converted into grasslands. She'd come with the full army behind her, standing atop a rock with her wings and tail feathers spread while the trees were cleared. The sunlight had splashed into green sparks against her plumage.

Her presence then had been a warning. Not realizing the precedent, none of the prides had thought to fight for the burnt forest. They had their own concerns. She'd better resembled a monument the eyrie had constructed to worship than an opinicus.

Looking at their situation now, Hatzel admitted to herself it would be a waste of time to attempt diplomacy. She believed in negotiating, but only from a place of power.

Right now, it was unclear what power the prides held. Even when it came to saving Satra, most were indifferent. Then the discussion turned darker.

When Askel said, "What if we blow it up?" it took a few moments for everyone to realize he was serious.

"We have a map showing us where to find crates of saltpeter," Triddle agreed. Hatzel knew she shouldn't feel disappointed that Triddle sided with Askel but still felt a little betrayed.

"Give them a taste of their own medicine," Merin agreed.

"Wait. The eyrie is huge. If the kjarr pride is two weald prides large," Hatzel estimated, "who knows how many opinici live in the eyrie? It reaches into the sky. We can't fight an army like that."

"Didn't your spy say that the wingtorn were supposed to be guarding the city while the main army helped the Crackling Sea Eyrie?" Merin asked. "If so, the moment Reeve Brevin deployed them to the fisherfolk villages, she left the Redwood Valley Eyrie defenseless."

"We don't know if that's the case," Hatzel said. "It's just a theory. Maybe the entire army is back except for a pawful of soldiers. Maybe the rangers and wingtorn left but the main forces stayed."

"We could always cut off the head of the serpent. With enough saltpeter diversions, we could slip in and kill Brevin." The owl pride leader's claws extended when he said *serpent*. When Strix used *we*, it seemed to Hatzel like he really meant *I*.

"Look," she said, flustered. "I agree we need to get in and get Satra. We can't let them have the kjarr pride. But there are so many there who have nothing to do with this."

"So many opinici," Merin countered.

"Yes, but so what?" Hatzel countered. "You can't just murder an entire population because you're afraid."

"Had one of Brevin's advisors only advised her similarly," Strix mused, "we wouldn't find ourselves facing this problem now."

After another hour of discussion, Askel and Triddle still wanted to blow up something. Askel suggested the eyrie. Triddle lobbied for the Snowfeather Dam and waterworks that brought water from Crater Lake up to the top levels of the eyrie.

Merin wanted to take the whole place down and, she suspected, expand his pride lands to include the Reeve's Hunting Grounds. Strix proposed a surgical strike to kill Brevin. Hatzel countered with a rescue operation to save the gryphlets and Satra while the prides evacuated to the mountains and shore. The other pride leaders were all on the fence, leaning towards a path of neutralizing the salt peter and waiting. It was their belief that, without the saltpeter fire, the eyrie would never send the military after them.

After Zeph arrived with news that the rangers had attacked Hatzel's nesting grounds, everyone agreed on one point. Whatever they believed would happen if the saltpeter were taken care of in time, they were no longer willing to allow the eyrie to have control over the wingtorn. Satra must be saved.

19

SALTPETER

The dusk sky was a crashing orange sea Kia swam through. She was only just aware of the dark splotches of gryphons flying near her since killing the opinicus ranger.

Most gryphons were hunters, she knew that, but Zeph had killed the rangers as though they were ground parrots. She was reminded of their first meeting when he'd walked her through how he hunted for food. The way he handled other sapient beings had been the same.

She'd seen him rise through the canopy with the accompanying dive, watched the first opinicus drop to its death. That's when she hurried to the nests. When the last ranger rushed in, she'd acted on instinct. Really, the ranger had rushed into her beak. It had only taken a little effort on her part.

No, that wasn't quite right. Her beak had broken through his rib cage. It had taken a *lot* of effort, though it had taken little thought.

The opinicus had spoken her name as he died. Had he known her? Or had he been sent for her? She thought back to the black cockatiel. He'd probably spoken to the head-master, who'd talked to the reeve. Or had the rangers been sent by the headmaster? It was hard to tell where Neider's sphere of influence ended. She may have put the pride in danger by coming here. She'd definitely put the rangers in danger. Her sister was a ranger, maybe even friends with the rangers she and Zeph just killed. Was Mia out there in the weald somewhere, waiting to light an explosive?

Kia looked out to the gryphons flying with her. The gryphlet who'd been used for bait was squealing happily at being carried through the air. She waved a paw at Kia, and Kia waved a talon back.

Would any of the gryphons understand what it felt like for her to kill? They grew up knowing it was something they'd do. Maybe killing an opinicus would feel different to them, but maybe not. Opinici were the *other* to most gryphons. What she'd done, it was more akin to a gryphon killing another gryphon. She didn't know if that happened. She wanted to talk to another opinicus, but as she was starting to realize, there was no going back to the eyrie.

They'd said Cherine was alive. She wanted to see him.

He should understand. When his grandfather died, he'd been surprised to find out that she'd never lost anyone. All her grandparents had been alive when she was born and were still living. She'd never even seen a dead opinicus before today.

She flew closer to the nearest gryphon. He resembled Xavi a little with his magpie-colored wings. While the word *gryphon* conjured up thoughts of Hatzel and Zeph first in her mind's eye, more than half their pride had Xavi's coloring. How had that come about? She wished someone had done a genealogy of the gryphon prides, but they'd been considered beneath scholarship.

"Do you know the way to the medicine gryphon's cave?" she asked the gryphon.

"Are you hurt?" There was real concern in his voice.

"No, but I think we can get more information about the rangers there," she lied. She was sure they had all the information Cherine had known, between his memory and the map. But she wanted to be close to her own kind.

"Sure, okay." The gryphon went and spoke to the head of their flight, then peeled off and led her south.

THE PLAN, Zeph thought, was like a parrot's shadow that turned out to be an unripe eggfruit gourd when pounced. He knew Hatzel would be dismayed if she knew that he shared the same opinion as the Parrotface and Feathermane Pride leaders, but he didn't see why they couldn't just fly away and settle elsewhere.

Starting a fight when their homes were all rigged to burn was foolish. It was hunting prey in a snowstorm instead of seeking shelter. Why help Satra at all? It would be easier to relocate their pride of thirty gryphons to some-place new and start over.

"Because the kjarr gryphons need our help." There was no hesitancy in Hatzel's voice. "Because without our help, the fisherfolk are in danger. Because if things go wrong, you and Kia need to warn the opinici or they won't be able to evacuate."

"Evacuation isn't part of the plan," Zeph said about the last.

The actual plan involved each pride hitting a different objective. Askel and Triddle had been distracted by the word *Nitrary* just outside the eyrie on Cherine's map. They believed it to be the dreaded flameworks where the saltpeter was made and wanted to blow it up or douse it in water, depending on which of them you asked. Either way, exploding it would buy Hatzel and Merin's gryphons time to evacuate Satra and the gryphlets. Strix had volunteered to provide them with a safe exit from the eyrie. He hadn't offered any details on what that meant.

Hatzel shook her head. "Evacuation *needs* to be part of the plan in case the flameworks' explosion is larger than Askel is thinking. You and Kia must get word to the right opinici up at the university to evacuate the eyrie."

"It's more than just the university," Zeph said. They didn't have a detailed map of the eyrie, but he'd given the prides all the details he remembered or had heard from Kia or Orlea. "There's a whole world of starving opinici beneath the main level. It's nasty down there, dry, overgrown. If any of the fire reaches that deep, the whole city could burn from the bottom up."

He'd made these same arguments in front of the pride leaders, but they weren't convinced. They hadn't seen what he had, and his safety concerns didn't stop there. While a fire starting in the bottom levels seemed less dangerous than if the high reaches of the eyrie caught fire, they'd all seen the effects of smoke.

It wasn't enough to avoid a forest fire. Gryphons had to be careful not to fly over it and needed to be mindful of which way the wind was blowing. When a fire was large enough, the smoke filled a large portion of the skies. More than one gryphon had died while watching a forest fire when the winds changed direction. He didn't have a better idea at a distraction than blowing the flameworks, but they had no way of knowing what would happen for certain.

He sighed. Hatzel was right. They had a responsibility to the opinici, too.

"Orlea seemed in better shape than Cherine," Zeph offered. "If she's able to fly, she should know how to evacuate the lower quarters if things go wrong."

Hatzel took a moment to consider. "Well, the medicine cave is on our way to the winter grounds. We can stop in and see."

KIA and her escort's initial flight towards the new shelter had cost them time when turning south for the medicine gryphon's cave. She'd tried to ask for directions, but her escort—she hadn't gotten his name yet—had just looked apologetic and said, "It's just a cave."

They backtracked over some of the same area, following the western edge of the weald where it bled into the mountains. The evening sky's vibrant orange had changed into the bright blue at the center of a candle before fading into the cool darkness of a deep lake. Many gryphons and opinici had excellent day vision or night vision, but almost none excelled in the transition. In fact, it was her companion's sense of smell that first alerted them. She'd been thinking about how easily that opinicus had died, and how easy it must therefore be for her to die. Her beak still ached, tasted of blood.

"Is something burning?" he asked, flying closer to her so she could hear him.

Kia looked around. Finally, she saw it—a small, thin line of white smoke coming up from the canopy. She pointed, and the gryphon caught sight of the smoke. They changed tracks and glided down to investigate.

Zᴇᴘʜ ᴀɴᴅ Hᴀᴛᴢᴇʟ arrived at the medicine cave to find two grumpy opinici and many exasperated apprentice medicine gryphons. Having spent every waking hour of the past few days together, Orlea and Cherine were both becoming friends and tiring of each other's company.

Orlea described Cherine as a "bloated, stuck-up opinicus with his head so far in the sky the clouds were obscuring his vision of the eyrie." Cherine thought of Orlea as a "narrow-minded poacher with no sense of the greater good." Their favorite topic of conversation was the conversion of the land around the eyrie, once full of ocellated turkeys, to only allow hunting by the rangers. Even the aneda forests of the nearby mountains were ranger-exclusive now, and about half of the grasslands had been taken over by farming or capybara herds.

Cherine's view was that the non-ranger hunters were killing too many animals, which hurt the overall production of meat for the eyrie. By carefully managing the Reeve's Hunting Grounds, they could produce the optimal amount of food.

Orlea's view was that Cherine was an idiot. Just how much of that meat did he think found its way down to the poorer opinici? They required the forest to get enough food to survive. They'd always lived off the land. Locking it away under arbitrary rules and ranger enforcement just made criminals out of the poor.

Cherine wanted to know why Orlea didn't just earn money some other way and buy the food.

Orlea wanted to know just how a hunter was supposed to get paid when the hunting grounds were closed off.

Hatzel wanted to know if they were interrupting, because she and Zeph could come back at a better time.

"Ah, my ress-cuer!" Cherine cheered. He had a bit more trill with the bandage on his beak.

"How're you recovering?" Hatzel asked.

"It's not so bad," he managed. "Whatever they gave me keeps me drowsy. When that doesn't work, I just talk to Orlea over there."

Orlea clicked her beak in annoyance. He clicked his beak back, causing the nearby apprentices to frown. Obviously, they'd given up on trying to get him to rest his beak until it healed. It had been a fool's errand from the start.

"How's your wing doing?" Zeph asked Orlea.

"It's not as bad as I thought." She moved it a bit to show it wasn't causing her pain. "The net just stretched it in the wrong ways. I'm not sure what they did to it, but it's just about as good as new. I've already flown a little, when the apprentices let me out to empty my bladder."

"If you're up for it, we need your help," he said.

"Oh? Need something poached?" Orlea asked with a look to Cherine.

Zeph shook his head. "We need an expert on the lower levels of the eyrie who can help us in case there needs to be an evacuation."

"What're they going to be evacuating from?" she asked.

"Probably us," Hatzel replied.

KIA and her escort's investigation turned out to be a short one. When they broke through the canopy line and got a close view of what was going on, they both fled as fast as they could fly.

Until now, she'd forgotten about the fallen opinicus, having been more concerned with his compatriots. She'd heard his cries for help and assumed he'd been eaten by the monitors. Down on the ground there was a long line of blood leading to a small camp, presumably the one the rangers had been using. Next to the tents was the unmoving body of the opinicus, minus a wing. In his foretalons were flint and tinder. The top of a box with a circle on it was on fire, and the flames were spreading and growing.

Kia and the gryphon launched themselves back up through the canopy and put as much distance as they could between them and the camp.

There was a moment where it seemed like the fire might have burnt itself out before reaching the saltpeter. Kia resisted the urge to look back. Her escort's willpower was not as strong, and he looked back just in time to see the explosion.

Both were rendered deaf and dumb by the concussive blast. The gryphon was also struck blind by the light.

The fire's effect was less like a typical forest fire and more like liquid. It was as though a giant flaming opinicus had crashed into the water, and the flames went up and then landed like droplets across the forest. As her brain recovered, Kia saw the flames dispersing and thought of the oil used in the braziers across the eyrie. Drops of liquid fire clung to the branches, incinerating the redwood foliage until they finally surrendered and burst into flames.

The gryphon's brain restarted first, but without his vision, he had trouble stabilizing. Kia's mind kicked in a moment later, and she called to him. Her own voice echoed in her head like it'd been shouted from the bottom of the Snowfeather Dam. She flew up to the gryphon and helped steady him. She stayed close enough to keep him going in the same direction they'd been headed originally, but she didn't know how they'd find the caves without his help.

As the shockwave's effects lessened, she felt a burning sensation across her body. She looked down at her forearm and saw small, smoking marks where the oil had splattered against them. Thankfully, she hadn't been looking at the explosion. Most of the oil was on her flank and back. None of what hit them had caught fire, but they were both smoldering with oil.

Her wings began to shake when a white shape flying from the direction of the mountains caught her eye. The explosion must have caught its attention. It rushed towards her and came into focus. Its head was like a gyrfalcon. No longer all white, she could now make out black bars that became black rosettes as they traveled onto his latter half. He looked from Kia to the gryphon, then slipped under the blind gryphon's other side and helped guide him.

Behind them, the fire fought to spread.

20

YOUNCE

Zeph, Hatzel, and Orlea were all standing at the cave entrance, looking out at the small flames blossoming far in the distance. Hatzel was the first one to spot the two gryphons and opinicus flying towards them and raise the alarm. She and Zeph flew up to greet them and helped bring Kia's escort down. Where the cave entrance narrowed to only allow three across, Hatzel and Kia helped the wounded gryphon through, leaving the taiga gryphon and Zeph alone.

Zeph noticed the snowy gryphon for the first time. Hatzel had mentioned one of the taiga pride was seen patrolling the border they shared with the weald, but she hadn't mentioned which one it was.

"Younce?" he asked.

"Hello, Zeph," the snowy gryphon replied. "We haven't seen you up in the taiga for a few years."

Zeph tried to resist the urge to bristle but found himself bristling regardless. Younce's tone was cold but not hostile.

Zeph had grown up with the taiga gryphlets until it became obvious that his feathers and fur were not able to withstand the extreme temperatures. They'd coddled him through his first winters but finally gave him to the weald pride his father had been from.

When the taiga gryphons interbred with weald or kjarr gryphons, it was always tough to tell if the offspring would be more suited to the warmer or colder climates. It was up to the mother who laid the egg to move the gryphlet to the father's nesting grounds if the gryphlet's fur and feathers weren't adapting well. Since his youth in the taiga had been marked with coddling, Zeph's hatchmates tended to think of him as sickly or weak.

"The summers have been busy," Zeph said. "Good hunting times. You could always come to the weald, you know. I can teach you to hunt ground parrots. They're less chewy than goliath birds."

"I'm in the weald now," Younce replied.

Zeph rolled his eyes. To the weald gryphons, the taiga began where the mountains started. To the taiga gryphons, the weald was everything below the elevation where the aneda trees grew. Hatzel's border with the taiga gryphons had always been easier than the one she shared with Merin's pride by virtue of the prey-free zone that divided them.

This did raise a question for Zeph. "What brought you so close to the border?"

Younce was scratching behind his rounded ear with a large, snowshoe-like back paw. "It's summer. I was patrolling for opinici. Sometimes they stray off the goliath bird pass between the eyries. It's become necessary to keep watch."

"I suppose no one comes after the taiga in winter," Zeph said.

"Oh, they do," Younce replied coolly. "We find them when they thaw in spring."

Only their shared childhood allowed Zeph to know

when Younce was joking. His delivery was as dry as the mountain air. This time, however, Zeph wasn't entirely certain.

"How's the pride holding up?" he asked.

"Not as well as it could be. I never liked the term pride, being as modest as they come. I prefer to think of us as an avalanche of gryphons." Younce's demeanor broke for a moment as he saw a twitch in Zeph. "Oh, I'm sorry, I didn't mean—"

"I have a favor to ask you," Zeph interrupted.

EVERYONE WAS ALLOWED a few hours of sleep, but it was important to get to the eyrie before sun up to join the counteroffensive.

The wounded gryphon, Kia's escort, turned out to be one of Xavi's many children. The gryphon's vision hadn't returned. Some of the burning oil had gotten in his eyes, and the old medicine gryphon was taking care of him. She reassured him that his sight could return in time. Until then, he would serve as Cherine's new chat partner while Orlea joined Zeph and Hatzel.

When Zeph awoke, he found the old medicine gryphon attempting to strike a deal for aneda extract from Younce. As best Zeph could tell, she was bartering her blue and yellow spotted assistant for an unnamed amount of the substance. Younce remained stalwart, but Zeph could see his bushy tail twitching in amusement.

Zeph woke Hatzel and Orlea, then asked Orlea to go get Kia without waking Cherine, if possible. Cherine's medication had knocked him out, but Kia had joined him after he was asleep.

"I never wake up to find someone in my nest," Hatzel complained. She began the grooming process, starting with her face.

"That's because you bite in your sleep," Zeph remarked.

She balked. "What? No, I don't!"

"It's why we put Orlea's sleeping nest closest to yours," he explained. "She's like a safe sleeping shield."

Hatzel did not dignify him with a response but instead returned to morning preening with redoubled efforts.

"Younce agreed to take us along the edge of the taiga up to the eyrie so we can come in from the goliath bird pass and reach the flameworks unseen," Zeph said between grooming between his paw pads. "The taiga pride's already holding the line against the Crackling Sea Eyrie on the kjarr side of the mountains. He doesn't want to swat the wasp's nest on this side, too. But he agreed to take Cherine up to the taiga and says Orlea and Kia can come. That should keep Cherine away from Merin."

Neither Zeph nor Hatzel was sure what the opinici would want, but it might give them a safe place to think it over, should the fisherfolk not get Xavi's word in time.

Having heard Kia's retelling of the previous night's events, he was certain that, however the rangers intended to use the saltpeter, lighting the box on fire was not it. The concussive blast had hurt Kia and her escort but hadn't spread the flames the way it could have. Much of the oil had been propelled from the explosion so quickly that it hadn't combusted. From what Zeph had gathered from his new opinicus friends, the saltpeter had to be prepared and a fuse lit to cause real destruction.

A scouting party had revealed a crater and a circle of charred trees, but the damage was contained. None of the other rangers were ready to go, or they had orders to wait, because no more fires started.

Kia returned with Orlea, and they began their own grooming. Zeph found it fascinating how the addition of foretalons instead of paws made some things easier and other things harder.

"It must be nice to see some old hatchmates." Hatzel motioned to Younce.

"Oh? Were you born up in the taiga?" Orlea asked. She looked at Zeph's eyes, which were a mix of brown and orange. "You don't look taiga."

He stuck his tongue out, fuzz from grooming still attached. "They only change to blue in winter, when the days get shorter. Look at Younce, his eyes are green during the summer."

Orlea looked over Kia to confirm the truth in Zeph's statement. Kia was still smarting from the burn marks, so Orlea was helping her preen and reapply the ointment.

"It is nice to catch up," he replied to Hatzel. *Or as close to catching up as anyone can manage with Younce.* "But I prefer the weald. Give me a plump ground parrot over a frozen frog any day."

"Oooh, that's not something you hear very often," Kia said. "I've heard it said that the frogs are delicious. One merchant tried to freeze them and bring them to the eyrie."

Hatzel looked up from cleaning between her paw pads. "I'm with Zeph, for once. They're too sweet. I can never eat more than one."

As they finished grooming, a sound came from outside the cave.

"Helllllooo?" it called.

Kia and Orlea looked alarmed, but Hatzel calmed them

down. "It's just Triddle and Askel. They're the ones who set up the plan to save Cherine."

She was correct.

Both came in with a bounce in their step, but only Triddle's beak was open in a grin. "Hatzel! Zeph! Kia! Cher-oh, I don't know you. You have a secret opinicus? Other than the other two secret opinici? Hello! I'm Triddle. This is Askel."

"Orlea." She stood up and bowed slightly, spreading her wings and tail feathers.

Zeph and Hatzel looked at each other, but Kia seemed used to this greeting, so they shrugged. Triddle returned it happily, his crest falling forwards as he bowed, and smacked Askel, who also did his best imitation, fanning his tail mid-curtsy.

"I wanted to check on Cherine before we went in, in case he had any information on the eyrie. It looks like you found more opies, though," Triddle explained. While Zeph was embarrassed by his use of *opies*, the opinici seemed unaware or ignored the fact that it was usually meant as an insult.

"Are you coming with us?" Askel asked Kia and Orlea.

They both nodded.

"How's Cherine holding up?" Triddle added.

"He'll be fine, but he's not ready to fly yet," Hatzel said. "He's asleep now, but he owes you his life. If you want to ask him something, I imagine he'd be happy to see you again."

Triddle's inner conflict danced from left forepaw to right forepaw in a little march as he came to an inner consensus.

Askel, who'd probably heard about the shape Cherine was in after being pulled through a river, stepped in. "No, he should recover his strength. Is he going to live in your pride after this?"

Hatzel shook her head. "No, it's too much of a risk if Merin recognizes him. He's going with Younce to the taiga once he's well enough to fly short distances. The mountains are too dangerous to be completely without flight."

Hatzel motioned to Younce, who now had the blue-and-orange apprentice with the spots on her back half standing next to him. He pulled some wrapped aneda resin and bandages from his harness and gave them to the medicine gryphon. The taiga was a dangerous enough place that harnesses on gryphons were a given instead of an oddity. It was one reason Zeph didn't have a problem wearing one to the eyrie when he traded. He'd grown up wearing one for the first few years.

"We should get going." Zeph chirped to let Younce know that they were ready. "We have a flight ahead of us if we want to get to the eyrie before dawn."

MEANWHILE, far to the south, Xavi jerked awake. He'd been flying for so long that he'd dozed off again. He was feeling the fatigue. There were a lot of gryphons who were better equipped for sky travel than he was. He'd always considered himself an average flyer. He'd only stayed awake this long because he still itched from the resin in his fur. Zeph had run off with Kia before finishing his grooming.

Xavi wished he'd thought to bring some food with him. There were a few harnesses in the pride for trips to the city. He could have filled one with supplies.

The fisherfolk often carried goods with them and broke the trip up over several days, but a fast and light opinicus might be able to make it from the eyrie to the southern shore in one go. His muscular gryphon build worked better for forest acrobatics than long distance flights. He'd already pushed himself past his usual limit and knew he'd pay for it when he finally reached the shore.

He could see the edge of the weald ahead, but he needed to rest his wings. It was too far for him to make it without a chance to rest, relieve himself, and drink something. Through a break in the canopy, he saw a small stream and began his descent.

He landed a bit off from the clearing, which was why he didn't notice that the branches had been broken to create the view of running water from above. He was thinking about his gryphlets, about Hatzel, about the return trip. He was practicing giving his warning to the fisherfolk in the most convincing way possible.

He was not looking for a trap.

The rangers' nets came fast when he lowered his head to drink from the stream. He flung one off and was making a run for it when he felt a scratch on his leg. It was a light, painless cut, but suddenly the weight of fatigue smothered him. His eyes lost focus as he looked back and saw an emaciated opinicus with a silver talon replacement dripping with some liquid.

"You caught another one, Rakesh," said a voice from the other side of the river.

Xavi prayed the fisherfolk discovered the wingtorn before the attack came.

21

THE PEAFOWL AND THE COBRA

Reeve Brevin's ceremonial home sat atop the center of the Redwood Valley Eyrie, lit by braziers all night. A no-fly zone was enforced because the reeve did not like to have anyone flying over her. The metalwork on the Reeve's Nest building, made from the first mine's discoveries before it collapsed, had always given her the impression of a large bird cage. As a chick living with her mom, she'd looked up at the government building and thought an impossibly large opinicus was housed inside. She was awed to find out that it was her own father who lived up there. It explained why he'd so rarely come to visit her. She'd understood that once she could fly, she was to go to him.

Brevin and Jonas were arguing logistics when a ranger burst in to give the news of the explosion. They'd been discussing the food situation at the Crackling Sea. A small fishing village had been set up across the sea from the eyrie to avoid the fish contaminated in the invasion, but it was too remote to properly guard. It was a stop-gap measure to stave off hunger. If resources had not been an issue—but what was all this about if not resources, she wondered—a new eyrie would have been built on the far side of the sea. As it stood now, if another invasion occurred, there'd be no way to protect it.

An alternative was to take the trained fishing opinici from the Crackling Sea and bring them south to the ocean coast, through the kjarr lands. Ideally, their fishing expertise would translate to ocean fishing. The problem was that there were currently no safe paths for goliath birds from the ocean to the Crackling Sea Eyrie. The kjarr lands were mostly peat bog. When the birds didn't simply sink into the squishy ground, they cried in distress until every sailfin monitor in a hundred yards came to try to eat them.

The Crackling Sea Eyrie was exploring the possibility of relocating to the fisherfolk villages to use that infrastructure to bring the fish north through the new grasslands—currently the weald—and then take the pass by the Redwood Valley Eyrie to get to the Crackling Sea. It was a long route, but with starvation as the other option, it was looking better with every passing day.

Jonas had proposed modifying the fishing rafts used as deep-sea fishing camps to allow the transportation of goods along the southern coast as a possible future option. An expedition was doing just that as they spoke.

The truth of the matter was that the only reason they were able to feed the Crackling Sea opinici now was that so many of them had died in the initial attacks. Using the kjarr pride as wingtorn had been a ploy of desperation in case the invaders returned. They didn't have the food to hold all the wingtorn at the Crackling Sea, so the gryphlets, Jun, and his most loyal kjarr wingtorn had been relocated to the forest for the time being to help with the grand plan to convert the weald into farms and ranches. It worked out well as there'd been fighting between the bog and kjarr wingtorn.

That left the question of what to do with the gryphons once the area was pacified. If the gryphlets converted well to eyrie life, Brevin could use the extra defenses. This assumed the attack on the fisherfolk villages left the wingtorn forces intact. In her experience, no plans ever went off without a hitch.

"Take a moment to catch your breath, then repeat that, please," she commanded the messenger.

The ranger did so, reiterating his message. "The northwest pride cache exploded. None of the rangers guarding it reported in. When we investigated, we found the nesting ground abandoned."

"Abandoned before or after the explosion?" Brevin asked.

He spoke between heavy breaths. "We don't know yet."

Jonas sifted through the parchment on the desk next to the table and pulled out the weald map. It unrolled to show a marker for the nest with a rough sketch of the pride leader, Hatzel.

Her jagged beak looked sinister in the brazier light. Brevin's scouts, prone to exaggeration about all things weald-related, claimed Hatzel could snap a goliath bird in half with it.

"That's the pride we suspect the spy came from," Jonas said. "The merchant, Parrotbane, entered the city under the guise of trading parrots and left with information. His hunting grounds put him close to the grasslands where the university researcher disappeared. We suspect the scholar was tortured to get information out of him, but that his tormentors couldn't read and left his field notebook behind."

Jonas's map included the locations of all the explosives, the locations of the pride nesting grounds, drawings of the pride leaders—with a few question marks by the southeastern plateau—and their best guess as to the population numbers.

He traced a talon down to the fisherfolk villages. "I wish we had better intelligence. Wolden's right, there's so much we don't know."

Brevin rolled her eyes. "Wolden would require the final feather count of each gryphon before we attack. Did you wait for accurate intelligence before cutting off the kjarr pride's wings? What're we supposed to do, send one of the wingtorn into the weald to ask questions for us? I hardly think their wingless state would lend itself to intelligence gathering. That just leaves the two kjarr gryphlets who fledged. Oh, and Satra. Would you trust her that far from the eyrie?"

Jonas shook his head. He'd often confided in the reeve that he thought keeping Satra unclipped was a mistake. There were rumors from their spies that she'd maimed one of her sisters and murdered a taiga gryphon. The fact that the taiga pride had not come to the kjarr's aid spoke to the truth behind the gossip. It was also possible that after the kjarr pride took over the bog pride, the taiga pride had worried they might be next and thought the world might be better off without the kjarr gryphons.

Brevin had watched Jonas do everything in his power to make sure Satra had been treated like a reeve, going so far as to make sure she ate better than he did. His greatest complaint was that she didn't act like a murderer, which hinted at something even scarier if the rumors were true.

Brevin turned back to the ranger. "What of the other rangers? The other explosives?"

"They're still setting up," the ranger replied.

"Did the Hatzel pride set off the explosion or was it an accident?" Jonas asked. "If they set them off, did they warn the other prides?"

"I saw a few others reporting in to Commander Wolden," the ranger said. "None of the rangers close enough to see the explosion had any gryphon trouble."

"Then we're fine," Jonas said with a shrug. "The fire should spread back up through the Hatzel lands. If they flee to the taiga, well, we have to deal with the mountain gryphons eventually. That's what the rangers occupying the kjarr nesting grounds are working on."

"If Parrotbane found out about the explosives ahead of time, he may know about the wingtorn. When do they begin their attack on the fishing villages?" She had no idea how long it took to traverse the length of the weald to the ocean by paw. It seemed like such a dirty place to walk through.

Jonas covered his beak to suppress a yawn. "They've recovered quite well here in the forest with proper nutrition. They were moving at a much faster pace than I anticipated. If they didn't arrive yesterday, they should be there today. They could've already won the shore."

"Or lost it." She dismissed the ranger and traced a talon down the old trail that went south from the Redwood Valley Eyrie to the ocean where two villages were circled. A drawing of a crane opinicus marked the leader of the fisherfolk there. She'd seen the crane opinicus come with their trade delegation several times. It disgusted her that this war would begin with the spilling of opinicus blood by wingtorn gryphons.

She'd sent Larren, the father of one of her seven children, to lead the assault. Wolden had insisted on sending rangers, but she'd wanted someone more expendable, someone she was certain would be expended.

Larren wanted the powers of a consort and had the adoration of her favorite child. This solved that problem and would also make Jun apologetic when he returned and had to explain that Larren had died in the assault.

Jonas seemed concerned by Reeve Brevin's hesitation. "If you want to save your opinici, you must do this. Do you think if we still had a reeve to turn to, we would have come here? Before we saw their soldiers, their assassins took apart our reeve. They prepared him like he was a ground parrot meal and left him on the throne. We found him less than an hour before the invasion came. We didn't discover the bodies of his children until much later."

She shivered. She'd wondered how the invaders knew the location and identity of all his children. She would not fight a war on two fronts like the Crackling Sea reeve had. She would secure the weald before the next wave came.

22

JUN THE KJARR

From the thick weald underbrush, Jun stood watch as the predawn morning gave way to daybreak. They'd made good time despite several setbacks. The goliath bird trail had become a footpath, wide enough for no more than two gryphons at a time. They'd reached the bridge only to find it buried under a layer of dead foliage, and they'd been forced to clear a path across.

With the mighty river dividing the weald, there was no other way south for the wingless kjarr pride. The tributaries from the Strix plateau and taiga spilled into the valley and met on their way south to form Glacial Run, which cut down through the weald and emptied into the ocean, creating a wide delta that presented a tactical issue for the flightless wingtorn. The water flowing out to sea was too swift to swim, though islands dotted the delta like stepping stones between the twin cities of Crane's Nest and Swan's Rest.

As the wingtorn neared the fishing villages, the four opinici who were meant to serve as Jun's jailors began to defer to him. While the rangers had escorted them through the weald, the guards had indulged in a level of self-importance. Larren, the main guard, and Maurle, his second, still maintained a pretense of being in charge while also agreeing with everything Jun said.

They'd served as city guards, not military, and were uncomfortable without the trappings of their station. Reeve Brevin had insisted they leave behind their uniforms and wear plain, black harnesses in case something went wrong. It was the only concession Commander Wolden had permitted to the possibility of failure. Larren, at least, had likely been incentivized to do well here in return for a higher station in the Reeve's Guard when he returned home. He kept a close watch on Jun while sending Maurle with the wingtorn approaching Crane's Nest across the delta.

Now, with the prospect of combat ahead of them, they deferred to "The Kjarr." Whatever they thought of Jun's current arrangement, Jonas had made Jun's prowess clear—this was Jun the Kjarr, leader of the kjarr pride who'd ravaged the Crackling Sea Eyrie, razed the markets, conquered the bog pride, salted the farms, and burned the goliath bird ranch. If not for the murder of his eldest son and capture of his youngest, his reign of chaos would have continued unchecked. And so, Jun's jailors deferred to his judgement, though this was his first time east of the mountains and his second time seeing the ocean.

They waited an hour's march—a detestable way to travel for a pride that once ruled the kjarr skies—from Swan's Rest. The night sky was long gone, but morning was not yet over. Several wingtorn shook dew out of their fur.

Across the delta, the other half of the army followed the western bank. They awaited his call to attack the sister town of Crane's Nest. Thenca and Urious, half-siblings who could've hatched from the same egg they looked so similar, served as communications officers for the raid. Both were bog stock, but where their relatives had always resented Jun's father for conquering their pride, Jun had befriended these two from a young age. He trusted them more than some of his mates and offspring. The rest of the bog pride, the ones who had made several attempts on his life during their wingtorn captivity, remained locked away in the bowels of the Crackling Sea Eyrie.

Thenca looked up at Jun. Her bog markings were clear, a dark beak gave way to a black band that went past her eyes, giving the impression of a mask. Neither she nor her brother were the best fighters, but both could imitate the call of a hundred wild animals loudly enough to be heard for miles. Jun's father had considered them both useless, a novelty and nothing more, but Jun had seen their potential. Being able to communicate from miles away under the cover of parrot *skraarks* made it easier to raid farms or launch surprise attacks on the goliath bird flocks. The fact that neither had children irked him. With an army of mockingbird gryphons, he could rule the continent.

Thenca's fluffy, ringed tail swished back and forth.

He shook his head at her. Not yet.

The opinici, taking their cues from her, became restless. Larren clicked his beak in an annoying manner. He remained irritated when the first scout, a thin spotted gryphon named Ari, returned and nodded her head. *All clear, no problems found.*

Another hour passed without further incident while they waited. Larren's clicking quieted when the second scout appeared, carrying the dead bodies of two children. One of the fisherfolk fledglings still held a branch of berries in her talons. The other, a gryphlet, shared similar markings. Siblings. The second scout nodded her head to confirm. Her section was now all clear, though the parents would come looking for their children.

The opinici—Redwood Valley opinici who were much more squeamish than their Crackling Sea cousins—looked at Jun like he was a monster. He laughed a little in the back of his throat. They'd heard the same orders he had: kill every opinici if you want your gryphlets to remain safe. Their lives for your lives, their children for your children. The midday light glazed the sand and rocks by the time the final scout arrived and added an adult opinicus to the pile with the same markings as the children.

Jun nodded to Thenca, and she let out a loud call that sounded like a parrot being killed by a monitor. They'd been practicing weald wildlife on the way over.

A few moments passed, then her brother's reply call of a mournful parrot came back.

The wingtorn stampeded towards the villages.

THE PLAN HAD BEEN to attack at daybreak, but the delay while they waited on the scouts removed their ability to strike from the dark. Jun never attacked without knowing the lay of the land, and to his mind a late morning attack worked just as well. Most of the adult fisherfolk should still be out on the sea.

Their floating docks, rafts anchored well off shore, were dark lily pads from this distance. The small huts and nests were built at the forest's edge, with rocks and sand buffering them from the sea. The fifty feet between the forest edge and the huts had been cleared of foliage. The wingtorn, now well-practiced at running—they hadn't flown from the Crackling Sea Eyrie to the Redwood Valley Eyrie, after all—covered the distance before anyone sounded an alarm.

Many fisherfolk followed the opinicus practice of raising children in the homes of the adults that birthed them. Jun would have preferred all the children be in one place, but he would make do. He exploded through the side of a reed hut, catching a crane-like gryphon off guard. The crane was dead before he could scream. His mate, a cobalt opinicus, managed to call out before Jun silenced her.

The kjarr pride leader looked out of the hut and saw a small crowd of fisherfolk from the shore hurrying inland. He cleaned the blood off his front paw so he didn't slip on the rocks. He'd heard tales of gryphons who went berserk after tasting the blood of their kin. They became unstoppable warriors, unthinking drones with names like *the swarm* or *the wasp*.

He wasn't like that. Blood was blood. His heart beat faster, but his mind grew calmer. He waited in the hut for the fisherfolk on the shore to reach him. His heart swelled a little with pride. His gryphons followed their training, waiting inside the huts and nests. None of them rushed out.

The fisherfolk approaching the huts slowed down, confused. No one came running out to them for help. When the first brave opinicus opened the reed hut to look inside, Jun leapt out and raked his claws against the opinicus's chest. It made a gurgling sound.

Three of the opinicus's friends attacked him, but a fourth flew to a pile of reeds a hundred feet from the village. Jun called out an alarm for Thenca, who relayed it. There was a cache of eggs nearby.

While he longed to handle the nest personally to spare

his gryphons the emotional damage of killing unhatched children, holding the attention of three fisherfolk was more important. They were hesitant, bewildered, unsure of his lack of wings, unsure of how to fight, unsure what was going on. He bellowed a growl that shook their feathers. Two backed up, but the third, a crane gryphon, let out a cry and stabbed at him with her long, javelin-sharp beak.

He shielded his face, barely protecting his eyes at the cost of bloodying his freshly-cleaned paw, and knocked her off balance. He bit her across the shoulder and neck, throwing her back at her colleagues. She was still alive but wouldn't be able to fight.

He risked a glance at the nest. Several fisherfolk were attempting to hold back the wingtorn as others gathered eggs and flew for the ocean.

He growled at the opponent on his left, then charged right at an alarming speed, barreling through the other. Without wings to depend on, his land speed had increased to an impressive rate out of necessity. While the wingtorn and fisherfolk jabbed and poked at each other, he leapt over both and landed between the fisherfolk and the eggs, a monitor among the parrots. The nearest opinicus grabbed an egg and tried to fly away, but Jun launched himself into the air and caught the opinicus's legs, pulling him to the earth.

The egg hit the ground with a wet *crack*.

Every fisherfolk turned to see what had happened, and Jun's wingtorn seized the opportunity to push their advantage.

Feathers and blood were everywhere. The benefit of being among wingtorn was there was no confusion. Any gryphon with wings was the enemy. All opinici were the enemy. His jailors watched from the woods, afraid to be too close to the traumatized wingtorn during combat.

While Jun, Thenca, and several others had adapted well, there were many wingtorn who had become unhinged since losing their wings. It was not a coincidence that no Crackling Sea opinici had been sent on this mission. They feared reprisal.

A few fisherfolk started to fly away, which is why Jun missed it at first. The light of the afternoon burned orange, but the sky darkened. He dove sideways as a spear was thrown down at him by an opinicus twice his size.

The fisherfolk from the rafts had made their way to shore and brought weapons with them.

THE OPINICUS LANDED between Jun and the remaining eggs. His back was black, his front was white, and his neck and chest were splashed with a vibrant red. With his long neck and beak, he towered over even Jun. Interbreeding with gryphons had created the largest opinicus in the valley.

Jun had read about the leader of Swan's Rest in the maps and scrolls. His village called him Rorin the Hunter. When the strange beasts of the ocean appeared, he was the one who sent them back to the depths. When the crowncrest sea serpent had come to feed on their schools of fish, he had made sure the fisherfolk dined on serpent that night, quipping that it was too gelatinous for his tastes. When other fisherfolk made kills, they splashed their chests with blood to look like him.

The hunter reared up on his hind legs and pointed a spear towards his adversaries. He didn't ask why Jun did these things to his people.

Jun appreciated the lack of chatter and was looking forward to killing him.

Rorin's harness held several fishing spears. They were long, thin, and light. Most were a treated wood, but at least two seemed to be the hollow spines of sea creatures. He brandished one at Jun now.

Jun had never known an opinicus to use a weapon before. Not like this. He'd seen the metal claws of amputees and the damage they could do in close combat. He'd seen the Crackling Sea opinici modify their fishing nets to be used on gryphons, a trick they'd brought with them to the Redwood Valley Eyrie.

He'd heard that the taiga prides used bolas sometimes, coated in aneda resin, but assumed that was just a tale. When the Crackling Sea opinici pushed past the kjarr and into the taiga, the rangers had been brought down and were forced to retreat. The snowy forests of the mountains remained safe, for now. If things went well here, he suspected his next campaign would be at a higher elevation.

Jun rolled left as Rorin launched a spear at him. Where once the contact of his back with the ground would have caused him pain, now there was only numbness where his wings had been. He launched himself at Rorin and managed a scratch before Rorin went airborne.

The other wingtorn fought their own battle. The fisher-folk were tired from fishing and rushing back, but each held a spear and could fly. The ones stupid enough to try to fight on land were taken down, but the wingtorn were at an impasse when the others took to the sky. Thenca, still unharmed, called to the trees for help from their opinicus allies.

Jun took a leap and nearly caught Rorin's leg, hearing Rorin's cry for the first time—it sounded like the rumbling of an iron bell, like chimes buried deep in the earth. Jun put some distance between himself and the opinicus. Rorin gave chase, and Jun led him back to the trees. Rorin was probably too smart to follow Jun into the forest itself, but at least he could buy the other wingtorn some time to clear up the shoreline problem.

He zigged, then zagged, careful not to provide a reliable target for Rorin's spears. Jun's feathers and fur were a sandy color similar to the rocks, but the black backs of his ears made for targets. Rorin was only willing to risk one of his spears, catching a patch of fur but no skin. He was smart enough not to pursue Jun into the woods and stopped just short of the tree line. What Rorin failed to intuit was just how high Jun could jump.

Jun leapt like he could still fly. From twenty feet up a redwood, across an impossible gap, he crashed straight into Rorin and brought the opinicus to the ground. Jun lashed out at Rorin, his claws catching on the tough harness. Rorin's harpoons spilled onto the rocky ground. They grappled, each attempting to catch the other's throat.

WHILE JUN AND RORIN FOUGHT, Thenca's cry brought the four eyrie opinici crashing down upon the remaining fisherfolk, driving them into the paws of the awaiting wingtorn. The ones who escaped with eggs were not pursued into the ocean, but those who remained were killed.

When Thenca realized Jun was not among the wingtorn and rushed to find him, what she found instead was his body impaled upon three spears. Drops of blood formed a trail leading out to sea. The most keen-eyed of the wingtorn could just make out Rorin flying past the floating fishing docks to an island in the distance where the surviving fisherfolk had fled with the eggs. She let out a call to the pride across the delta and heard back a sound of victory. Crane's Nest had not received backup and was destroyed.

She returned her brother's cry with one of her own, one of mourning.

23

WINGTORN

The fisherfolk retreat was short-lived, and Thenca was under siege long before her half-brother Urious and the other wingtorn returned from razing Crane's Nest and rejoined the main forces.

She'd managed to build a small pyre for Jun's body after seeing that crabs were scavenging the dead. Just after one of the guards managed to light the driftwood, the counterattack arrived.

Rorin himself was not in attendance, but small groups of six to twelve opinici would fly in, exhaust their supply of fishing spears, then retreat. Then the wingtorn would come out from the forest and try to scavenge what they could from the huts and make sure no caches of eggs remained. It was obvious they wouldn't be able to hold the shore without flight or cover.

One of the four opinicus guards, Maurle by the look of his orange talons, tried to get advance warning of the raids by flying out over the ocean and keeping watch on the docks and distant island. His build was slight enough that he could, if not hover, come close to it. He wove back and forth, watching the skies. This taught the besieged wingtorn a new lesson: fisherfolk could swim.

While two crane fisherfolk flew just in view at a far anchored raft to hold the guard's attention, a third of a new type swam from under one raft to the next, hiding beneath it and catching her breath. Though the wingtorn had once played along the banks of the river that gave the kjarr its name, and while the eyrie opinici had splashed and swum in Crater Lake from time to time, neither would have considered it possible to swim the distance between the rafts without coming up for air.

Thenca did see a dark shape moving under the water, but it looked like a dolphin. It slipped between Maurle and the shore, then swam down. The tip of a dark tail broke the surface, but by the time she realized it had feathers, it was too late.

The aquatic gryphon exploded from the water below the guard and pulled him under. Thenca's first thought was that Maurle had been eaten by a shark. It was only after the gryphon emerged from the water, shook off the blood and gore, and flew back out that she realized it'd been a gryphon. The next volley of spears came right after.

And so, Urious arrived just as Thenca led the last of her wingtorn back into the forest for cover, her jailors fearful and rambling about "the shark."

EVEN FROM ACROSS THE CAMP, Urious could hear the three remaining guards arguing amongst themselves as the sky changed from blue to black and the stars came out.

Larren insisted they hold the beach at any cost. They'd been given explicit orders. The other two pointed out they'd also been given orders to destroy all the eggs at the beach, and that hadn't worked out.

They hushed when Urious and Thenca came over but perked up when Urious handed out some fish scavenged from Crane's Nest.

"It's cold but good," Thenca apologized. "We can't risk a fire. They may or may not have someone with good night vision, but they can certainly throw their javelins at a bright light."

Larren's thanks were a courtesy, but the other two guards had the good sense to ask about the well-being of the wingtorn.

"They mourn Jun," Urious said, "but this was a better death than he expected after his surrender to the Crackling Sea Eyrie. Those opinici had to steal children to hobble him. At least these fisherfolk have fight in them."

Ari, a yellow kjarr gryphon with black spots, had seen Jun's leap in the fight against Rorin and had spread the word of his heroics. Jun had taken a special interest in encouraging her after she'd lost her wings, and this was her way of repaying the debt. Even now, Urious could see her talking with another group and mimicking Jun's leap.

Urious stayed while Thenca left to make sure the lookouts, four wingtorn who could see fairly well at night, were in place. The guards talked tactics in a half-hearted way that included amazing aerial battles.

Not much chance of us pulling that off. Urious stared at the ocean, and his mind wandered back several years to the kjarr. Neither him nor Thenca had children that he knew of, but the thought of escaping had been too much for them. They couldn't bring themselves to flee after Jun surrendered. Giving up flight had been a terrible cost. Getting to serve with Jun had been worth it, Urious thought. He'd never asked Thenca if she regretted going back to the kjarr to surrender. There'd been rumors she had a suitor she'd met where the kjarr lands and the taiga pride's hunting grounds interlocked. Even if it were true, the taiga was a cold place. Would she have gone and lived there if he hadn't suggested they turn back?

While he mused, he kept watch on the water. There'd been some movement along its surface, but nothing had come ashore. The star-laden sky reflected blue light upon the ocean. Strange, he thought, but he'd never seen water like this before. The Crackling Sea was grey and choppy. The ocean felt different. The blue starlight collected, intensified, and flowed towards the shore.

He stood up, alarmed. "Do you see that?"

The opinici looked out at the glowing mass that seemed to grow closer to shore without moving. His first thought was of the bog wisps that appeared sometimes in the kjarr, but there were so many, and they were an intense blue, like the rarest flowers of the deep bog. The spots of light concentrated on the bodies of the dead wingtorn and fisherfolk on the shore. Where the water touched the corpses, the blue flowed over them. The outlines of gryphon, opinicus, and wingtorn alike became terrestrial constellations.

24

SHARKLIGHT

Turresh, Tresh to her friends, kept her wings half-folded when she swam, imitating the diving petrels she resembled and had modeled her technique after. They had the benefit of webbed feet to move them along, but with the help of an enterprising opinicus tinkerer, she'd managed to develop some simple webbed additions for her back paws that helped a lot, and a slightly less useful version for her forepaws that still allowed her to kill things.

She climbed up the anchored raft, shivering, and dried off in the starlight. She could fly coming out of the water, but it would burn energy she wasn't sure she had. A day of hunting fish, swimming, and fighting wingless gryphons left her tired to the marrow of her hollow bones.

She grimaced as she preened her feathers dry. The scars on her beak ached in the cold, and her feathers tasted like the salamander blood she'd used to lure the bioluminescent shrimp to the shallows to scavenge the bodies of the dead. The giant salamanders on Luminaire Island, named after the shrimp, were ideal for this work. Few ocean predators other than the shrimp would eat salamander. That limited the chance the trail of blood would attract sharks before she finished guiding the glowing scavengers to the dead. The shrimp wouldn't be enough to clean bodies in one night, but perhaps this would allow the spirits to leave the bodies and ascend into the sky ocean.

She hissed softly into the wind as she watched the shrimp do their work. So many dead, why? It was hard to think of the chicks and gryphlets. Her nieces and nephews had been at Crane's Nest. As the tide came in, the shrimp gained access to more of the dark shapes on the shore. Many of the new bodies were small, too small to be adults.

She thought she recognized the outline of her brother in the sand between the water and his hut, but it could've been her mind playing tricks on her. She wasn't as close to her brother as she'd wished. She'd been too serious-minded for him. He loved the sea, loved tending to the gryphlets.

One day, when a swarm of flying fish had kept everyone busy, he'd flown all the way out to Luminaire and picked up a sleeping salamander. He carried it from raft to raft, pausing to douse it with fresh water at each stop. When he reached the shore with his new pet, the chicks and gryphlets had gone wild for it. Not yet fledged, none of them had been to Luminaire or seen a salamander before. Soon, it became a challenge to see who could carry the largest salamander across the water.

Rorin had laughed his songlike, resonate cry when asked to join in. "Let me leave some glory for the others!" he told the gryphlet and begged exemption from the antics. He later helped them set up a pen for the salamanders far enough up the river that the amphibians could stay safely moist. The enclosure had to be fixed every few days or the water would erode it away.

Now the young would play as stars in the heavens, the giant salamanders would eventually escape their enclosure, and she would have to return to Rorin to report in lest he worry about her.

THE RAFTS ANCHORED as stepping stones to Luminaire revealed the set of shallows connecting the once-peninsula to the shore. Before the last great storm, a strange low tide had revealed the path to the island, and the rafts had settled on the ground. Tresh would not have expected this to be their refuge now, but she wouldn't have foreseen an invasion by a legion of flightless gryphons, either.

She called a greeting as she flew close to the island. Even in the dark, her outline should be obvious to all the fisherfolk. She was jet black with a white stomach—her nickname of Tresh was bolstered by her resemblance to a thresher shark—and her beak had several small chips in it from a childhood encounter with a rock crab.

The crustacean had been as big as her, but she'd still managed to kill it. Once it was dead, smashed by a rock she'd pushed down a hill at it, she chipped her beak trying to get inside it before she went for more rocks. The grooves along her beak matched the small spikes on its shell more than shark's teeth, but fisherfolk enjoyed an interesting scar and a good nickname almost as much as they enjoyed a good story.

Her beak may not impress the fish, but it'd impressed several suitors, including a beautiful slate blue opinicus who'd suggested they build a nest together. She told him she wasn't that sort of gryphon, which wasn't entirely true. She just wasn't that sort of gryphon for him.

The fisherfolk weren't immune to the biases of the weald and eyrie. They still called their offspring gryphlets or chicks, as one example. Maybe a quarter of the adults had been part of a pride or an eyrie before coming here. They turned away from their biases on a conscious level, but some of it still bled through in their stereotypes. Especially the ideas that gryphons didn't want to be tied down and opinici were only interested in nesting.

Neither was necessarily true, of course. Gryphon-gryphon pairs did nest out here. Some of them had left the prides because they wanted a place where their relationship could be recognized. Still, the stereotypes lived on, often in arguments between couples, but the day-to-day reality was closer to parity.

Tresh had always seen herself as having a nest full of sharp-beaked, slick-swimming predatory gryphlets that she'd take hunting while someone else took care of the boring task of grooming them. Nesting didn't work that way —it was supposed to be more of a partnership—but she could dream.

The sentries acknowledged her reply, and she landed on the island.

They'd built a small encampment here years ago. While most salamanders were docile, they did grow up to six feet long, so the encampment was made on a stony protrusion on the west side as a safety measure. The rocks reached into the ocean like the claws of a rock crab, and a large tidal pool could be laced with salamander blood to lure in shrimp and illuminate the camp. It was a nice place to get away and think, but it wasn't designed to house a hundred gryphons and opinici.

The few rescued eggs were guarded by those most incentivized to protect them, parents. Some eggs had marks for parents who were now dead. Those were guarded as securely as the rest.

The communities of Swan's Rest and Crane's Nest were close. A fisherfolk may not be friends with everyone but would still probably recognize most on sight. That made it all the more heartbreaking that no one had heard if the third fisherfolk community, Sandpiper's Dune, had been attacked, too. While trapped on Luminaire, they had no way of knowing if the dune fisherfolk were in trouble.

The fisherfolk's medicine opinicus, black circles around his eyes, tested the water. It was fine for drinking, but no one was sure if the spring could support so many. There were several spots in the salty shallows where fresh water erupted from the rocks. Rorin had called Tresh crazy when she'd told him that, but she'd challenged him to swim down with her and taste it. Sure enough, fresh water springs under the ocean. She hoped the water on Luminaire was from a similar spring and not dependent upon rain.

Rorin was talking with a few of the survivors from Crane's Nest. His wounds had been cleaned and treated with a poultice of aneda. The advantage of gryphons and opinici loving fish was that the fisherfolk had been able to trade with everyone. The aneda trees formed the bulk of the taiga but didn't grow in the neighboring weald or kjarr.

The fisherfolk who'd first braved the taiga had hoped to return with sugar frogs. That proved impractical. They still ate their fill, having to delay their departure a day because of upset stomachs, but ended up trading their fish for aneda leaves and resin. These had proven more valuable than frogs for preventing infection. Aneda resin worked on sting ray barbs and most jelly stings.

When the wingtorn attacking Crane's Nest had retreated to meet up with the wingtorn across the delta at Swan's Rest, several fisherfolk had slipped back into Crane's Nest hoping to find eggs. Only two eggs were found, but they located the supply of aneda and brought it with them.

"Is it done?" Rorin asked her.

Tresh smoothed her feathers. "Yes. Their spirits turn to light and join the sky ocean."

"Thank you for doing this," Rorin said. "It's too easy to forget tradition in the face of adversity."

She was unsure how to respond. Their interactions had never been this formal or about tradition in the past. She'd always been one of his best, even though she wasn't one of the hunters who learned from him and painted their throats red. Those hunters celebrated him and sought to learn from what he did well. She'd flown—well, swum—a different current and had her own disciples who'd heard she was back and were making their way up. She kicked off her webbed boots, and another petrel gryphon took them to be mended.

Her relationship with Rorin hadn't been emotional, and she didn't like to see him morose now. "So, some wingless snakes from up north decided to come to our nest and soil it. What do we do now?"

Rorin shrugged, but there was a hint of a smile. "Tonight, we sleep. In the morning, we get more spears and make a plan. In the afternoon, we kill them. Then, when they're dead, we figure out who they were."

"I like a straightforward plan," she said.

25

THE MAP

Thenca found herself with a strange reprieve the next day. Larren, flying high above the forest and nowhere near the water, reported seeing two flights leave the island for the mainland. They went west past Crane's Nest instead of east towards the wingtorn camp.

"Is there another village west of here?" she asked the Reeve's Guard captain from her perch atop a redwood branch.

"How should I know?" Larren turned his beak up at her.

"*You* actually live here," she challenged.

He snorted. "No, I live in the *eyrie.*"

Her tail twitched. "You live in *an* eyrie. It's not the only one. And I meant you live here, east of the mountains. I've heard that the fish at the eyrie are mostly caught here, yes? You must know something."

"No one knows anything about the fisherfolk," he replied. "They're just sick opinici who can't integrate with the eyrie proper and run off to live at the edge of the world. Perverts who want to *nest* with gryphons."

His sneer and candid speech belied a blind spot she'd seen among the Redwood Valley opinici: they no longer thought of the wingtorn as being gryphons anymore. In truth, most wingtorn felt the same way. What alarmed her was that opinici might think of the kjarr gryphlets as gryphons instead of integrated eyrie citizens.

"How did you know where to find Crane's Rest?" She deliberately mixed up the absurdly similar town names.

"Crane's Nest," he corrected. "That's how it was written on the map—" before she could interrupt, he caught on. "Maurle had the map. He's the one the shark got. I don't know if it had more cities."

She looked out at the shore. The tide was low again. If last night's high tide hadn't washed Maurle out to sea, they could still get the map. If the fisherfolk were about to bring in reinforcements, the wingtorn needed to flee now. There'd be no way to win.

"Did either of you get a good look at Maurle's map?" Larren tried to yell down to the other guards. They seemed caught up in their conversation with Urious and ignored him.

She rolled her eyes and then did an exact impression of Larren at a much louder volume. "You two! Over here, NOW!"

Larren and the two guards all started, then the guards flew over.

Urious smirked.

"Yes, sir?" the guards said in chorus, one echoing the other.

"Did you two see the map?" Larren asked. They nodded. "Good. Now, is there another village west of here?"

"I think I saw an 'X' far west of here, south of the taiga," the first guard said.

"No, I think that was just the artist's way of drawing the peaks of the mountains," the second guard offered.

"Does the taiga extend all the way to the ocean?" Larren asked.

They all looked at Thenca.

She stared back. "I don't live here, remember?"

"But on the kjarr side?" the second guard asked.

The kjarr side was all mangrove swamp along the coast. She thought back to the pretty owl-faced taiga gryphon she'd spent so many hours talking with. Hadn't he said he'd flown to the mountains' end once? And found sand?

"I think there are dunes," she said at last. "I don't know if anyone lives there, but a taiga gryphon told me he played in hills of sand where the mountains end and the ocean starts."

Larren worried a talon, his way of coping with annoyance. "We need to make a try for the map to be sure."

ARI WAS LONG, sleek, and covered in small black spots. Urious had found the fastest wingtorn for the map retrieval task. Black streaks like tear stains flowed down her eyes and around her black beak. She looked a little like the sand in direct sunlight, which might help.

Thenca sketched a replica of the shore with a circle where Maurle had died while Ari looked on.

"If there's no map," Urious explained, "just head back. I think we're seeing his body there, but it can be hard to tell."

Ari nodded. She removed her harness and stretched. Her positive attitude had made her popular before losing her beautiful orange wings. She'd been the den mother of the kjarr pride once. Two of the gryphlets being held at the eyrie were hers. Since becoming wingtorn, her popularity had only increased.

She'd been a good flyer, but she was a wonder at running, something she'd never have discovered living with wings at the edge of a peat bog. Jun had calmed her many times, reassuring her worries about the gryphlets, complimenting her ability to run. *Fortune in misfortune* was the mantra he'd used. There was little of that to go around, but the eagle's share had gone to her.

While Larren was on the ground, the other two guards kept watch from atop the redwoods. There'd been no sign of stirring from the fisherfolk since two flights left the island around dawn. There were still some debris along the shore —driftwood, barrels, and a tall post that rose above the water line even at high tide that held water skins, spears, and other supplies.

The wingtorn couldn't help but notice that the fisherfolk villages had been designed as if to protect them from the ocean side. Ari didn't know what that meant, but she would have loved an opportunity to sit and talk with one of them, find out how they lived.

An opinicus guard gave the all-clear, and Ari made a dash for it.

The distance from the forest to the huts: cleared in a flash.

The loose rocks before the sand: cleared, but not as fast.

The sand slowed her down, but she kept at it. Around forty yards from the corpse they thought was Maurle, she heard an alarm. From her left and right, further down the beach, two all-black gryphons crawled out from beneath driftwood. If they weren't the same shark-gryphon who killed Maurle, they were cut from the same cloth. They wore wooden masks resembling sea creatures. Their back feet looked strange, webbed, as though they were backwards opinici, and they wore harnesses made from something waterproof. When she realized they were both gryphons, and thus wouldn't be throwing spears her way, she continued her dash for the map.

Instead of going after her, they attempted to go towards the rocks to cut her off from the camp.

Her paws shook as she checked the body. The tide may have withdrawn, but the entire ocean seemed full of possibilities that ended poorly for her.

She had one bit of luck. The body *was* Maurle. She snapped his harness off and held it in her beak.

She tried running left and right, but the sand slowed her down too much to let her go around the gryphons. When she sprinted, one of them flew to stay between her and the forest. If there were more, they were probably coming from the water. She could see Urious and Thenca running out, but they weren't her first choice for backup.

She needed Jun, but Jun was dead.

Another call of warning from the tree tops: gryphons from the water. There was a third gryphon, more brown than black, but with the same flippers and build, flying from a raft to the shore.

Ari called out for help. The two fisherfolk hissed at her. They saw Urious and Thenca coming from the forest and decided to make their move. One of them started to fly when a spear flew past its head.

The two guards had abandoned their station as lookouts and had joined the fight with as many spears as they'd been able to scavenge between raids. Their aim was poor, but it was enough to shift things in their favor. The two black gryphons split, one going east, one going west, then they cut south to the water and disappeared. The third gryphon watched them from the edge of the water. He seemed to be going to check Maurle's shrimp-eaten body to see what was so important about it.

The guards escorted Ari back into the forest, and they picked through the harness looking for the map to try to determine just how much trouble they were in.

26

SERPENTS

The Redwood Valley Eyrie was quiet. With the impending shore invasion and weald fire, Brevin took a moment away from Reeve's Nest to tuck her children in. They'd grown up in the same nest she'd lived in as a chick, away from the politics of the official housing. If she'd taken a consort, they would have lived here and watched the children. Despite the parallels to gryphon culture, reeves were often expected to have several eggs with different opinici to protect the family line. She'd been considered unusual in that she was an only child.

Even the Crackling Sea Eyrie's reeve, whose consort and interests were exclusively male, had felt the pressure to father a small flock of children. She understood that pressure. She'd never been attracted to another opinicus—the power dynamic complicated issues further—but she'd found time to lay seven eggs.

On most nights, a team of nannies would watch over her brood, but since the Crackling Sea Eyrie's attack, she'd also assigned guards to keep an eye on her youngest. Three of her oldest offspring had homes and mates of their own now, so all of Brevin's eggs weren't in one nest, so to speak. She didn't know what good it would do, but she couldn't send them away from the eyrie. There was nowhere safe to go.

The only way to live in a safe world was to reshape it, pacify it. It was why she'd made the decisions she had. Her father's only indulgence to the eyrie's isolationist policies was to keep the goliath bird pass open to the Crackling Sea. Living at the far corner of the world, past a frozen taiga, against the untamed ocean, had been an effective strategy for independence for many years. It had allowed generations to be born, live their lives, and die without interference. If the Crackling Sea Eyrie's diminutive size and lack of prosperity was any indication, the Redwood Valley Eyrie had done well for itself by comparison.

Her youngest child, the one she'd had with Larren, chirped for a story. She was the only opinicus in the room not wearing a harness because she refused to wear her sisters' hand-me-downs. Under protest, all of Brevin's offspring were all sharing the same room with soft nests lined against the walls. The feral goliath birds of the taiga had feathers that resembled fur, and each of her chicks had a bed made from the feathers of a different goliath, ranging in color from white to grey. The reeve sat on a cushion and settled in for story time.

She told them about their ancestor killing the great cobra to save the lord of all eyries. Seven snake pendants, all different species, had been crafted to remind them of their lineage. Whoever became reeve after her would inherit her cobra necklace as she'd inherited her father's on his passing.

They asked about the types of snakes across the continent, snakes that hadn't been seen by any of the Redwood Valley opinici in her lifetime. Cobra were a world away. The taiga formed a barrier that kept most snakes out. She didn't know if sea snakes existed off the weald shores. They were excited by the idea of snakes that swam but seemed unimpressed that gliding snakes were a rarity outside the weald.

She'd have to ask someone at the university about offshore snakes when she had a moment. *I should have asked that apprentice, Kia, when I interrogated her. She didn't provide any other useful answers.*

The scholars kept a taxonomy of all wildlife. They'd insisted on updating it with capybaras after the grasslands experiment—the tome's first new addition since squirrels. During her last meeting with scholars, she'd feigned interest, and they'd regaled her with reports of massive snakes crossing the grasslands, a few large enough to eat an opinicus whole. Still, she told her children the stories of serpents as her mother had told them to her.

She finished up the story of the krait, her youngest's favorite for being more venomous than a cobra without drawing attention to itself. The last to ask for a story was her middle child, Ivess. She had a dorm at the university but had been called back, under protest, after word of the Crackling Sea's invasion arrived. Unlike her sisters, Ivess had a native favorite, the leaf-nosed snake.

A leaf-nosed snake was far too small to eat an opinicus whole. It didn't have the venom of a sea snake nor the flair of a cobra. It couldn't fly. Still, Ivess loved it. This was not a story Brevin's mother had told her, so Brevin's telling of it was her own creation. It'd become a game they shared.

"What does it do if I were to come after it?" Ivess would ask.

"It rises up and flattens its neck like a cobra," Brevin would respond.

"But what if that doesn't scare me? I am reeve's blood, after all." Ivess's questions hadn't changed in all these years.

"Then it puts its tail into some leaves and shakes them to sound like a rattlesnake." Brevin put her talons under some loose parchment and shook them for effect.

Ivess laughed in spite of herself. "But what if I take that as a challenge?"

"Then it flips over and plays dead," her youngest chimed in, unable to restrain herself any longer.

Much like politics, Brevin thought. Being a cobra was enough to keep most problems away. Other times, a warning served. Lulling your opponent into thinking they'd won was sometimes the only way to survive. The Crackling Sea Eyrie was clearly on its back now. The army was stationed there in case the invaders returned to finish them off. A leaf-nosed ploy.

"May I come with you to the meeting again tonight?" Ivess asked.

Brevin thought of the reeve's children found after the Crackling Sea Eyrie invasion. Would Ivess be any safer by her side? She didn't know.

"Yes, but only for a little," she conceded. If all went well, the fighting would be a day's flight away at the closest.

THE SMALL LEDGE below the Snowfeather Dam overlooking the flameworks and Redwood Valley Eyrie was crowded. Zeph, Kia, Orlea, Askel, Triddle, Hatzel, and twenty gryphons they'd picked up from their pride on the way all huddled and kept low in the pre-morning darkness. Their goal was to unleash Triddle on the flameworks—no one trusted Askel inside anything with *flame* in the title—while the rest would infiltrate the eyrie from the ground and use the confusion to smuggle Satra and the gryphlets out of the city.

After departing the medicine cave, Askel and Triddle had put on harnesses that contained saltpeter wrapped in a dry covering. The saltpeter had come from the crate they'd found Cherine with. The dried leaves were the same type Zeph used to wrap the ground parrot meat when it was time to bring it to market. Askel and Triddle had been understandably nervous about bringing the explosive with them into the medicine gryphon's cave.

The additional saltpeter caches the prides had found with Cherine's map were moved to a pile just north of the weald in the grasslands. It wasn't an ideal location, but there was a small pond for the capybaras, and no pride wanted to house anything combustible in their territory.

Merin and Strix's groups were in position, waiting on the flameworks diversion to begin. The harpy eagles were at the ground-level eyrie gate Zeph had used to escape. It was safer to have two groups going after Satra in case one ran into trouble.

The owls were in the east. Because Strix's plateau was the only safe place for the eastern prides to flee to, most of his kin stayed behind to help with the evacuation. They were trying to find a safe path up for the wingtorn. Only Strix's children, six owl gryphons with black and red markings, had come with him to help find Satra. He'd said he would clear the route out and make sure they weren't disturbed by guards. The other pride leaders had not come themselves, opting instead to attempt to find the other caches in the weald.

Merin considered it cowardice, but Zeph understood. What good was any of this if all the prey animals in the weald burned? The redwoods would survive, even thrive once the fires burned down. But if there wasn't enough food to support the prides through the winter, tensions would rise even higher than they were now. A few stragglers had shown up despite their pride leader's commands to the contrary. Zeph recognized at least one feathermane. In total, there were almost fifty gryphons against an eyrie of thousands.

Younce had guided them through the mountains to get to their vantage point unseen, then left. He'd promised to bring the orange and blue medicine apprentice with him and ask his pride leader if Cherine and Kia would be welcome.

The apprentice had been sent because after the monitor sickness, the old medicine gryphon wanted to check on the health of the prides and pool knowledge. Her young assistant would do just that, if she could survive the cold and Younce's grumpiness. While Zeph would never admit it, he did miss Younce's taiga pride grit, just a little bit.

Everyone knew the plan, so Hatzel's only words of wisdom were simple. "Everyone know what to do? Good. Now go do it."

They split into groups, and Triddle led the first into the flameworks.

27

FLAMEWORKS

Triddle and four copper hawk gryphons made their way into the *Nitrary,* as the map referred to it. He'd interacted with the members of Hatzel's pride from time to time but never could tell them apart. Most of the ones who weren't magpie-plumed liked Xavi resembled those with him now, a nondescript brown with a slight build that presumably made hunting easier but made it impossible for Triddle to distinguish them from each other.

He'd only learned how to identify Zeph because of the way Parrotbane held himself. His plumage wasn't flashy, but he was always interacting with Hatzel, and Hatz was easy to spot. Once Triddle knew to look for her giant, saberbeak form, he could always locate Zeph hovering nearby.

With these four, Triddle could only identify them based on the colors of the pads on their paws. One had all black, one had grey, one had a mix, and his favorite had a single back foot with pink pads while her other feet used black.

They landed at the edge of the flameworks, and it was only once they were on the ground that he found the failure in his cataloging system. With all their feet on the stone floor, he couldn't tell Pink Paw from the others. Depending on how things went tonight, he may need to work out a better system for identifying Hatzel's pride. He and Askel had decided that it would be better to eat parrots with Hatzel's pride than to get stuck in an evacuation camp in Strix's territory if the weald fire got out of control.

Triddle, Pink Paw, and the other three gryphons padded around a field that smelled of manure and saltpeter, then crept to the flameworks' entrance. It was the first building Triddle had ever seen composed of stone instead of treated redwood, and he loved it on that merit alone. He and Askel used to sneak up to the water mill to see how the opinici got the water all the way into the sky. The waterworks used treated redwood and thick bamboo to move the liquid. The flameworks, by contrast, was designed to limit accidental flammability. Unfortunately for them, Triddle thought, it had not been designed to prevent someone from coming in and trying to blow it up.

Askel is going to be so jealous that I got to blow something up.

There weren't any guards. The stone entrance slid open without a squeak. No alarms sounded.

No oversized ground parrots had been specially trained to defend against attackers—Askel's pet theory for how eyrie buildings were defended at night. Triddle had devoted exactly one pouch to parrot treats just in case. Neither of them had managed to train a ground parrot to do, well, much of anything, but both were inspired by stories of peafowl being taught to kill cobras. Now it looked like he'd brought the parrot treats with him for nothing.

A brazier hanging from the ceiling lit the entryway. Whatever they were using to light it wasn't the usual oil. It produced almost no smoke. The wall had a black outline of an opinicus with a plaque that read: *Felicio the Phoenix is remembered for his contributions to the wellbeing of the eyrie. Miner, pioneer, inventor, father. He lived as he died, consumed by flame. -Bario*

The four gryphons with Triddle couldn't read, so he read it to them and explained what a blast shadow was. They looked askance at the wall.

Past the entryway, a thick wall divided the flameworks into two sections. Taken together, they were around the same size as a nesting ground. The larger half to the left contained storage and packing. It was full of crates of saltpeter. The far side was open to the fields where it looked like they were trying to create saltpeter by leaching water through a mixture.

He'd listened to Askel interrogate Kia on the flameworks and saltpeter on the way over. As best Triddle understood it, Felicio had been in charge of the early mining attempts, and they'd come across a mine of saltpeter while looking for copper. When the mine was around half played out, an incident caused an explosion that closed off the mine and created the blast shadow in the entryway.

Bario had been more interested in creating saltpeter by other means, but as long as the mine was productive, there was no money for research into alternative methods. Though the loss of his father was tragic, it provided him with the funding and resources he needed. What he did in the flameworks was seen by the common opinicus as more witchcraft than science, but the addition of the braziers to the city had been a boon to industry and nightlife. If the scent-free, smoke-free example by his father's shade was any indication, Bario had continued to iterate on the design.

Triddle took off his harness and detached the saltpeter he'd brought with him, still wrapped like parrot meat. He stuck a claw into the top and showed the gryphons how to create a trail of saltpeter from the warehouse through the entryway to the outside.

While they got to work, he went to look inside the right door. He mostly trusted the explosion to take out both sides —just look at what several crates had done by Hatzel's nesting grounds—but it didn't hurt to be safe. And, if he were honest with himself, he really wanted to know what Bario's laboratory looked like. Askel would have so many questions about it.

Unlike the entryway door, this one was thick and emitted a metallic squeal when Triddle pushed it to the side. The lab had clearly been designed to keep any explosions contained. The wisdom of building a flameworks that was both laboratory and storage was dubious at best, but if the door hadn't been effective at keeping explosions isolated on the laboratory side, Triddle wouldn't need to be here blowing it all up.

The room was full of strange mechanisms and pots of different powders. There were metal gizmos of every shape and size. He wished Askel was here to see it with him. Triddle had never seen so much metal before in one place. It remained too precious to be traded outside of the eyrie. The few pieces he'd acquired had been scavenged from harnesses in the eyrie trash heap.

The door rolled shut behind him, probably a safety precaution, and he looked around for a brazier to light. His eyes adjusted a little, and he saw one across the room. He reached for his—well, Cherine's—flint and tinder, but they were in his harness in the entryway. He heard the sound of someone else striking the flame.

"Hello? Is someone there?" asked a sleepy, trilling voice.

WHILE STRIX HAD SAID he would wait on the eastern side of the eyrie for the explosion, that had been a lie. An explosion after sun-up? Who wanted to kill people in the light? No, that simply would not do. Not when he already knew the eyrie so well.

When the other pride leaders had chirped and chuffed about how no opinicus rangers could have snuck through their hunting grounds, he'd laughed to himself. He'd been sneaking through their hunting grounds for years. Though, at night, weren't they really his hunting grounds?

He'd matched wits with all manner of game over the years. If a species flew or walked and lived in the weald, he'd stalked and probably eaten it. Some of that was his devotion to excellence. Hunting different game taught him to be a better hunter of all game. Some of it was a hunger within that only became satiated by novelty. He could only match wits against a type of animal so many times before it became boring. The rush of the first kill halved with each subsequent.

He believed this was a problem most gryphons faced. Their intellectual curiosity required constant maintenance. He'd seen it in gryphlets. They'd hunt small lizards and squirrels around the nesting grounds until there were none left. Then the gryphlets would hunt each other. All play, of course. Strix even organized games several times a year that allowed for gryphons to hunt other gryphons for prestige and recognition. It helped focus their minds.

Old gryphons that became too weak to hunt or play went mad with boredom. He'd have gone mad long, long ago if restricted to his little plateau. So he'd ranged across the weald until it, too, made him bored. Then he'd ranged into the eyrie's hunting grounds to kill turkeys, the northern mountains to hunt feral goliath birds, the kjarr to dismember sailfins, to the bog to pry open matamatas, and finally circled back.

Yes, he'd eaten the strange, fuzzy herd beasts on the grasslands. He'd grown fond of the taste.

Then he'd infiltrated the eyrie itself. First, he came in through the forgotten ground-level gates and looked around. Owl opinicus and gryphon front legs were both so shaggy that he wasn't worried about being identified from a distance. He'd never been teased about his lack of ears, but it pleased him that they helped hide him in the city.

He'd stolen a harness that looked official and worn it inside the city. The upper levels were lit by braziers, but the underbough was not. It was a dark place, and no one detected his presence. He'd seen the wingtorn, their hostage gryphlets. He knew about the waterworks that held Triddle's attention so. He'd smelled the awful saltpeter operations at the flameworks. He just hadn't felt like he needed to share that knowledge with the other prides. They'd want to know what he was doing in the eyrie, which was none of their business.

More than the plateau, more than the weald, the eyrie had become his hunting grounds. Opinici came in all shapes, sizes, and combinations. Thus far, no two had been quite the same. He'd not eaten them, of course. Well, he may have tried a little. Capybaras had ruined him on other game. This hunting was just to assuage the hunger in his mind. But he was running out of combinations in the lower levels. He'd managed a Reeve's Guard and a ranger, but he wanted a reeve. He'd overheard the wingtorn talking about how an opinicus had killed the reeve of the Crackling Sea Eyrie, and the idea had stuck in his mind like a parasite.

The soft calls he made were imperceptible to all but the most sensitive of ears. The reciprocating sound he received back was calming, like the absence of other noise. He counted to three, then slipped through the opening in the Reeve's Guard Headquarters' roof with six of his pride. There were no sounds. Strix and five shapes slipped back out of the roof and disappeared into the city in all directions. Strix made his ascent alone towards Reeve's Nest.

SEVERAL MINUTES LATER, a Reeve's Guard came back from patrol. Possibly from having been admonished for using the roof entrance several times, he came in through the door. His mind only had the barest amount of time to register the carnage inside before the seventh gryphon, left behind, took care of him. There was a thud and the sound of the owl-gryphon dragging the body to the others, then the quiet scraping as she closed the door and waited for the next Reeve's Guard to return from duty.

Ninox, Strix's daughter, licked the blood off her paw. *Too salty*, she thought. It was her first time for opinicus. Already, she missed the taste of the capybaras they'd stolen from the grasslands.

TRIDDLE STEPPED behind a stone bench to hide his forepaws.

"Hello, who's there?" Bario called.

"Hello! My name is Askel," it was the only name that wasn't Triddle's that he could think of on short notice. "The reeve sent me. I was told you had a report concerning the explosion last night?"

There was a small makeshift nest in the corner. Bario probably had quarters in the eyrie proper but preferred to stay here when he worked late. "What? Oh, yeah. I wrote down a few notes. I, er, didn't know the reeve would be wanting to read them. A ranger was here earlier. Are you part of the rangers?"

"University scholar, assigned to help the reeve temporarily." Triddle did his best opinicus accent, the one he used when explaining things to Askel.

"Oh, okay. Hmm." Bario rubbed sleep from his eyes. "It was an interesting explosion. Most likely the crate itself was lit while the oil was still packed in its protective jar. The concussive blast is fascinating. It had the effect of actually limiting the spread of the flames. Explosives to stop fires! Can you imagine?"

Triddle could absolutely imagine. He'd heard Askel suggesting such things for years now. This was all Askel tended to imagine. Triddle decided he liked Bario despite the rumors regarding his father's demise.

The junior phoenix finished wrapping a scroll of vellum with his findings and handed it to Triddle.

Triddle reached out with his paw to take it.

They both looked down at their paw and talons holding the vellum, and then Triddle headbutted Bario as hard as he could.

The opinicus fell, unconscious. The gryphon still stood but now had a headache. He reached up to smooth down his crest feathers. Askel had always said that their heads were their greatest hunting assets.

Triddle propped the door open with the stone bench and shouted, "Pink Paw." Evidently, this was something she'd been called in the past, for she showed up with an unhappy expression on her face. Still, she helped him drag

Bario out of the workshop while the other gryphons finished spreading the saltpeter around. They returned but seemed reluctant to bring Bario along. Triddle couldn't bring himself to let the opinicus stay here and burn.

While the Hatzel pride gryphons worked together to fly the unconscious opinicus to safety, Triddle retrieved his harness. Askel had worked out a system of dry vines he thought could serve to delay the explosion and sent them with Triddle. As he placed them down, he recalled seeing something similar from the workshop. He side-stepped the bench and looked around. There were many metal talon models, some of which allowed a kind of poison sac to be secured to them. There were fuses. There were all sorts of goodies. He grabbed as many odds and ends as he could stuff in his harness and the longest fuse he could find, then went back to the entryway. He had no way of knowing how effective this new saltpeter was, but he wanted enough time to fly as far as he could from the blast. He struck the flint and tinder fungus using his beak and paw, and as soon as it caught, he flew out of the flameworks and made a break for the hills.

The blast shadow of Felicio overlooked the burning fuse as it crept from the entryway, down the hall, and into the saltpeter storage facility.

28

THE POACHER AND THE PHOENIX

Hatzel led her gryphons—with Kia and Zeph bringing up the rear—as they followed Orlea, their opinicus poacher guide, through the underbough of the Redwood Valley Eyrie towards the hatchery where they hoped to find Satra. Hatzel wanted to be in position when the blast hit so they could evacuate the gryphlets in the confusion.

The last saberbeak found the undergrowth to be disgusting. It was a combination of opinicus waste, vines, decay, and bugs. She hoped the flameworks explosion would remain contained and the eyrie wouldn't burn, but these bottom levels were in desperate need of a purging fire.

Knowing Triddle would likely get distracted in the flameworks looking for shiny prizes to bring home to Askel, Hatzel motioned to Orlea and the others to stop and help her scrape away some of the vegetation. Hatzel inspected one of the redwoods that formed the pillars of the eyrie and found rot both in the tree and in the iron vines that rein-forced it. Given enough time, she thought, the eyrie would come down under its own weight. It was unfortunate they couldn't afford to wait that long.

When they reached the hatchery, they didn't find Satra. Instead, they found Merin and his pridemates waiting for them.

"Take the scenic route?" Merin quipped. "We have a problem."

There weren't thirty gryphlets, as Kia had seen earlier, but nearly a hundred. Merin's pride had come in from a different direction and found two more hatcheries. He had twenty gryphons with him, eighteen of whom were wearing special harnesses designed to carry gryphlets.

"What are you wearing?" Hatzel asked the harpy eagle pride leader.

He gestured to a set of racks along the wall. It seemed Satra was one step ahead of them, and she'd had the harnesses made here at the eyrie for this exact contingency.

Hatzel had another twenty gryphons with her, but she could tell it wouldn't be enough. A few of the kjarr gryphlets were no longer gryphlets—they were now fledglings, young adults who could fly. Like Crackling Sea opinici, they wore harnesses with a pink fish emblem.

To the fledglings' credit, they hadn't raised an alarm. Satra must have prepared them for the possibility of escape. Still, it didn't help with Hatzel's predicament. Even if every weald gryphon on the rescue team carried a gryphlet, they'd need twice their number to evacuate the hatchery.

"Where's Satra?" Hatzel asked. She'd meant to ask Merin, but one of the new adults spoke.

"The reeve wanted her close until they heard from the shore," the kjarr fledgling answered, "in case there were any problems with Jun."

Hatzel considered this. "We can't do this without

bringing her along. If we bring them and not her, the wing-torn may think we're kidnapping their offspring."

"We can't search the entire eyrie for her," Merin countered, but his mind seemed to be catching up to Hatzel's. There were too many gryphlets for the few wingtorn who had been stationed here.

Most gryphons didn't lay an egg every season. If each pair of parents that had a gryphlet had become wingtorn, that was still two hundred gryphons. Counting the old, infertile, newly fledged, and adult gryphons who may not have chosen to have gryphlets, the number of potential wingtorn grew.

There could be as many kjarr gryphons as all the weald prides combined. However many wingtorn had been housed here at the Redwood Valley, there could be hundreds more enslaved at the Crackling Sea Eyrie. If Hatzel's gambit left even a quarter of the gryphlets behind, they could have made enemies of hundreds of wingtorn parents. They had no way of knowing right now.

Hatzel frowned. Had Satra withheld the accurate number because she thought no one would try to rescue a hundred gryphlets? It was too late to back out.

"Jonas will be with the reeve or in his quarters," the other kjarr fledgling said. "If you need Satra, you only have to go where Jonas is, and she'll come to you."

Merin and Hatzel looked at each other.

"Why is that?" he asked.

The two kjarr fledglings looked at one another. They still seemed unsure of their rescuers. One shrugged, and the other spoke. "Jonas did not cut the wings off the gryphons himself, but he was the one who developed the method for cutting the wings and keeping the gryphon alive. He was the reeve's consort. He wielded massive power before the eyrie's fall."

"Okay, new plan," Hatzel said. "I'll go investigate Reeve's Nest and see if Satra is inside. You find this Jonas and wait there."

To her surprise, Merin agreed without argument. He ordered the eighteen gryphons with harnesses to fly their gryphlets to safety. That left Hatzel with eighty gryphlets to worry about.

The two kjarr fledglings recognized Orlea from her babysitting efforts and chirped a greeting. Orlea grabbed Kia, Zeph, the fledglings, and Hatzel and pulled them into a circle.

"Do you know where Jonas keeps the goliath birds?" the poacher asked the kjarr fledglings.

One of them nodded.

"Kia, Zeph, would you go with her and see if the goliath birds are still here?" Orlea asked. "If so, we may be able to pack these gryphlets up and ship them out. I'll stay behind and clear the goliath bird trail south of town. There'll be at least one gate to break."

Hatzel nodded and sent Merin's two remaining gryphons and ten of hers to help Orlea. Hatzel could only hope that being outnumbered five-to-one would keep Merin's pride from balking at obeying orders from an opinicus.

With the new plan in place, it was time for her to leave. Afraid to climb the rotting trees, she jumped as high as she could, beat her massive wings, and began her ascent to find Satra. A moment later, the concussive blast of the flame-works shook the eyrie and cracked the hatchery walls.

WHILE MERIN HAD KEPT Hatzel and the others occupied, Askel had slipped away and met two of Merin's most loyal offspring by the waterworks. The aqueduct system pulled water from Crater Lake and the Snowfeather River below up to incredible heights. It was a testament to the construction that when the entire eyrie shook and swayed in the blast, the aqueducts stayed in place. Askel's assistants were splashed with water.

He hadn't told Hatzel that Merin had his own plans for the eyrie just like he hadn't told Merin anything about Hatzel's opinicus allies. Askel was good at keeping secrets. He knew that his pride had not evacuated west to the taiga border, but instead had gone east. He hoped he'd be able to join Hatzel's pride, but he was keeping his options open.

He was here to create an explosion, but Merin had been specific. When they'd discovered the rangers had used fire suppressant powder to keep the weald's wildfires from gaining purchase, Askel had pointed out that the eyrie was also a forest that hadn't had a good wildfire in years. The eyrie's redwoods had been kept from burning for far too long. He knew all about that because he'd been placed in charge of starting small weald fires to clear out underbrush. It kept the weald healthy.

Now, Merin had told Askel, the eyrie needed him. It was time to cleanse the bad and let the forest regrow healthy and strong. The opinici may evacuate and find safety elsewhere, but the eyrie as a construct and institution needed to go.

Askel had ordered his two pridemates to remove the safety powder next to the braziers before the flameworks went up. He could just kick the braziers off the sides and see what burned, but he couldn't be sure of how that would go, so he'd come up with a different plan.

He went out behind the largest butchery and called for help in his best opi trill. When the butcher came out, the gryphons subdued him. Askel now had access to all the oil used in the braziers for this market level.

When the flameworks exploded, a moment later there was a smaller explosion from the middle of the market, courtesy of some of the saltpeter he'd brought with him. The gryphons with him looked confused at the hole. What was the point? He ignored their questioning looks and sent them out to get ready to evacuate the residential areas. Merin hadn't asked for an evacuation, that was Askel's touch, but the gryphons just assumed it was part of the plan.

"How will we know when to start the evacuation?" one asked.

"Look for the flames," was all Askel said.

Once they were gone, he lit the butchery on fire. The oil burned bright and high but remained contained. Then he went up to the aqueduct above the butchery and set the second, smaller explosive.

The explosion was tiny, but it took out a length of the bamboo. He squawked an apology to Triddle for harming his beloved waterworks. The redirected water spilled into the butchery and spread the flaming oil across the market square, where it hit the large hole in the center and spilled down into the depths of the eyrie, a waterfall of flame.

Askel sat atop the aqueduct and watched it burn, the fire and water mixing together and spreading. Was there a better way to describe his relationship with Triddle? He hoped Orlea would be able to evacuate the lower levels. He didn't want anyone to get hurt. But when Merin took him aside and suggested this plan to him—just him, no Triddle —he knew it would have to happen. He'd never get another opportunity like this in his lifetime. He was made for this moment.

Some Reeve's Guards located him an hour later, still staring at the flickering orange light coming from the hole in the market floor. His wings and tail were spread, absorbing the dancing light and heat. They pulled him away, put a leash on him, and led him to the jail north of the market to question later. Even as they locked him up, they seemed unaware that the oil had spread to the lower levels. The fire had yet to reach up to their glistening spires, but it would come.

Yes, the flames would come.

29

INSURRECTION

When a kjarr fledgling led Kia and Zeph to the goliath bird ranch, they expected to find the birds unattended. They did not expect to find Headmaster Neider and his cockatiel packing up a saddle full of books to make their escape with. Despite the fact that he may have been the one to send the rangers after her, the owl opinicus still seemed to be Kia's best bet for notifying the university all at once. Before Zeph could do his hunting thing, she flew straight to the scholar.

Kia could smell smoke in the air. Had cinders from the flameworks reached the underbough? "Headmaster! Wait, you need to notify the dorms and get everyone out of here."

Neider turned around and started in surprise. He looked around, perhaps for a guard, but saw only Zeph. The kjarr fledgling had begun putting pack harnesses on the goliath birds.

"Kia? What brought you back to the eyrie? You need to go," the headmaster said.

The cockatiel looked around nervously. He had patches where he'd groomed away his fur and feathers. His harness was packed, and he was trying to hold a book in his talons, *The Complete Genealogy of the Forest Reeves.*

"We, we, we need to go, headmaster," the cockatiel chattered. They must have cut off his supply of red fern after what happened with Kia. "They'll be expecting us when word gets to them about what hap, hap, happened here."

The acrid scent of smoke emanating from the eyrie center filled the stable.

"You have to help us evacuate. The eyrie is on fire," Zeph said. "The weald may already be burning. We have to get the opinici north."

It was like a switch had been flipped in the headmaster's brain on the word *north*. He laughed. "Zeph Parrotbane, in the flesh! The world is already burning, didn't you know? We were just the last to ignite."

"I don't understand—" Kia began, but the opinicus interrupted her with a wave of his talons.

"Save yourself, Kia. Go run off with your gryphon and escape to the taiga. Maybe they won't want the heights? They've ignored other pockets of gryphons. Or come meet me, in the north. You remember the circled eyrie, yes? They've promised, promised so much, in exchange for just a little information here and there."

The cockatiel dropped the book and shook the headmaster, snapping him out of it.

"Kia, I'm so sorry about Cherine. Goodbye." He and the cockatiel fled north before Kia could tell him that Cherine was still alive.

"What can we do?" Zeph asked her.

"The chimes outside his office," Kia replied. "They won't reach far, but when students come, we can send them to spread the word. They're designed to reach across the campus."

He nodded. "I'll do it. You help save the kjarr gryphlets."

"No, the upper levels won't be safe for you alone," she protested.

Zeph held up his forepaws. "You're going to be able to secure the harnesses faster and safer than anyone else. Get the gryphlets out. I'll find the chimes."

Kia barely had time to agree before he'd disappeared up the nearest tree and glided off into the darkness. She flew over to where the cockatiel opinicus had dropped the book and picked it up. This was an original, not one of the forger's copies, as best she could tell. She opened it. The first pages contained a genealogical tree with sketches, all past reeves and their descendants. Starting on the third page was Reeve Brevin's father. All the living members of her family, including her seven children, were circled in red ink.

"What is it?" the kjarr fledgling asked.

"Nothing." Kia shut the book. "It's just...weren't the reeve and his children killed prior to the invasion of the Crackling Sea Eyrie?"

The kjarr gryphon nodded. Kia frowned and stuffed the tome under her harness.

"Let's get the goliath birds to the gryphlets." If the genealogy survived the night, Kia would give it to Cherine to ponder.

To their credit, Merin's gryphons followed Orlea's orders. Neither of them had been in the eyrie before tonight, and both seemed reassured by her confidence. Orlea would never deny the underbough was decay and rot, but it was that and so much more—it was her home.

Her red beak and wings made it easy for the gryphons to keep track of her as she led them past old haunts and hiding places.

After her mate had died poaching from the forest, she'd abandoned their nest together and moved to the outer edges. It gave her a better view of game animals who came close enough to the eyrie to scavenge from the trash heaps, allowing her to trap them without alerting the rangers. Despite her offer to help the gryphons infiltrate the under-bough, she'd been avoiding all but the outskirts of it for over a year. Even now, she felt reassured to be at the edge, dismantling the dilapidated gate.

Things were going well until the gryphons smelled smoke. At first, she thought they must be looking in the wrong direction. They were facing the center of the eyrie. There was no way a spark from the flameworks could reach that far. The shaking from the blast must have knocked a brazier down.

Then she had another thought. If she couldn't smell it yet, that meant the other opinici living down here may not be able to, either. She grabbed two gryphons—they happened to be from Merin's pride—and gave them new orders: raise the alarms.

How does one decide who to warn first and who to warn last when the world is about to go up in flames? she wondered.

These were questions for scholars. Despite her arguments with Cherine, or perhaps because of them, she thought of the university as a place where the hard decisions were weighed and measured.

There was a way to warn everyone that maximized the number of opinici likely to survive the night. Therefore, there was a right choice. She didn't know what it was or how to figure it out in the little time she had. Her best guess was to have the three of them fly to the center of the eyrie and then spread out warning the underclass about the fire.

What the university was designed to counter was the heart of every opinicus. While she would follow that plan, what she really wanted to do was to go to her mate's family and warn them first. She felt like that's what he would have wanted. It would not be the optimal solution, but it would let her sleep soundly in the nights to come that may stretch on to years. She would rather fail doing what she felt was right than risk succeeding at the cost of his family. They'd dealt with enough already.

Orlea and the gryphons reached the center without interruption. The Reeve's Guard stations were eerily quiet. Whatever Strix's pride had done, the bottom levels were free of guards and rangers alike. She told Merin's gryphons what to shout to get opinici to listen. The underbough residents might ignore a warning of invasion as a fanciful fiction, but they'd probably believe there was a fire. She hoped.

"Forest fire! Get out of the eyrie!" should do it, she said. She made them repeat it.

"Can you do anything about your accents?" she asked. "They're really thick. I don't know if they'll understand you."

They looked aghast at being told—in an opi trill, no less—that they had accents.

"I guess you can't help it. I don't have time to teach you how to talk. Let's do this." She sent one southwest and the other southeast. She didn't know how long they had, and she wanted them out of the city as soon as possible. That left her with more than half the eyrie to talk to. She thought of her mate and flew to his mother's nest. If things went well, they'd help her spread the word.

Their chimes had long since been stolen, so she rapped on the door.

Her mate's mother answered with bloodshot eyes and red stains around her beak, hinting at heavy fern use after her son's death. His family grew it along the inside edge of the eyrie where a little light reached. It didn't take much for the fern to grow. Orlea saw several of her mate's brothers and sisters asleep inside.

"Orlea?" came an old, raspy voice.

She had not seen or talked to them since her mate died. She'd started the poaching when the hunting grounds closed. It was her fault he was dead. Even now, she didn't know why she'd made it out and he hadn't.

Orlea looked at her mate's mother. "The eyrie is about to burn down. I'm heading north to spread the word. Please, hurry east and west and get people out of here."

"Orl, you're not well…" her mate's mother began, but the smell of smoke was heavier here, and with the door open, she heard it.

A moment later, something gave way on a level above them, and the waterfall of fire crashed upon the forest floor and spread. Her mate's family rushed off, carrying two chicks to spread the word. Orlea headed north and hoped that her beloved's spirit had been appeased.

30

STRIX

Reeve Brevin returned to find that Jonas had gone home to sleep, for which she was grateful. She'd concede that he knew politics and logistics, but when it came to military strategy, she'd rather have that conversation one-on-one with Commander Wolden.

The commander had been dispatched to the Crackling Sea Eyrie to aid them against the kjarr, making him one of the few opinicus military commanders in either eyrie who had seen combat and was still alive. The Crackling Sea opinici had a strange disfigurement of honor that required them to go into battle with their troops. Wolden's own vanity had been appeased by the loss of his digit to a monitor when he was still young. As she understood it, he'd hung onto the lizard's back for dear life, and the talon had been torn off. Since then, he kept up his talon-to-talon combat training but never stuck his neck out when it didn't make tactical sense.

Wolden arrived with a contingent of the Reeve's Guard. The main bulk of the military forces were helping establish a raftworks and new fishing outpost on the far side of the

Crackling Sea. The rangers who weren't at the weald had been deployed north to watch for anything suspicious, minus one group of the brightest who stayed here to advise the commander. It seemed most likely that the next invasion would go after the weakened Crackling Sea, but it was too much to hope that the other eyries had forgotten about this last, little outpost tucked away in the Redwood Valley.

With the wingtorn—hopefully—subduing the coast, the eyrie's defenses were left to the Reeve's Guard. The city division of the guard were trained exclusively to manage small disputes and find illegal fern growers. Had they been competent tacticians, she wouldn't have sent three of them with Larren to watch the wingtorn. The guards assigned to defend Reeve's Nest were meant to look impressive, which made them the natural escort for Wolden. Not that she expected to need the Reeve's Guard, but the Crackling Sea reeve had been torn limb from limb, after all.

The commander stuck one of the shoreline maps to the wall. Swan's Rest, Crane's Nest, and Sandpiper's Dune were circled. The rangers were stationed at Sandpiper's Dune. The opinicus who led the far west fisherfolk settlement had been eager to join the eyrie and receive citizenship. According to the ghastly ranger who held the area, Rakesh, they'd purged their gryphons. Brevin was unsure if that meant the gryphons had been kicked out or killed.

Her middle daughter, Ivess, sat in on the meeting. Of all Brevin's daughters, Ivess was the most driven to learn how to run an eyrie. She attended every meeting she was allowed to attend. She'd spent time at the university learning the history of the eyries and the names of each one. Brevin had considered her daughter's pursuits a waste of energy back then, but current affairs had proven Brevin wrong.

Her only complaint, a nitpick, really, was that Ivess took

after her father. Her plumage was far too blue to give her the iconic look of past Redwood Valley reeves. She'd tried to dye it as a fledgling and had only succeeded in turning the fur-covered half of her body green. Having been teased by her sisters, all emerald-plumed like their mom, she'd finally devoted herself to being better than them. There was no rule that the reeve had to be the eldest child—as Ivess herself often said in front of her older sisters.

Their talk was interrupted by an innocent-sounding *thud* outside the front door.

Before Wolden could send a Reeve's Guard, Brevin said, "Would you go check on that, dear?"

Ivess hopped up and fluttered to the main entryway. She was still dainty enough to fly short distances indoors and have it considered cute instead of impolite. She opened the door and was lifted off her feet by the talons of a large owl gryphon.

"My name is Strix," the gryphon seemed to speak without opening his slight beak. Brevin was reminded not of the cobra or rattlesnake, but of the tiny krait which made no noise, gave no warning, before it bit and killed.

"Reeve, stay back," Wolden warned.

"I would like a word with you alone." Strix tightened his claws, drawing blood from Ivess. "I am not patient."

Brevin's heart went out to Ivess, but none of her daughters were ready to lead the eyrie if something happened to her. The eyrie needed Brevin, not her offspring. Still, it was impossible to watch a child she'd hatched in danger. Brevin knew her father would never have saved her, but she wasn't her father. She took a step forward, and Wolden took the decision out of her hands.

"Reeve's Guard, attack!" he yelled, and they rushed the gryphon.

Strix flung the limp body of Ivess at the guards. Brevin couldn't tell if her daughter was alive or dead. Wolden tried to escort Brevin through the back, but the door had been barricaded from the outside. Strix slipped between the Reeve's Guard and dashed at Brevin. Only Wolden's last minute intercession saved her. Strix showed no sign of annoyance, made no comment. He just stared at her and Wolden, then renewed his assault.

ZEPH ARRIVED at the university grounds ahead of the fire. It took him a moment, but he found the open door of the headmaster's study and flew inside. There were chimes of a hundred sizes and materials. He wasn't sure what to do. Ultimately, he just shook all them, surprising himself at just how loud they were.

Several opinici who'd been awakened by the blast from the flameworks heard the chimes and flew over. They didn't look twice at Zeph's forepaws. His infamy did not extend past the guards to the common opinici. He explained that the eyrie was on fire and they needed to evacuate, but to spread the word on their way. Soon, the skies began to fill with opinici heading out of the city to the hills.

"Where now?" Zeph wondered aloud. The smoke was only going to get worse. He needed to get out of here soon. Maybe he should look for more chimes in the other districts.

His thought was cut off by the collapse of the market spire. The mushroom-shaped structure collapsed in on itself and toppled over, knocking the top off a neighboring building. Zeph launched himself into the air and fled south before the university spire gave out.

By the time Kia arrived back at the hatchery with the goliath birds, the way had been cleared, and most of Hatzel's gryphons had returned and were helping corral the kjarr gryphlets. Kia and her fledgling helper had found packs for fifteen of the goliath birds. The other three wandered behind the others, not wanting to leave the safety of the flock. Since they were designed to bring large quantities of fish from one eyrie to another, they smelled terrible but could fit two gryphlets in the left harness pouch and two gryphlets in the right side of the saddlebag. The goliaths stood nine feet tall, dwarfing the small gryphons and lone opinicus. Kia hadn't found a cart to attach them to but thought this would handle most of the gryphlets.

The two adolescent kjarr fledglings took the reins and led the flock while Kia and the weald gryphons each grabbed a single gryphlet and followed the trail. They'd made it forty yards when Kia looked back and could just make out the top of the hatcheries catching fire. She hoped they weren't taking the gryphlets out of the eyrie just to find the weald and grasslands aflame.

Hatzel approached Reeve's Nest with trepidation. The grounds and walls were decorated with blood. She didn't see any gryphons, but Reeve's Guard corpses littered the grounds. This looked less like a surgical strike and more like a war had been played out against an unseen enemy. The silence unnerved her, and she wasn't reassured when it was broken by an opinicus calling for help. She flew up to an open balcony and looked down upon the chaos.

The Reeve's Guard inside had fared little better than the guards outside. The maps on the table suggested the reeve had been talking strategy when Strix arrived. The commander's escorts were dead. She counted twenty bodies, all opinici. They were next to the throne, and Brevin was nowhere in sight, so Hatzel assumed they'd been killed buying time for the reeve to escape.

A small blue peafowl opinicus was slipping out the main doors, but before Hatzel could decide what to do about that, the light of a brazier flickered off a shape across the room from her. The metal badge on the harness of a ranger watching from another balcony glinted in the firelight.

Strix himself clashed against Wolden. Hatzel recognized the opinicus from Kia's description. The two flew against each other, Wolden with a war cry, Strix with silence, and then separated. Wolden's breastplate lay in tatters. The lacerations on his chest looked extensive. It took Hatzel a moment to realize Strix was similarly wounded. The talon scrapes across his chest were hard to spot in his dark plumage, but sticking out of the wound was a metal claw that had been pulled off Wolden's talon.

Across the room, Hatzel saw another ranger with a net join the first one in appraising the situation, preparing to come to the commander's aid. As they pulled themselves up and got ready to launch, Hatzel flew into the building and cried out a warning for Strix. She caught one opinicus mid-flight and crashed with him into the maps on the wall on the far side of the room. Strix slipped around the other's net like oil on water and slashed the opinicus's throat as though it had been an adolescent lace monitor with an inflated sense of self.

"Nice of you to join me, Hatzel." Some of the softness of Strix's speech had been sanded away by his wounds.

"I'm looking for Jonas," she responded. "Did he escape with the reeve? Long-necked, duck-shaped bill, Crackling Sea harness."

"There was no duck here when I arrived." Strix looked around, his eyes pausing momentarily on the location where the blue peacock opinicus had fallen and was now absent. "The reeve escaped but is on her own. I will take care of her once he is dead."

Hatzel wanted to help Strix but was unsure of how this had come about. He was supposed to be guarding their escape route. Had he left his kin there? Her thoughts were interrupted by his speech, which came slow, labored.

"Now, if you wouldn't mind?"

She took the hint and grabbed the map of the cache locations from the wall and held it in her beak. She left through the balcony she'd come in from and risked one glance back at Strix and Commander Wolden. She flattened her ears. She needed to find Satra and get out of here before things devolved further.

31

PREDATORS AND PREY

Satra watched Jonas sleep. His chest rose and fell. She pulled herself close to him and pushed him onto his back. No response. She traced her paw along his stomach, letting one claw down to draw a line of red blood across his soft underside.

Nothing.

She worried she'd given him too much. It was the same drug they'd used to cut off the wings of the kjarr gryphons. Her father had refused it, of course, but most of the others had taken it. They slept and awoke wingtorn, all except for those who died in their sleep. She'd been worried that Jonas would be the one in a hundred who never awoke.

Lying around them were his tools, tools she'd stolen and bribed a metalsmith to modify to let her use them with her beak and paws. She'd even stolen several of the pink Crackling Sea harnesses to tie him down with, just in case he awoke mid procedure. She hadn't planned to let him live, but she'd wanted him to get a taste of what it was like to live without flight.

He'd observed the wingtorn, the stitches where their

wings had been still bleeding, and told his assistants to take notes on their *mood* and *resilience* and *adaptation*.

He'd shown no compassion when some wingtorn, unable to cope without their wings, flung themselves off the cliffs of the Crackling Sea Eyrie. Resilience, adaptation—he didn't understand what those words meant. How could he, growing up in an eyrie, eating fish others caught? To be a kjarr gryphon was to survive. The kjarr was not a kind place to live. It was frozen taiga on one side, bog on the other.

To be kjarr was to survive. Her father had told her that. A poor taiga gryphlet had taught her that. This would not be her first murder, but it would be the first she'd planned.

The other had come from that very same taiga gryphon. They'd been young and playing on a frozen lake. Both were adults with their own hunting grounds. Both were *new* adults with their *first* hunting grounds. The taiga gryphon had seen her try to pounce a bog hopper and miss. The light snow had concealed the ice underneath, and Satra had gone sliding. The taiga gryphon's name was Mignet, but Satra hadn't known that yet.

Satra had heard the laughing and growled—well, squeaked, her voice giving out—a challenge. Mignet had flown down and landed daintily on the ice. She'd been beautiful, graceful. While taiga gryphons included several designs and shapes, she'd been the one most strangers conjured up if asked to describe the taiga pride: white with black bars and rosettes. She was Satra's first, and only, crush. Satra had pounced at her and sent them both sprawling across the ice.

Times were not as lean back then, and Satra had spent her mornings hunting and her afternoons with Mignet on the frozen pond. In retrospect, things had always been moving towards this particular end. They'd played and slid, preened and talked. If Mignet had seemed coquettish, Satra hadn't minded. She'd just liked having a friend outside of the kjarr pride. They'd played through into the spring.

In the angry phase that had come later, Satra had thought that Mignet should have known better as a taiga gryphon. The weather had warmed ever-so-slightly, and one day the ice had broken with both of them above it. The water below had been still cold enough to cause shock. They'd called for help and struggled, their legs and wings losing feeling, their soaked fur weighing them down. The ice that'd been so solid for months now rebuffed their claws and refused them purchase.

Satra had no way of knowing their cries had been heard. She'd been certain she was going to die, so she'd used the only thing she could get purchase on to give her the leverage she needed to get above the ice: Mignet.

To be kjarr was to survive.

The taiga gryphons had arrived moments later. They'd seen blood in the water and no Mignet, whose voice had brought them here. They'd only seen Satra, with her paw in the water. They'd had no way of knowing she was searching, hoping to pull Mignet out. Had it not been for Thenca's arrival a moment later, Satra wasn't sure what they would have done to her. Trade with the taiga gryphons had fallen off after that. Her father had predicted that the taiga gryphons would never come down from the mountains to anyone's aid, but Satra had always suspected that his comments were meant more to soothe her.

His words had been prophetic. The taiga gryphons had not come to help the kjarr when the Crackling Sea opinici raided their nesting grounds.

She looked from the metal saw to Jonas's wings. Despite what her pride thought of her, despite the monster the taiga gryphons thought she was, she was frozen with indecision. Jonas was evil and deserved much worse.

Staring at the soft fur of his stomach, listening to his heart beat, it required a different gryphon to have the strength of will to operate the saw. She was not that gryphon, and not a day went by when she didn't wish she'd pushed Mignet up at the cost of her own life. The way her pride treated her had made her cold and cruel like the ice that'd taken her lover, but Satra had not become that gryphon.

She stood up and kicked the saw away from Jonas with her bloody paw.

Merin burst through the door and found her standing among the tools with Jonas, stomach still bleeding from her scratch, next to her. The saw was bloody from her paw. Jonas's wings were underneath him at an unnatural angle.

Merin did not comment on any of these things. "You need to meet with the prides south of here as fast as you can and get to the shores with at least one of the gryphlets."

She understood why she needed a kjarr gryphlet with her. She needed proof that she hadn't left her pride's gryphlets to die. It seemed word of her past had spread across the mountains.

From outside the hut, she heard another gryphon calling for Merin. He pushed Satra out the door and closed it.

"I found her!" he called out.

The gryphon who landed dwarfed Satra and was half a head taller than Merin. Could a gryphon that large even fly in the forest? Satra knew who it was from reading Jonas's maps. The saber-toothed beak and eagle-like features gave her away. There was only one pride leader who fit that description.

Hatzel landed. Her claws reflexively dug into the posh,

northern quarter flooring. Part of it crumbled. She set the map down at her forepaws. The ambassador's quarters were at the northern tip of the northern quarter, the last district not covered in smoke. The rest of the city burned in the night sky. There was no longer a clear path out of the city anymore.

"Satra?" Hatzel asked. Satra nodded. "You need to get to your father as soon as possible. Can you get her out of here, Merin?"

"Where are you going?" he countered.

Hatzel pointed to the map. "I know where the explosives are. I'm going to meet up with the rest of my pride and get the word out. Triddle and Askel should be meeting in the west. They might have some ideas about this. You remember how they handled the fires that one summer."

Merin nodded. Satra just looked on without a word. When he lifted off, she joined him. Hatzel went in the other direction. Satra didn't know what would happen to Jonas, but that was up to fate now. Maybe this was better than tainting her own paws.

While they flew, she did her best to groom the blood out of her left forepaw. No need for the gryphlets to see her this way.

FROM THE JAIL window in the northern district, Askel watched as the flames spread across the eyrie. Removed from the immediacy of his fiery waterfall, the heaviness of what he'd done sunk in. He hoped the eyrie had been evacuated in time but no longer held any certainty that everyone would make it out okay.

He was sorry for what he'd done, and as the smell of

smoke began to reach his cage, his own mortality settled upon his wings. He didn't want to die. He wanted to be with Triddle again. He wanted to talk to Hatzel. He wanted to watch Zeph hunt parrots. He wanted to ask Triddle about the flameworks and help him trace the underground river and map it.

The opinicus in the cage next to Askel was rambling. The guards had told him not to mind "mad 'ole Impir here, our resident scholar." Impir, a painfully bright blue peacock, was talking about a formula he'd invented to allow only the maternal or paternal appearances to pass along to opinicus chicks.

"Designer chicks!" he'd laughed. He claimed that the proof of the potion was the reeve's chicks—six emerald, only one blue. "She forgot the potion for that one, you see. It was my own fault. We were up in the mountains, and she just couldn't resist my charm. Or maybe I couldn't resist her charm. Ha-caw!"

Askel preferred to spend his final hours staring out the window, despondent. He wasn't worried about making friends in a jail that was going to burst into flames and collapse. Contrition was a better use of his time.

There was a knock at the door. The guards—he had to admire the sense of duty that kept them here, if not their reasoning skills—looked at each other. Finally, they opened it. A blue peafowl opinicus with bruising and lacerations across her chest walked in with several other opinici in tow, including a ruffled red one with a bump on his head.

She looked around and came to Impir's cage. "Let him out."

The two guards protested, but she spoke again.

"My mother is missing. I'm in charge now. Let him out."

They opened the cage but backed away, afraid to get near Impir.

"You can go," Ivess told the guards.

"Try not to burn, Askel. Ha!" Impir called to him. The strange red opinicus next to Ivess broke out of his daze. A look passed between him and Impir before he turned to Askel.

"You're Askel? You were caught here tonight?" He seemed to be trying to remember something but was shaken by the events of the evening.

Askel nodded.

The red opinicus looked from the top of Askel's crestless head down to Askel's feathered tail as if things weren't quite matching up. Finally, he shouted "Wait!" at the guards. "Toss me the keys."

Ivess gave him a questioning look. "Are you mad, Bario?"

"This is the gryphon scholar who dragged me out of the workshop," Bario said. "I must know what they know. We hadn't even considered that there might be gryphon scholars before tonight."

"Nor had we considered gryphon assassins," Ivess retorted. "Fine, bring him along."

Bario unlocked the cage.

"Now we're even," he whispered.

HATZEL FOUND a collection of weald gryphons and underbough opinici waiting south of the eyrie in the grasslands. Some of her pride parted to give her room to land, and she went searching for Triddle.

She found him in a muddle of feathers and fur, discussing options. Kia and Zeph waited outside the collective and listened to them talk intently about something with a red and black owl gryphon. Strix's daughter asked if they knew what had happened to her father and brothers.

Hatzel thought of the last time she'd seen Strix and decided to keep her mouth shut. With opinici around, it was probably better not to mention the carnage at Reeve's Nest. No one else answered the owl gryphon's question.

Hatzel thought she caught a glimpse of Askel's plumage, but the nonfeathered tail meant it must have been one of his relatives. She asked one of her pride what had happened with the gryphlets and was told the goliath birds had met with more of Merin's pride, and his gryphons were escorting them down the trail and then east at Glacial Run to get to Strix's plateau. The best they could hope was that they could reach the owl gryphon nesting grounds without being cut off by the weald fires. She forced her way into the circle and found Triddle. His ears dropped and his crest lay flat.

"I know you're worried about Askel," she said, "but he probably had to evacuate the city on the other side. I need your help."

She handed him the map of the weald she'd stolen from the eyrie. There were dozens of circles on it. For the under-bough opinici, this was the first they'd heard of their ranger kin building a network of bombs.

"This is a lot of explosives. We didn't find half this number." Triddle preened in agitation.

"Can we get to them before—" Hatzel began. Another explosion occurred, this one far outside the eyrie. She could just see the flames licking the northern border of the weald, just south of them. "Okay, no, we can't. What can we do?"

Triddle counted and mumbled to himself. "I can't save the whole weald. But I think I can save some of it. We need to get to the caches the other gryphons caught with Cherine's map. They were supposed to leave them for us in the grasslands along with some of the fire suppressant powder from the camps. I sent someone to the medicine gryphon caves for some of the goo they soak their fire keepers in, too."

Everyone leaned in closer while Triddle began to lay out his plan for saving their homes.

32

BIRDS OF A FEATHER

There was something therapeutic about having room to spread his wings to their full span, Merin thought. The weald rarely afforded a gryphon of his size the opportunity to glide like this without running into a branch or getting caught up in vines. He didn't know how Hatzel stood it. Did she feel as constrained as he did?

"We'll help you get the kjarr nesting grounds back," he told Satra. They ducked between fleeing opinici who were oblivious to the gryphons in their midst. Most of them went north and then west to the goliath bird pass that led to the Crackling Sea Eyrie.

Satra's eyes were on the Redwood Valley Eyrie. Flames blossomed along the bottom levels, spreading out to the surrounding forest like roots. The smoke interwove the different spires and districts together, creating a giant ashen tree expanding into the heavens and disappearing from view. Where would all the opinici go? Was the Crackling Sea Eyrie large enough to take them in?

He wondered what the following weeks would bring but decided that depended mostly upon the state the weald was left in. As far as he knew, the kjarr was in one piece. Only its people had been maimed. Had the opinici set up a camp there? If so, perhaps the taiga pride would help him clear it out.

When Satra finally spoke, it surprised him. "I don't want the kjarr."

"You need somewhere to settle. You're welcome with us, but I don't know how much of the weald will be left." He didn't know how many gryphons would be left, either.

Satra had finished cleaning Jonas's blood from her feathers but was still coated in the ash of the fallen eyrie.

She looked Merin in the eye. "You misunderstand. The kjarr was a hard life. I will not live that way again. With the wingtorn at my back, I'll conquer the entire Crackling Sea if it takes me generations. I won't see my kin scrape to get by ever again. I will not see them at the mercy of any opinicus."

He smiled in spite of himself. He often worried he was the only one of his generation with ambition. Now, it turned out only a mountain range had separated him from the only other gryphon who shared his vision.

The weald may end up reduced to ash, but the kjarr and sea awaited. With the kjarr gryphons in his pride—or his gryphons in the kjarr pride, he wasn't as egotistical as some believed—they could make that happen. Satra's kin lacked flight, which he could provide, but that would change as the kjarr gryphlets grew up.

He would never have more leverage with her than he had right now, right here. "When you get your pride, come northeast. Follow the coast to the plateau and look for me. I'll make sure the sea is yours."

She gave him an appraising look. He knew what she saw. He was strong. He was able to show discretion. He would provide new blood for the pride. He knew how to lead.

"Not mine. My father's," she said, but it sounded half-hearted to him. Would they want a landbound leader? Did her father share her ambition?

Merin and Satra hit the edge of the eyrie and cut south. In the distance, the two kjarr fledglings led a parade of goliath birds. His pride escorted them to safety and carried any gryphlets who wouldn't fit in a saddlebag. One of the fledglings trilled a greeting to Satra, and both flew up to escort her down.

While they preened her and worried, Merin caught up with one of his pride. They were taking the kjarr gryphlets southeast to the plateau. There was no way to know when the forest was going to go up, and they hadn't wanted to wait. That turned out to be prudent, as he and Satra heard the caches explode from the far side of the eyrie. The weald burned in several places.

He hurried to her. "You need to go south before the whole weald is aflame. You can't fly over it once the smoke gets bad. This is the only chance for you three to get to the shore and stop the bloodshed. I'll take you."

"No," Satra replied. "You make sure the gryphlets are safe. I'm placing their well-being in your care. I'll go to my father, but I have to know they're in good paws. I can find the ocean. I've spent hours studying the maps. I need you, personally, to guarantee their well-being."

He nodded. "We'll be at the plateau."

One of his pride brought harnesses with food and aneda wraps and helped the kjarr fledglings into them for the trip. Satra changed into the new harness but held onto her Crackling Sea Eyrie one, too. As they flew off over the weald, she dropped it over one of the small blossoms of wildfire.

Merin watched them go, then spoke. "Okay, enough resting. Let's get out of here before we're cut off. Did you leave the caches on the grassland? Excellent. If Askel and Triddle need them, they know where to find them. If not, it won't make much difference now, will it?"

He grabbed the reins of the lead goliath bird in his beak and led the flock down the path, deeper into the weald. With luck, Askel had finished his mission in the eyrie and was now helping safeguard the weald.

A TRAIL of blood led into the smoke. Strix was too angry about losing Brevin to let Commander Wolden get away. When part of the Reeve's Nest collapsed, Wolden had fled, leading Strix on this chase. The owl gryphon spared a single thought for his own children who had come with him tonight. They were smart enough not to linger once the fires spread.

He hoped Ninox, his daughter—not that family meant much to some gryphons—had escaped from the Reeve's Guard headquarters and gotten to safety. She had orders to leave as soon as the smoke started, but she had a tendency to get lost in her work. As a gryphlet, she'd once focused so hard on a squirrel that she'd missed the branch between her and it. That single-minded focus was a trait she'd picked up from him.

Her trouble with trees must have come from her mother, a fantail.

With his forepaws tucked under his body and his back legs obscured by the fan of his tail, he looked more like a long owl than a gryphon. He was a black shape with red wings flying through the smoky haze. Several opinici fleeing upwards from the underbough nearly crashed into him. He didn't waste his time expressing his annoyance but continued to follow Wolden's trail.

When the net came at him from above, Strix dodged it with less ease than he expected. The throw was solid, and his body had never been taxed like this before. Wolden dove after the net and managed to graze him. Droplets of Strix's blood fell into the dark smoke and disappeared into the abyss.

He pivoted and rushed Wolden. Wolden reared back and guarded his chest with his claws as though he was expecting a body shot, but Strix went left and managed to take out a pawful of feathers. They continued this back and forth with as much grace and strength as they could muster while their lungs filled with smoke.

Buildings crackled, cracked, and collapsed around them. An asphyxiated opinicus, its feathers ashen, fell past them and disappeared into the labyrinthine underbough. The sky was lost in the smoke. Embers hung in the air like bog wisps. Where trees were artificially raised into platforms, the platforms toppled.

Strix coughed, the only sound he'd made since his conversation with Hatzel. Wolden's ability to fly was in question, but he made one last leap.

The platform Strix was standing on gave way, sending them both into the hungry furnace below.

33

CONFLAGRATION

Triddle's plan for the caches was twofold. With the jars of oil removed, they could be dropped on the new fires. The concussive explosion should have the same effect as the one detonated by Hatzel's nesting grounds, suffocating the flames and preventing the fire from spreading. They could also be used to create a barrier by destroying the trees and starving the fire of fuel.

He drew a map in the dirt as best he could. It was summer, so the mountain runoff wasn't at its spring high. The large river running down from the mountain, Glacial Run, met the runoff from the plateau and cut the weald into two. The top half made up just under a quarter of the weald, but the prides had found four caches up there already. Then there was the one by Hatzel's nesting grounds.

Merin's pride had confiscated the saltpeter crates they'd discovered Cherine investigating. Those were now resting at the bottom of the cave that'd been his prison before Triddle and Hatzel's rescue mission. Since Cherine's map came from his own exploration, its information hadn't strayed far from the border with the grasslands.

If they were going to save any of the weald, Triddle thought, they needed to use the natural barriers and hope the winds stayed on their side. Winds from the north might push the eyrie's fire to the northern weald, and winds from the south might allow the southern weald fire to jump the river.

Glacial Run was wide enough to keep the fire limited to the south. There was only one section that might be a problem, where the fisherfolk trail crossed it. A decrepit bridge wide enough for twenty goliath birds had been built long ago and abandoned in recent generations.

As time passed, seeds landed on the bridge and found purchase until it became an extension of the weald itself. The varnish protecting the planks wore down. Vines took root, spread across the bridge, died, then dried in the sun. Chances were good that, whether or not Triddle managed to stop the fires in the north, if the fire in the south made it to the bridge, it'd carry the flames back north.

All of this, he explained, depended on the fire from the eyrie not crossing the grasslands. He was saved from having to make a plan for that by the fortuitous arrival of Orlea. With her she brought a flock of opinici who'd heeded her warning and didn't know where else to go. While Hatzel led teams of gryphons and opinici to carry the caches and drop them on the northern weald fires that'd sprung up, Orlea's opinici brought something more valuable, the powder the guards used to put out fires. They'd been using it to rescue opinici trapped in flaming nests.

Orlea's reminder of the fire suppressant triggered something in Triddle's brain. He scrambled to grab his map. The squared circles were caches, but the triangles might be the camps the rangers set up between pride hunting grounds. Any smart ranger transporting explosives would have brought some of the suppressant powder with them. In fact, he was now certain the strange white ash found at the site of several lightning strikes had been the rangers making sure the weald remained ripe for a massive fire at the end of the summer. He shouted after the teams that they should check the ranger camps for powder before returning.

"What do you need us to do?" a speckled blue opinicus merchant asked. It had been her idea to grab the powder.

Triddle pointed to the map. "If the fire gets to the grasslands, it'll be nearly unstoppable. Can you keep the eyrie fire from crossing the Reeve's Hunting Grounds?"

"It's well-kept by orders on high, so there's not much underbrush," the merchant chirped. "If it's possible, we'll do it."

"We'll do it," Orlea confirmed.

Most of the gryphons and opinici were now deployed. All that remained were Zeph, Kia, two of Triddle's pridemates, and Strix's daughter. Also, two caches of explosives.

Ninox, the owl gryphon, stepped forward, and Triddle realized that what he'd taken to be a dark red design in her plumage was dried blood.

"Where do you need us?" Her ears remained still, not moving the way a normal gryphon's would to indicate mood and subtext. He'd never seen an owl gryphon with ears. Combined with a nocturnal lifestyle, she must not get to talk to the other ear-expressive weald gryphons often.

He motioned to Zeph and Kia first. "You two, take that cache and blow the dam. With any luck, it'll flood part of the Reeve's Hunting Grounds and some of the grasslands."

Zeph nodded. Triddle showed them how to use one of the fuses he'd picked up from the flameworks. They struggled a little to get the crate into the air, but it had rope handles on each side. Kia's adrenaline must have been in overdrive because she had no trouble lifting it. Triddle appreciated their skill set and knowledge, but he'd given them the smaller of the two remaining saltpeter crates because Zeph was too slight a gryphon to handle the heaviest. The task of carrying the larger crate fell to the two Merin pride gryphons.

Once Zeph and Kia flew off, he motioned to his two pridemates. "You two, grab that last cache. We need to get to the bridge as fast as we can."

He looked directly at the owl gryphon. Specifically, he was staring at the blood on her left ear. "Can you keep me safe?"

Ninox licked her paw, wiped some of the red off her face, and nodded.

The Snowfeather Dam had been built before anyone's memory, possibly even as a precursor to the Redwood Valley Eyrie itself. A peacock statue topped one side with a cobra bookending the other. Their construction used a white brick that may once have been the same color as the dam, but generations of aging revealed their differing compositions. It must have been imported at the time of construction or traded from a different eyrie. Whatever the stones were, there were no quarries in the valley. Zeph couldn't imagine what you would trade to get enough stone to build a dam. As far as he knew, parrots were the most precious thing around.

As the Snowfeather River flowed through the northern mountain range and passed through the glacial crater, it fell twenty stories to continue along the northern border of the weald, eventually diving underground and passing by Cherine's former cave prison. Runoff from the snow kept the river flowing during the summer months, but in the winter, it slowed to a trickle. The falls had been nicknamed the Summer Falls due to their seasonal temperament. The dam, as Kia relayed from her reading of the eyrie histories to him on the flight up, had been built one winter to allow water to accrue for eyrie use, creating Crater Lake. A few fishing huts stood at the far side of the lake across from them.

Slits along the left side of the dam allowed the summer runoff to flow down the falls instead of flooding the settlement on the lake. Zeph and Kia were panting by the time they lifted the saltpeter crate to the top.

"Where do we set it off?" she asked.

"It shouldn't matter, should it?" he responded. "It should blow up all this easily. You were there when the last one went off. The crater seemed pretty deep."

She clicked her beak. "I guess. I'm just worried that if we detonate it up top we won't get the full lake to spill out. If we detonate it at the bottom, assuming we can find a place to set it, it might cause the rubble to block the way."

"We could set it atop Brevin's beak. It wouldn't be effective, but it'd feel pretty good," he thought aloud.

She looked up at the peacock statue, and her eyes widened. "It really does look like her! I never noticed before. I must have flown by here a hundred times. It must be based on her ancestor. That beak has definitely been passed down."

Zeph was struck with how much the bird looked like her. He couldn't remember seeing another bird statue or carving that resembled someone before. He'd never, say, seen an owl carving based on a gryphon or opinicus with owl features.

Most of the gryphons and opinici did have features that

matched with a specific bird, though he couldn't identify all the avian influences, and there were birds he'd never seen a gryphonic version of. He'd never met anyone who resembled a seagull, for example. Maybe if the weald burned down he'd go try to find someone who looked like a seagull.

While Kia pontificated on the best location for the explosives, Zeph continued his mental feather-gathering. If their front halves were near matches for birds, at least sometimes, what were their back halves?

The furriest animals he could think of were the small squirrels that glided through the trees. Their paws weren't like his. Or the herd rodents, the capybaras, where had they come from? There hadn't been any in the weald before the grasslands were created—someone had brought them here. He knew his view of the world was limited, but talking to Kia and Cherine had made him realize that the eyrie scholars were as ignorant as he was on some of these questions. If he saw Satra after this, he would have to ask her who lived beyond the kjarr.

Kia chirped to get his attention.

"Sorry," he apologized. "Ideally, you want the rubble to be blown outwards, right? It's too bad we can't put it on the water side. The saltpeter doesn't work wet, right? I don't remember if they let Triddle throw it in a lake or not."

Kia snorted. "The flint and tinder aren't waterproof even if the saltpeter is, though I'm pretty sure it's not."

There were some refugees gathering across the lake at a settlement. Their harnesses were blue and gold.

"I don't think we have a lot of time." Zeph looked closer. Those were definitely guard harnesses. There were four outside and at least one more in the hut.

"Okay, there's a ledge partway down," Kia said. "Let's put

it there and get this done. We can't risk the grasslands catching fire while we make birdsong up here."

One of the guards seemed to notice them and was pointing. Zeph and Kia slipped over the fall's side and lowered the saltpeter into place.

"How long do the fuses take?" he asked. They couldn't risk the guards coming over and clipping it off.

"We don't actually spend a lot of time blowing things up at the university." Her voice showed the stress. "We should light it and fly."

Zeph flew up a little and peeked over the edge. All the guards—seven in total—and an emerald peacock opinicus were flying across the lake. "They might extinguish the fuse if we leave it. I can't take that risk. You light it and get out of here. I'll draw them away as best I can."

She frowned but nodded.

Zeph flew up just as Reeve Brevin alighted on the dam.

TRIDDLE HAD no problem finding the bridge over Glacial Run. The goliath bird trail went straight through the area Cherine had scouted, mostly Merin's territory. By the lack of smoke, Triddle felt pretty sure his pridemates had taken care of any explosives.

Off in the distance, Hatzel dropped a cache to stop a forest fire while several opinici used the fire suppressant powder to smother the few remaining sparks. The path beneath Triddle had the footprints of a flock of goliath birds that cut east before the bridge.

He could just make out Satra and two fledglings flying far south of them towards the ocean. They had their own mission, but it was a relief to see she'd been rescued successfully. The kjarr gryphlets should be on their way up to the plateau. There was no way to know what the shore looked like at this point, but those were not his problems. His problems began when he arrived at the bridge.

Three rangers, probably stragglers who'd lost their way, were trying to follow Glacial Run out of the weald. They were surprised to find four gryphons attempting to blow up a bridge. The four gryphons attempting to blow up the bridge were surprised to be found.

Two of the rangers dive-bombed the saltpeter crate, causing the harpy eagle gryphons to drop it and leap out of the way. A third rammed Triddle and knocked him to the northern edge of the bridge.

The first two opinici grabbed the cache and were overcome by its weight. They were dragging it towards the edge of the bridge when Ninox struck.

One ranger dropped the cache and ducked while the other took her claws across his face. The two large gryphons rushed in to finish him off.

Triddle felt drowsy. He saw a little blood, but no serious injuries. The third ranger landed, and his front left talons clicked as he walked, metal on the joints of the bridge. Triddle remembered the glove with the poison sac from the flameworks. They must have been produced for the rangers. Desperate, he reached into his harness for his last saltpeter bomb but instead pulled out a pawful of parrot treats.

He was saved only by the intervention of his owl bodyguard. Without a sound, Ninox crashed into the opinicus, and they both went flying over the edge. He wanted to shout for her to watch out for the metal claws but he was having a hard time opening his beak. The world was moving slower now.

The last ranger held off his two gryphons remarkably

well. None of his metal claws glistened with poison, but he moved like a snake, dodging slashes and returning kind with kind. The fire was starting to spread on the other side of the river, and they needed to blow the crate before the flames crossed the bridge.

Two gryphons charged, only to be repelled. One was bloodied, the other made wary. The unwounded gryphon roared and the opinicus stepped back.

Before the ranger's back paw could set down on the edge of the bridge, Ninox's gryphonic claws reached up from under the bridge and caught it, pulling him over the edge. The splash told Triddle that the opinicus hadn't managed to right himself before hitting the rapids.

While the healthiest of the Merin pride attempted to figure out the fuse and flint and tinder, Triddle still lay paralyzed, waiting for the toxin to wear off. Strix's daughter sat a way off, inspecting the metal glove. She removed the talons from it and tried to get it on her paw without success.

Triddle's pridemates chose a long fuse but were having trouble working out how to get the flint and tinder going. He wanted to shout at them, but his beak wouldn't open. Two curious ground parrots snuck out from the underbrush and began to eat the treats from his paw. A third one nuzzled under him to pull the treats out of his harness pocket. A small bit of drool leaked from the side of Triddle's beak.

Ninox finally noticed the trouble on the bridge and came over to light the fuse. They were talking, but Triddle couldn't make out the words from here. She tilted her head to the side. The two gryphons looked back and forth, then mimed a huge explosion and crater as they talked. Her eyes widened. She nodded, they lit the fuse, and then they ran to get Triddle, waking the gluttonous parrots that had cuddled up next to him.

The gryphons were too weary to fly with him, so they took turns carrying him on their backs as they hastened away. It was fortunate that they chose the long fuse, because when it went off, they were still close enough that it knocked them all to the ground.

THE VERSION of Brevin that Zeph was experiencing here was different from his previous interaction. Her long train of tailfeathers remained tucked. When she glided down and backbeat her wings, he'd seen only brown with a hint of green. Gone was the jewelry and glittering harness. What she wore now was practical. Her only indulgence was a small cobra necklace and metal talons on her left foreleg. Her right foreleg had long, sharp claws. Since most upper-class opinici filed down one set of talons to allow them to better write and use instruments, the metal glove was an interesting adaptation. She knew she may have to defend herself.

"Zeph Parrotbane." Her voice was too smooth for her to have flown through the smoke. She must have escaped before the fires hit their worst.

"Reeve." His natural inclination was to fight or flee, but he needed to keep them occupied until the dam exploded. If Jonas and Cherine were any indication, some opinici liked a good conversation.

Unfortunately, this opinicus only had one question for him. "Who sent you?"

It was a silly question. Who did she think sent him? Hatzel? Merin? The truth was easier and might buy him some time. "I just hunt and sell parrots."

"No one just sells parrots." She looked from his lack of a

harness to his drab plumage. From an opinicus point of view, he wasn't much to look at.

He stood a little taller. "They should. It's a good life."

From the distance came the sound of a district collapsing. Only the expensive living quarter in the north had been intact last he'd looked. There would no longer be any safe districts left.

"I suppose all the beads I've collected will be useless now," he mused.

With her neck fully extended, she towered over him. "Saving up to buy eyrie lodgings, were you?"

"No, just fish and books. I've acquired a taste for both." He'd paged through *What Does Your Plumage Say About Your Personality* while waiting for a merchant. It was not kind to brown gryphons with black bars. He'd always thought of his inner plumage as being a vibrant red: good for risk taking and love making. This was according to the author, a male cardinal opinicus.

The guards were starting to spread out and move to his sides but still maintained a healthy distance. He didn't want any to get close enough to look over the ledge. He didn't know if they'd seen Kia, too. Her plumage was bright enough that there was no missing her if they'd looked over earlier.

If they knew, there was no indication in their posture. They were all focused on Zeph, only Brevin seemed distracted by the fire. The Redwood Valley Eyrie's spires had all collapsed. Only smoke and burning redwoods remained.

"Was this destruction worth it?" she asked.

He kept his eyes on her. "That wasn't my intention. Someone needed to save Satra."

"You let your weald kin burn thousands of opinici to save that little murderer?" Her laugh was high-pitched. "Say you save the wingtorn. Well done. We stuffed the weald full of saltpeter. It'll burn for weeks, burn to ash. You may scatter to the mountains. Maybe the shore is even saved. What do you think happens next? I have an army enslaved for me at the Crackling Sea. There are hundreds of wingtorn waiting on the other side of the mountain pass. Enough of this—"

Zeph's pounce caught all of them off guard. Brevin pivoted too quickly for him to catch her long neck in his beak, but she took the brunt of his tackle across her chest and fell into the frigid water while he kicked off from her stomach and dashed low across the lake to pull the guards as far from Kia as he could get.

34

FLAMES

Orlea was sure the entire world was going to burn. She was certain they would run out of the fire suppressant powder. Having seen the size and scope of the Snowfeather Dam, she was certain it would withstand a single saltpeter crate. She was also sure that all the opinici would band together to save their eyrie home.

She was learning to live with being wrong.

What she had not made any predictions about was the number of gryphons who would come help stop the spread of the eyrie fire. As gryphons finished their bombing runs on the weald fires, they retrieved boxes of the suppressant from the ranger camps and brought them to Orlea, who then made sure the powder was sent where it was most needed.

At the present, that was the northeast corner. When there were fewer options, she'd considered letting the aneda forest north of the eyrie burn. Now that the powder supply had tripled, she was no longer willing to risk the fire spreading from the mountains back into the grasslands. She sent a pack of four gryphons led by an opinicus to take care of it. The opinicus, Foultner, was a northern poacher Orlea had crossed paths with several times, so she trusted her old rival to know the terrain.

Another explosion racked the forest. Several factories and storage facilities full of explosives had remained insulated from the initial fire but had later fallen into the depths. She looked over to see two scythe-beaked opinici wounded from debris. She started to rush over, but two gryphons covered in the flamekeeper's grease from the medicine gryphon's cave materialized out of nowhere to help. The slick gryphons glistened in the firelight but were unhurt by the falling embers.

Orlea's mate's sister put her foreclaw on Orlea's shoulder. As strange as it felt, she understood. Someone needed to coordinate the firefighting efforts, and everyone had decided to report to her. For once, she was grateful for her bright red beak. On several hunting expeditions, she'd had to rub black smear on it to keep from being spotted by the rangers. Now, it made her an easy target to find and request orders from.

Seeing gryphons and opinici working together eased her fears for the future only slightly. Gryphons had destroyed the flameworks. Nothing had suggested that the fire would be this extensive. She'd helped them because she'd believed the eyrie would remain untouched. The way the fire spread to the ground level suggested that someone had wanted the eyrie to burn, and when the flameworks failed to get the job done, they'd taken matters into their own paws. As gossip spread, relations would grow even more strained.

Yet, the current whispers she was hearing told a different narrative. A brave opinicus—with a description matching Kia or Cherine, depending on the telling—found out about the reeve's plan to burn everything and stole a map to warn the gryphons before it was too late, gryphons who then returned to evacuate the eyrie before it was burned down. The fact that the upper crust of opinicus society were fleeing to the Crackling Sea just confirmed that they'd known what was going on.

Just because Orlea didn't know the truth, it didn't mean she didn't know a lie when she heard one. For tonight, the lie was helping smooth over relations between disparate groups working together to stop the fire from spreading. The eyrie would need the weald, and the weald would need the eyrie in the days to come. Long term, she wanted to know exactly what caused the burning waterfall that destroyed her home and the homes of her loved ones.

She leaned down to speak to her mate's sister. "Go to the grasslands ranch and find out how much food—living and processed—is there now. Bring your brothers. Relocate that food to the ranger staging area in the hunting grounds without being seen, if possible. The grasslands don't belong to anyone right now. I want that food under our control."

Her mate's sister, an opinicus who'd fought with her every time they encountered each other from the moment Orlea mated her brother, just nodded and disappeared. More than her departed mate, what they shared in common was knowing what it felt like to starve.

More gryphons arrived, and she assigned them to the western border.

THE SNOWFEATHER RIVER climbed into the mountains, meeting the first straggly aneda trees. Zeph climbed with it. Right behind him was the leader of the remaining Reeve's Guard who was, Zeph could not believe, wearing a circlet that resembled a tiara. The captain's stomach and throat were chestnut with a black head, feathers, and rear half. Zeph wondered if the opinicus had won that tiara at the Reeve's Guard annual races or if all captains had one.

The captain had left his fellow guards far behind to catch up to Zeph. He took a bite at one of Zeph's tail feathers.

Zeph dropped down, letting his paws push off from the ground and buy him a little altitude as the captain adjusted. He would much prefer to have the element of surprise or the time to figure out this opinicus's strengths and weaknesses, but every moment the captain lived was a moment his guards were catching up.

Zeph flew straight up or as close to straight up as his wings could manage.

The captain was gaining on him again, but this time, Zeph twisted and pulled his wings in before the falcon opinicus crashed into him, giving Zeph four paws to defend himself with. He kicked at the captain's stomach but took a left hook across his chest before they separated.

Zeph watched a shower of blood and feathers fall to the tree tops and did a quick check. He didn't feel any pain, but adrenaline did weird things to pain perception. He'd seen gryphons fly with injuries that should have prevented it only to pay later with permanent wing damage. He looked down at his chest where he'd seen the captain hit him. Some damaged feathers, no blood. He risked a glance back.

The captain was losing altitude quickly. He held his stomach with his left foreleg, the talons of which had been sanded down. His position in the Reeve's Guard must have been too prestigious and required too many hand-written reports for him to leave his left talons sharp. It must also have paid too little for him to afford metal talons, to the benefit of Zeph's health.

Zeph slowed and landed near the opinicus, who was now coughing. The captain was unsure what to do about his injures. He was unstable in his footing. Zeph pulled the bark off a nearby aneda tree. Infected with beetles, no use. He found another without any bugs.

"Hold the sticky side against your stomach. It'll keep it from becoming infected until you can get help," he told the captain.

Overhead, two of the other guards flew past them. Zeph looked at the captain and mouthed for him to keep quiet.

"Down here!" the captain shouted with the last of his energy.

So much for the kindness of strangers, Zeph thought.

He slipped into the forest heading north and quietly tried to backtrack once he was out of the captain's view. If it were just the two opinici, he'd kill them and be done with it. But there were other guards on Zeph's trail. If these called out for help, soon there'd be too many for him to fight. The lower range of aneda forests, as he knew from his gryphlethood, were too sparse to allow for the kind of forest combat he was used to.

He made it to the shoreline undetected and looked across Crater Lake to the dam but didn't see Brevin. Had she been with the guards chasing him? That didn't seem like her. In fact—

He jumped straight up.

There hadn't been an odd feeling. There wasn't a prickling on the back of his neck. His ears hadn't picked up on a strange sound. There was just a moment where he realized his back was to the one place someone could hide along the shore, the fishing hut.

The reeve's metal talons missed his tail by a squirrel-length.

Pursued by an angry, long-necked opinicus bent on killing him, he flew to the one place where he shouldn't have, the dam. She was lithe and quick. Had her talons been poisoned, he'd already be dead. Her neck moved like a snake. He couldn't seem to catch it with his own beak or dodge her when she struck at him. Nothing he hunted in the weald fought like this. She was serpent, monitor, and gryphon all in one.

Just as he made a leap up to try to dive down the cliffs and escape to the weald, the fuse ran out. Both he and the reeve were caught in the shock wave. Consciousness faded from Zeph with twenty stories of air between him and the ground.

KIA COULDN'T BRING herself to start the fuse at Zeph's command. Instead, she waited until she heard a splash and the shouts of the guards flying after him before lighting the longest fuse Triddle had given her.

She remembered the last explosion and Xavi's offspring recovering at the medicine gryphon cave. This time, she wanted to be as safe as she could make herself. She knew better than to be airborne. It was also probably not safe to be along the cliff itself. If things went well, the grasslands and hunting grounds would be flooded. That left the edge of the weald.

The grasslands were narrowest here where they met the weald, mountains, and Reeve's Hunting Grounds. An avalanche or falling debris could still reach her, but the more time she spent flying away, the higher the chance she'd get caught in the air.

Once she arrived at the weald and found a good vantage point—careful to look away until after the explosion—she was left with time to think. With the reeve gone, assuming Zeph was able to get the upper paw, Kia might be able to follow the refugees to the Crackling Sea.

While she held no loyalty to the Redwood Valley Eyrie itself, she couldn't see herself fleeing north to try to find the eyrie the headmaster had gone to. She didn't want to throw herself at the mercy of a culture that employed spies. The fisherfolk might be the easiest option if they'd survived the wingtorn, but she knew nothing about fishing. Had they need of a scholar? Could she be happy cataloging fish?

Then there was Zeph's pride. No, Hatzel's pride. She didn't like the way gryphons didn't form lasting romantic relationships. It wasn't necessarily that relationships didn't happen from what she could tell, it was just that they weren't respected the way two mates might be respected in the eyrie. As an opinicus among gryphons, she didn't want one more reason to be an outsider. She also didn't know what Zeph's intentions were. They'd been through a lot together but didn't have a common language for feelings.

This just left Cherine. Long ago, she'd broken his heart, and once she thought he'd died, she felt like she couldn't live without him—until he turned up alive and recovering well, at which point she found she didn't care for him that way again. She'd felt no jealousy at his newfound connection to Orlea. The two of them had grown close in that brief time, but Cherine developed a relationship with everyone he met. It was what had driven Kia crazy when they'd been together.

Her plan, if she were being honest with herself, had

been to rekindle her relationship with Cherine and run away together, possibly among the taiga gryphons. Now that everything was reaching an end, she realized Cherine may not want that and she wasn't sure she did either.

That's when her revelation came. She didn't want a mate, she didn't want chicks or gryphlets, she didn't want a place to belong. She wanted to know what had gone wrong. If the world were really on fire as Headmaster Neider had said, she wanted to know why. She wasn't sure how to fix what went wrong here, but she might be able to figure it out if she had the view from the sky.

The fuse on her musings reached its end as the fuse on the saltpeter explosives did the same. She was far enough away this time that her hearing and sight were unaffected. When she looked up, she saw that a chunk of the dam had been blown upwards along with two bodies, one emerald, one brown.

It was a testament to the sturdiness of the dam that it resisted the initial blast as well as it did. Water came flowing over the top, but the bottom half remained whole.

She flew as quickly as she could to try to catch Zeph. She wasn't sure she could carry him on her own. She crashed into him, ignoring Brevin's unconscious body as it fell past.

Kia hung on tight, trying to get him beneath her, but his wings hung limp and kept causing him to twirl. She finally pinned them against his body and wrapped her foreclaws and back paws around him. Her wings weren't strong enough to keep them both aloft, but she was trying to slow their descent as safely as she could. She was lucky this was Zeph and not Hatzel or Merin. The pain in her wings was already excruciating even with his slight figure.

With the last spin, she'd had a glimpse of the dam above

her. Huge cracks spiderwebbed from the blast site. One crack spread straight beneath the statue of the cobra, causing that section to fall apart under the weight. The cobra toppled down, bringing an entire side of the dam with it.

Kia steered Zeph into the river fed by the Summer Falls. They hit with a splash. She struggled to keep them both above water. She saw the drenched figure of an emerald opinicus right at the base of the waterfall. She tried to call out a warning but there was no time.

The cobra statue crashed down, creating a tidal wave that erased the green figure from Kia's view. The surge of water sent Kia and Zeph into the weald. With some sputtering, Zeph came back to his senses and caught a tree branch. She hurt too much to fly. Instead, they climbed higher into the redwood forest and watched the destruction.

Crater Lake was gone. Only the far side of the dam still stood: a wingless, beakless alabaster peacock on the edge of a mountain. The water had spread across the northern border of the hunting grounds and into the grasslands. How far it reached was difficult to tell this late in the day with the smoky haze over the valley. The fire that had started to slither out across the hunting grounds to the grasslands was gone, and that was enough of a victory for her. Where the invading army of the north had failed to take the Crackling Sea Eyrie, a hundred gryphons attempting to save their kjarr kin had burned the city-state of the Redwood Valley Eyrie to the ground.

There was movement from the rubble of the snake statue, and a glistening emerald opinicus pulled herself out of the water.

ZEPH SHOOK as hard as he could, spraying water everywhere. The bottom six feet of the forest were underwater. With the flood washing away the topsoil and filling all the nooks and crannies, the water writhed and hissed. Xavi's snake-clearing efforts had missed the underground nests.

Having closed the distance from the rubble to the trees, Reeve Brevin came straight at him with her own writhing and hissing.

He fled deeper into the weald, hoping she wouldn't stop to attack Kia, whose wings were at their limit. He needn't have worried. The reeve had eyes only for him.

They raced past the animals of the forest making their evacuation—gliding snakes, squirrels, songbirds, and even leaping forest spinners filled the air. Beneath them was a soup of snakes, monitors, and ground parrots. The rest of the dam crumbled, and the last of Crater Lake spilled into the valley, raising the water level further.

Brevin was not in good shape. Her beak was scuffed, and many of her tail feathers were missing or broken. She was bleeding from a dozen small cuts caused by rocks. Her wings remained intact, but she was in worse shape than Zeph.

His rescue by Kia put him at an advantage. As Brevin flew faster and harder, he slipped lower into the canopy. Her large, beautiful wings would have dazzled against the smoky sky, but here in the weald, vines clung to her, and branches raked against her like claws.

The collapse of the last of the dam caused an avalanche that surged the water ten feet. She was forced to fly up to safety, getting tangled in vines before disappearing from view.

He was caught by the wave but grabbed a branch and pulled himself around to the back of a large tree and clung to it. While the reeve attempted to catch up, he folded his wings, turned around, and climbed backwards into a thick clump of rimu needles.

The reeve flew around, trying to see if he'd escaped further into the forest. When she didn't see the shape of a gryphon flitting between the trees, she returned to investigate the site of his disappearance. Most of the animals had been washed away at this point, leaving just the two of them.

He watched her search, afraid to attack for fear of her agile strikes at the dam. She'd moved with a second sense for what he planned to do. He calmed himself with the patience of Hatzel, waited, and prayed.

When the reeve was almost directly below him, his chance came. She saw feathers and lashed out with her metal talons. From the foliage, an owl emerged. Whatever she saw in the owl's features, whatever gryphon face she thought she detected, it was enough to paralyze her in place.

Zeph released his dewclaws and fell straight down, crashing into her with all of his weight, sending them both into the flood.

The water pulled them deeper into the weald. She fought, scratching and biting at him, but his assault had worn her out. Just as he thought they might both drown, the current slammed them into a redwood, peafowl first. As the water knocked her head back into the thick trunk, he caught her neck in his beak and ended it.

He stayed there, frozen—her neck in his mouth, his body pinned against her corpse, her blood drawn downstream into the weald—until the floodwaters subsided, dropping him to the forest floor.

EPILOGUE

When Satra the Kjarr arrived at the ruins of Swan's Rest with the smoke and fire of the weald at her back, her father's corpse had already been given a proper burial. Not everyone had agreed with Jun's decisions years ago, but the dissenters had died fighting rather than lose their wings. All who remained of the kjarr pride believed he had done what he had to do to save their children. When Satra showed up with two of their fledglings in tow, along with promises that the others were safely with Merin's pride awaiting their return, there were tears of joy and tears of despair: what had been the meaning of the last few days?

Two of the Redwood Valley opinici were quick to prostate themselves before Satra. The third, their leader, hesitated.

Satra killed Larren where he stood.

While the parents of the two fledglings who had flown with her had a tearful reunion, the other wingtorn packed up what supplies they could find. The opinici insisted they take some of the light spears with them in case sea hunting became a necessity. Satra was given several of her father's feathers. Not his wing feathers, as was traditional, but some from his neck ruff.

Once they were packed, she said they were headed east along the shore first, then north to a plateau. "The weald burns. The Redwood Valley Eyrie burns. We can't cross the taiga on foot, even if we could get to it. We'll meet with the rest of Merin's pride where the weald ends."

She walked with her people, never disrespectful of the sacrifice they'd made. She allowed the two fledglings to fly up and scout for them as necessary. These gryphons had loved her father, and even the ones who resented her wings were starting to say that the golden streak of feathers on her head looked like a crown.

THENCA LOOKED out at the ocean. There was some movement at the closest raft, but the fisherfolk didn't pursue the wingtorn as they left. Not today, at least. The blood of some crimes would follow her wherever she went. She'd learned that when she'd salted the farmlands and watched the Crackling Sea opinici starve. She nuzzled Urious, and they fell in line behind Satra.

AFTER DAYS OF BURNING, the Redwood Valley Eyrie now smoldered under the watchful eyes of the underbough opinici, led by Orlea. Most of the weald south of the river still burned, but the northern weald had been spared.

Despite the persistent danger of the fire jumping the river, old and new nesting grounds had been reopened to house opinicus refugees from the north and gryphon refugees from the south. The flooding from the Crater Lake explosion had subsided, and the ground had finally begun to dry.

Hatzel walked between gryphlets and opinicus chicks playing together. The medicine gryphon's apprentices worked long hours to bind wounds, treat coughs caused by the smoke, and mend broken limbs. Everyone made way for her.

Where once her pride's plumage was composed almost entirely of brown hawk and blue magpie gryphons, now every shape and color of gryphon and opinicus filled her nesting grounds—all wounded, all hungry. Orlea sent forces into the eyrie ruins for supplies, but Hatzel had to send out her healthiest pridemates to try to catch the animals fleeing the weald into the mountains. What she needed now more than ever was an adept hunter to lead them.

A small brown gryphon walked into the clearing side-by-side with a beautiful blue, red, and green opinicus. Her wing was over his back for support, and as they entered, some of the refugees recognized him. Hatzel ran to the missing pair, but a medicine gryphon reached them first and began to work on Kia's hurt wing.

With all the mud, the medicine gryphon could be forgiven for missing what Hatzel saw now. Zeph was bloodied, bruised, and in poor shape. Kia had been supporting him as much as he'd been supporting her.

Hatzel cocked her head, wondering what had happened to him. Instead of a story, he dropped the cobra necklace from his beak. It landed at her feet where the refugees could see it.

"Zeph..." Hatzel began but was interrupted by a splotchy blue merchant.

"Zeph Reevesbane," the opinicus said, then motioned for the other refugees to back away and allow the two gryphons as much privacy as a crowd could provide.

Want to know what happens next to Satra and the wing-torn? Wondering how Orlea will handle all the Redwood Valley Eyrie refugees? Worried about Askel? Curious about Younce and the mismatched medicine gryphon who followed him to the taiga? Need more Zeph? Purchase *Ashen Weald* today!

AUTHOR'S NOTE
WHO WROTE THIS? AND WHY GRYPHONS?

Hello! My name is Vale, and I wrote this book. I debated for days whether or not I should include a note about myself at the end. I talk about myself too much as is, and I wasn't sure I wanted to commit that bad habit to print. What finally convinced me is that I'm the sort of person who loves to read an author's note when I finish a book. If I finish a movie and love it, I start it over with the audio commentary on. I can't help myself. So, for the readers who made it this far and can't help themselves, either, this is who I am and why I wrote *Eyrie*.

Eyrie isn't the first book I've written, but it is the first book I've published. My writing shelf, where I hide all of the writing I haven't published, starts with "Attack of the Snowmen," written as a third grader, and continues to the more recent literary fiction, fantasy, and horror novels.

I've told stories for as long as I can remember, but I wasn't serious about getting them out into the world until I woke up in a hospital for the second time in two years and wondered how long it would take the doctors to get all of my organs working this time. That's a story for another Author's

Note, but once I was released from the hospital, I knew I wanted to be the person who could introduce themselves as "Hi, I'm the author of a series of books about gryphons." And now I can.

So why gryphons? Well, because they're the best mythological creature. It's okay if you disagree with me. Honestly, I had to be persuaded as a young child, too. Gryphons weren't on my radar until one day it seemed like they were everywhere. *Frankie* was probably the youngest gryphon story I'd read: a young kid wants a little brother or little sister and instead gets a gryphon. *The Black Gryphon* by Mercedes Lackey and Larry Dixon was the sort of book everyone had a copy of and loved when I was in middle school.

I imagine for most gryphon fans, Lackey and Dixon were the start. A common complaint I began to hear from friends was that there weren't enough gryphons in fantasy. Why all the dragons? Do we need another unicorn? Why does Harry Potter have a hippogriff instead a gryphon? I didn't pay them much mind then, not until after I awoke in the hospital after the second embolism.

"Fantasy has a million races to choose from but I'm forced to read about humans over and over again, who are always the most boring part of the world-building," my spouse said one weekend after reading several books in a row.

I'd spent the same time slush reading for a literary magazine, so I was just grateful there hadn't been anymore Bigfoot erotica in this week's submissions. We started looking for fantasy books without people and found that most of it is in Young Adult. (*Song of the Summer King* by Jess E. Owen is a great YA series with gryphons as the main characters if you're looking for YA gryphons.) Time went by again while I wrote a horror novel, then a literary fiction book for my honors thesis. I loved fantasy, but I hadn't had a chance to do more than dabble with it yet.

Coming home from the doctor's office with a scan of my lungs, which looked like someone had filled a shotgun with blood clots and fired them into my chest, I sat down at the computer and decided to try to write a book that had everything I wanted to read.

How would I sell myself on a book? It'd need to have gryphons. My spouse had been right, humans could be boring if you had other options. Could I stick to only gryphons?

Most gryphons are magical creatures, sometimes created by mages. Well, no human mages in my world. I made the decision not to include magic in any form. If my gryphons were part of nature, I wanted all of the other parts of my world to be based on real animals and plants. I'd become interested in New Zealand, an ecosystem without any terrestrial mammals until travelers brought rats, cats, and other critters there. Birds had evolved to fill those roles.

What would that look like? I made the decision not to restrict myself to extant species, instead grabbing everything that interested me. New Zealand's kakapo became my ground parrots. The strange basilosaurus became my serpentine whales. I wondered about the spread of mammals, so I included squirrels as an invasive species. I now had the world I wanted to read, I just needed the characters.

I'm always torn between writing a safe book and having shades of morality. For a lot of readers, knowing that they're reading a book where the main character will not die and the female characters are not under constant threat of rape helps them enjoy what they're reading. I can respect that. I've put down several books when terrible, graphic things happened to characters. On the other hand, or paw if you prefer, I didn't want a story where the characters were slotted into black or white categories. I like understanding character motivations. It's okay to like some people more than others, to disagree with motivations, but as I wrote a character I found myself becoming more and more sympathetic with them. I wanted to know more.

As a small child, moral complexity in books and media isn't as common, or wasn't when I was little. Yasumi Matsuno video games filled that role for me, instead. I loved getting near the end of the game to realize that I had become the villain, but not necessarily a bad guy. Finishing one of his games and moving on to the next would have the protagonist become the antagonist, with player sympathies shifting slightly to the new character. I switched my reading habits to adult books to find storytelling that compared, though I did spend one hospital visit replaying his games as an adult a few years back.

The promise I make for *Eyrie* is this: bad things will happen, people will feel forced to make bad decisions, but you'll come out of this okay. None of the characters you love will die on a whim, though I can't promise they'll all survive. Ground parrots will be eaten. It's okay for you to love the bad guys along with the good. I do, too. We'll skirt the darker edges sometimes, but always fly away.

Now, if you're interested, move on to the next book. I'll be waiting in the next author's note for everyone who can't resist reading an author ramble awhile.

-Vale

ABOUT THE AUTHOR

K. Vale Nagle is alarmingly hard to kill. While he's written his entire life, after surviving a pulmonary embolism and multiple organ failure, he began to take his writing more seriously and worked to get a degree in creative writing while recovering.

During that time another embolism struck and failed to kill him, at which point the doctors discovered an undiagnosed autoimmune disorder and patched him back up. Having used up two of his nine lives, he began publishing short stories and novels. When the doctors said that lung surgery was a 95% certainty, he dyed his hair dark blue, which is when he discovered that he was so unwell that his hair wasn't growing. A year later, and a switch from dark blue to teal, and his hair has finally started growing again (albeit silver instead of its pre-embolism black) and he's writing like a fiend.

Now, Vale writes feral fantasy—books with mythological creatures and nature-based settings, often involving gryphons and conflict.

He can be found online at kvalenagle.com, via his news-letter, or on Patreon.

facebook.com/kvalenagle

twitter.com/kvalenagle

bookbub.com/authors/k-vale-nagle

patreon.com/kvalenagle

instagram.com/kvalenagle

CHARACTER LIST

Hatzel's Pride

Hatzel. Haast's eagle + saber-toothed tiger gryphon. The last saberbeak in the weald.

Zeph Parrotbane. Cooper's hawk + cougar gryphon. Born in the taiga. Trades parrots with the eyrie.

Xavi. Black-billed magpie + panther gryphon, denfather.

Pink Paw. Cooper's hawk + cougar gryphon. Has one paw with pink pads instead of black. Close to Xavi.

Merin's Pride

Merin. Dark brown harpy eagle + lion gryphon. Second largest gryphon in the weald. Hooked beak.

Askel. Chestnut-colored golden eagle gryphon. Feathery tail. Likes fire.

Triddle. Blue harpy eagle + lion gryphon with a crest of feathers. Likes water.

Merin's Eldest Son. Disappeared on an expedition to find the starling prides.

Carru. Blue harpy eagle + lion gryphon. Huge. Left the weald to become a fisherfolk.

Redwood Valley Eyrie

Kia. Red-winged parrot + orange tabby cat opinicus. Apprentice scholar. Used to date Cherine. Paints green markings on her tabby half so she matches. Interested in flora and fauna. Good with plants.

Cherine. Golden eagle + cougar opinicus. A scholar specializing in food. Lost his little brother to the monitor plague. Worked as a butcher before he was given a scholarship by Neider to attend the university. Dated Kia for a few years. "Is kind when it is not easy to be so."

Orlea. Female cardinal + house cat opinicus. Used to be a hunter with her mate until the Reeve's Hunting Grounds were declared off limits, then she became a hunter. The Reeve's Guard killed her mate.

Reeve Brevin. Emerald peafowl opinicus. Several children, no consort. Destroyed part of the weald to create farms and grasslands.

Commander Wolden. Golden eagle + lion gryphon. Leads the Redwood Valley Eyrie forces. Lost a talon to a monitor, wears a metal one in its place.

Headmaster Neider. Eagle owl opinicus. Leads the university. Pretends to be forgetful. Often travels for research. Has a library of forbidden books.

Cockatiel Forger. Black cockatiel opinicus. Name unknown. Red fern addict. Is able to handwritten documents and books. Hangs out at the university.

Ivess. Blue peafowl opinicus. Brevin's middle child. Her favorite snake is the leaf-nosed snake. Plans to be the next reeve.

Levin/Lei. Emerald peafowl opinicus. Brevin's youngest child. Her father is Larren, a Reeve's Guard captain. Just finished fledging. Her favorite snake is the krait.

Reeve's Guard Captain Larren. Peregrine falcon opinicus. Father of Levin. Hopes to be declared consort some day.

Fisherfolk

Rorin the Hunter. Japanese crane + van cat opinicus. "When the great beasts of the sea arrive on the southern shore, it is Rorin who sends them back to the depths." Leads Swan's Rest. Likes spears.

Turresh the Shark. Peruvian diving petrel + fishing cat gryphon. "Tresh" to her friends. Has angular breaks on her beak that give it a shark-tooth appearance. Excellent swimmer. Only gryphon born into a family of opinici.

Gressle. Blue heron opinicus. Emigrated from the Crackling Sea long ago. Often trades with the eyrie and weald.

Kjarr Pride

Jun the Kjarr. Hawk + caracal gryphon. "The Scourge of the Crackling Sea." The opinici caught his son stealing from the farms and strung him up as an example, so Jun salted their farms and began his own private war against the blue opinici. Was ultimately captured by the Crackling Sea Eyrie.

Vitra. Shrike + caracal gryphon. Bog mother. Disappeared into the bog with her mother. Used blue feather and fur paint. Presumed dead.

Satra. Golden-crowned kinglet + caracal gryphon. Jun's youngest. Held hostage at the bottom of the Redwood Valley Eyrie. Often referred to as a murderer due to an incident with a taiga gryphon.

Ari. Cheetah gryphon. Kjarr pride den mother.

Bog Pride

Thenca. Mockingbird gryphon. Urious's sister. Can

imitate almost any sound or voice. Was one of the last eggs to hatch before the bog pride was integrated into the kjarr pride. Loyal to Jun. Helped raise Satra. Used to have a snowy owl gryphon lover in the taiga she would visit. Helps keep the bog pride in line.

Urious. Mockingbird gryphon. Thenca's brother. Can imitate almost any sound or voice. Was one of the last eggs to hatch before the bog pride was integrated into the kjarr pride. Scarring on his tail. With his mask pattern and bushy tail, slightly resembles a raccoon. Has always had a crush on Ari. Helped raise Satra. Helps keep the bog pride from rebelling against the Kjarr.

Strix's Pride

Strix. Black and red owl gryphon. Unlike most gryphons, no cat ears. Hunts at night. Was friends with Jun. A little off. Was the first owl pride leader to start having his pridemates learn the common language in addition to owlish.

Ninox. Black and red owl gryphon. Like most gryphons, but unlike most owl gryphons, she has cat ears, though she doesn't remember to move them like a gryphon does. Her mother was a fantail. She runs into a lot of branches. Appreciates a smart gryphon or opinicus. Still has trouble speaking common. Has many brothers.

Parrotface Pride

Parrotface Elder. Kakapo + cougar gryphon. Since kakapo sort of always look old, no one is sure her age. Prefers walking to flying. Tends to scavenge rimu olives and eggfruit rather than hunt. Owns most of the northern weald. Paints her fur with violet berry juice and wears small rocks and beads.

Fantail Pride

Erlock Fantail. Unnamed bird and cat mix, but she has 42 tail feathers exactly, and there's a hint of starling in her dark plumage. Leader of the fantail pride, who control the southeast weald. Unlike most gryphons, all of the fantail pride have long, flowing tailfeathers.

Feathermane Pride

Zrim Feathermane. Golden eagle + lion gryphon. Huge, bushy mane. Disapproves of the 'younger' prides like Merin's and Hatzel's. Controls the southwest weald which borders both the dunes, taiga, and fisherfolk shore. Is good at roaring.

Old Medicine Gryphon. Golden eagle + cougar gryphon. Losing her eyesight. She treated the original monitor plague victims, setting up the medicine gryphon caves where the three "plagueborn" survivors grew up. She prefers to teach now that her sight is poor. While the medicine gryphons are technically neutral, she would control the Feathermane Pride if something happened to Zrim until a new leader was selected.

Biski. Blue jay + jaguar gryphon. Called the "mismatched medicine apprentice" in Eyrie, but is named in future books where she has a larger role. Bossy. New adult who doesn't have her eponymous mane of feathers yet.

Crackling Sea Eyrie

Crackling Sea Reeve. Killed by a blackwing assassin. While he had a male consort, he still had many children to continue his line. They were all killed in the same attack. His eyrie now stands without a reeve.

Jonas. Royal spoonbill + Russian blue cat opinicus. Once a merchant who owned the largest goliath bird ranch on the

Crackling Sea, he became the reeve's consort and had to give it up. After the reeve's death, he took over the eyrie. It was his decision to kill Jun's son and subjugate the kjarr and bog prides. He opened a fishing village on the far side of the shore and is working with the Redwood Valley opinici to try to fix the food shortages. Many at the Redwood Valley are unaware of his importance, believing him to still be a merchant.

Ranger Lord Grenkin. Blue heron + Russian blue cat opinicus. Missing an eye and several digits from his left foreleg, bitten off by Ari when he captured the kjarr pride's gryphlets. He leads the Crackling Sea's military efforts, the rangers in particular.

Ranger Captain Ellore. Blue heron + snow leopard opinicus. She's the ranger captain assigned to hold the old kjarr nesting grounds.

Ranger Captain Rakesh. Bird and cat species unnamed, but a combination of grey and green. Emaciated. He was sent deep into the bog as a cadet and came back changed. Was once Ellore's best friend. Assigned to the combined forces sent to the dunes. Has a metal talon weapon with a moth on it that Ellore gave him as a gift when he was made captain.

ALSO BY K. VALE NAGLE

THE GRYPHON INSURRECTION

Eyrie

Ashen Weald

Starling

Reevesbane

The Ruins of Crestfall

The Crackling Sea

Opinicus

Pridelord

SHORT STORY COLLECTIONS

Blue Eyes and Other Tales